SINS *of the* DAUGHTER

a novel by

Carolyn

Huizinga Mills

Cormorant Books

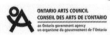

The publisher gratefully acknowledges the support of the Canada Council
for the Arts and the Ontario Arts Council for its publishing program.
We acknowledge the financial support of the Government of Canada through
the Canada Book Fund (CBF) for our publishing activities, and the
Government of Ontario through Ontario Creates, an agency of the Ontario
Ministry of Culture, and the Ontario Book Publishing Tax Credit Program.

LIBRARY AND ARCHIVES CANADA CATALOGUING IN PUBLICATION

Title: Sins of the daughter / a novel by Carolyn Huizinga Mills.
Names: Mills, Carolyn Huizinga, author.
Identifiers: Canadiana (print) 20220255253 | Canadiana (ebook) 20220255261 |
ISBN 9781770865945 (softcover) | ISBN 9781770865952 (HTML)
Classification: LCC PS8626.I4563 S56 2022 | DDC C813/.6—dc23

United States Library of Congress Control Number: 2022938939

Cover photo and design: Angel Guerra / Archetype
Interior text design: Tannice Goddard, tannicegdesigns.ca
Manufactured by Houghton Boston in Saskatoon, Saskatchewan in August, 2022.

Printed using paper from a responsible and sustainable resource,
including a mix of virgin fibres and recycled materials.

Printed and bound in Canada.

CORMORANT BOOKS INC.
260 SPADINA AVENUE, SUITE 502, TORONTO, ON M5T 2E4
www.cormorantbooks.com

To Scott — for believing,
from the very beginning

JANE LILY ❧

LILY CALSLEY FEELS SURPRISINGLY little emotion as she kisses her husband goodbye. She is standing at the kitchen sink when Andrew grazes her lips in the perfunctory way he does every morning.

"Have a good day," he murmurs.

"You too," she says.

"I shouldn't be home late. My committee meeting was moved, so I can leave right after my lecture."

Lily only nods; Andrew doesn't wait for her to answer anyway. He will drive to UBC's campus and be so caught up in his day that he won't spare her another thought until he gets home.

When she bends to kiss the top of Danah's head before sending her little girl out the door to school, Lily grabs her and hugs her. Danah looks up in surprise, and Lily is relieved when after a heartbeat of hesitation Danah wraps her skinny arms around Lily's waist and squeezes back.

They stand rooted like this, awkwardly clinging to each other. Lily rests her chin on the impossibly straight part in Danah's hair and breathes in the scent of her shampoo. Strawberries and kiwi. For a fleeting instant, she wonders if she will be able to let go of this sweet-smelling tangle of limbs. But she does, and Danah skips away from her, down the steps toward the sidewalk where her friend is waiting.

"Bye," Lily whispers, waving from the porch. Danah looks back but doesn't wave. As the girls disappear around the corner, something inside of Lily collapses.

She takes a deep breath to steady herself. Then she walks back inside, down the hall, past her daughter's pink and white room, and into the bedroom she has shared with her husband for ten years. Andrew has left the radio on again, and Madonna's "Take a Bow" is playing. It's always playing. Lily has heard the song at least once every day for the last month. Whenever Madonna sings the line about saying goodbye, Lily's heart does a stutter-step. It's not just this song either. Yesterday, during breakfast, when "Let Her Cry" by Hootie and the Blowfish came on, she had to leave the kitchen.

She shuts off the radio and sits on the bed, staring at the wall. She needs to get ready. She needs to pack and call a taxi and get to the airport. But she is having trouble making her muscles cooperate. Her body feels numb.

Packing should be simple. She knows exactly what she is taking: the envelope of cash hidden in the linen closet, a few pieces of clothing, and the dolphin figurine on her dresser. She only decided on the figurine at the last minute, a tacky souvenir Danah brought back from a trip to the Vancouver Aquarium. It's small and not too sentimental.

Like her.

She was expecting lightness, not these heavy limbs that she has to drag down the basement stairs to get her suitcase. She has been waiting and waiting for this moment. So why is it suddenly so hard?

It wasn't like this the first time.

DANAH 🌱

I USED TO WISH my mother was dead.

I went through a phase where I spent hours constructing elaborate fantasies about how she died, each one more detailed and tragic than the last. It wasn't that I actually wanted her to be dead; what I wanted was an explanation for her abandoning me, for sending me off to school one morning, then disappearing from my life like a wisp of smoke.

Mothers aren't supposed to abandon their children. It goes against gender norms. I know a lot about norms and the kinds of people who break them. I study deviance. Not because of what happened, though. Choosing to pursue a Ph.D. in sociology had nothing to do with my mother's cold rejection; I chose this discipline because of my dad. I wanted to follow in his footsteps, big as they are. Still, what kind of mother walks away from her only child? Fathers, yes — they have more latitude in the parenting department. But mothers? They're supposed to stay.

I remember her standing on the porch. Her long, curly hair fell in waves over her shoulders, and she was wearing a loose T-shirt with a pair of whitewashed jeans. It must have been one of her mornings off. She wore nicer clothes on the days she worked at

Noble's Florist. She was smiling. I remember that too. It was her smile that tricked me. I thought it meant she was happy.

For months, I sucked on a morsel of hope, waiting for news, for her to come back, for something — anything — to happen. It didn't seem real that she was gone. That she had just up and walked away from me, from us. My father never said as much, but I got the sense he was waiting for something too. I could see it in his eyes, the way they darted in the direction of unexpected sounds. We were both holding our breath. But it didn't matter. Nothing ever came of all that hoping. Instead, my mother's presence just sort of evaporated from the house. And as the last of my sweet-tasting hopes dissolved on my tongue, they were replaced by a thin film of guilt.

The deaths I daydreamed about were melodramatic. Drowning in the Fraser River, Mom's long curls plastered to her face. That was a good one when I wanted a cold, lonely way for her to die. Or standing on a corner, clutching a present for me in her arms, then a bus swerving around the corner, killing her on impact. I let her die quickly in that one because of the gift. Also, falling out a third-floor window, lying broken on the ground, whispering my name with her final breaths. Her death here was slow and laced with regret. I relished the idea of her being sorry.

It doesn't take a Ph.D. in sociology to understand the motivation behind those morbid fantasies. If I could convince myself that my mother was dead, it would be easier to forgive her. Not just her — also myself. I wanted forgiveness. Badly. Although I'd be lying if I didn't also admit to taking some pleasure in dreaming up all those deaths. I found them comforting. I had no other way to punish her.

That was all a long time ago, though. Eighteen years. I've done a lot of growing up since then: I'm no longer consumed by wishes and what-ifs and tricking myself into believing my mother is dead. Or maybe I don't care anymore.

It's not like I never think about her. I do. She floats somewhere on the edge of my consciousness, and on days like today, when

I'm making my way up *her* mother's front walk to fulfill my obligations as a dutiful granddaughter, I can't help but be aware of her once-upon-a-time existence. I don't mention her on these visits, though.

I know better.

It's already four-thirty, which is later than I planned to get off campus, and if I didn't think Edith would get all bent out of shape by me not showing up, I would've gone straight home. The sky is thick with low-hanging clouds, and I cross my fingers that we're finally going to get some snow. I've had enough of the rain and dead grass and rotting leaves that have pretty much defined November. No wonder people think Hamilton is ugly.

I rap lightly on Edith's front door before letting myself in. "There's no need for you to stand there waiting for an invitation," she told me once. "You know how a door works, surely?"

The narrow front hall of Edith's tiny bungalow is dark. I unzip my boots and throw out a tentative hello. No answer. I scoop up a pile of mail from the floor and take a few steps further inside. The air, which usually smells like fresh bread or something sweeter — sugar and cinnamon — is strangely stale. I turn toward the living room, where I see Edith, stretched out on the couch, her body as still as a corpse.

"Headache?" I ask, as if there might be some other, less predictable, explanation. She has a blue washcloth draped over the top half of her face, and her normally perfectly arranged curls are sticking out in every direction.

She lets out a sound like a strangled goat. "Migraine. It's this weather." She pulls the cloth away from her eyes and tilts her head toward me, wincing with the effort.

I nod with what I hope looks like genuine sympathy. Edith's migraine means a short visit, which suits me perfectly. My mind is already wandering to the stack of student papers sitting on the front seat of my car, waiting to be marked.

"Sorry I didn't come earlier. Can I do anything for you? Get you some water, maybe?"

Edith mumbles something that I interpret as a yes, then raises her hand to her head, indicating, as far as I can tell, that even this helpful interference on my part is a bit too much for her right now.

I take her cue. I'll get her some water, then get the hell out of here. Papers aside, I'm entering a crazy vortex of colliding deadlines, and, like the rest of the second-year Ph.D. candidates in my program, I'm feeling the first twinges of pressure.

I drop the mail on the counter, and as I'm pulling back my hand, I notice a creamy white envelope addressed in a spidery script. Curious, because who writes letters anymore — and more to the point, who would write to Edith? — I glance at the return address. *Lily Wilder.* The name Wilder means nothing to me, but Lily rings like an alarm bell in my brain. My mother's name was Lily. Is Lily. But this letter can't be from her. That wouldn't make any sense. And this person, this Lily, is writing from Edinburgh. Who the hell does Edith know in Scotland?

Could it be her? Something like hope blossoms in my chest for the briefest moment, but I quash it quickly with practised skill. Still, even as I'm convincing myself that Edith will have some perfectly reasonable explanation, a shiver of anticipation runs across my skin.

I wait for the tap to run cold, then fill a glass for Edith, taking the envelope with me into the living room. As soon as I see Edith's limp body on the couch, her eyes still buried under the washcloth, my half-formed hopes disintegrate. Clearly, my grandmother's in no shape for questions.

And truthfully, even if Edith weren't lying comatose on the couch, I wouldn't know where to start. We have formed a habit of careful silences. Besides, if Edith were in touch with my mother — in Edinburgh? — she would have told me. Wouldn't she? She might not be the most forthcoming person in the world, but still, I hardly think she would keep something like that a secret.

I set the glass of water on the coffee table, on one of the wooden coasters Edith insists I use. I hesitate for a second, then return to the kitchen and shove the letter under a Home Hardware flyer.

I'll ask Edith about it tomorrow when she's feeling better.

I return to the living room and stand for a minute staring out the window at the heavy drops of rain splattering against the street. So much for snow. I pull Edith's thick drapes closed, shutting out the encroaching darkness.

"I should go." My voice sounds strange, higher pitched than usual. "I'll stop by after my tutorial tomorrow to check on you."

Edith ignores me. I almost change my mind then. I almost speak the question that is quivering on the edge of my tongue, but in the end, I don't have the courage.

I DRIVE HOME THROUGH a blur of rain, my thoughts just as murky as the road in front of me. My mind runs over and over the possibility that my mother has resurfaced. And if she has, what then? What am I contemplating? A reunion? Mommy coming back, finally, for her little girl? I need to get a grip. What would Dad think if he could see me now?

The SUV crawling in front of me comes to a sudden stop, and I slam on my brakes, skidding to a stop inches from its bumper. My tote bag flies off the seat, spilling my laptop and several student papers onto the floor. I smack my hand against the steering wheel hard enough to sting. "Asshole," I mumble. I blow out a breath as a black squirrel scampers across the road and disappears into somebody's front lawn. The SUV creeps forward, then makes a left turn, leaving me alone with my racing thoughts.

What the hell is wrong with me? There's no way that letter was from my mother. When she left, she broke contact with everyone. She disappeared completely. Or at least, that's what I've always been led to believe.

Even before she left, she never had anything to do with Edith.

7

Hell, I didn't even know I had a grandmother until after, when seemingly out of nowhere she started sending me cards and money.

"Write her a note to thank her for the birthday card," Dad would insist. Or, "Tell her what you plan to buy with that Christmas money."

"Why is she all of a sudden sending me stuff now? Why didn't she ever send anything before?" I asked once, annoyed at having to write to this stranger on the other side of the country who had nothing to do with me or my life in Vancouver.

"Maybe she did," he said. But when I looked up at him, confused, he had already turned back to the journals on his desk.

My windshield wipers whip back and forth furiously, and I have to squint to see through the rain. It pummels the roof of my Camry, blocking out the sound of the engine. It does nothing to drown out my thoughts, though. Damn Edith and her stupid headaches. I should have just asked her about the letter. Then at least I would know. Although maybe knowing would be worse.

I squeeze my car into the narrow space between my landlord's car and the neighbour's fence, leaving myself just enough room to open the door and shimmy out. But first, I reach for my phone and call Trevor.

"Hey, babe. What's up?" He sounds distracted.

"Any chance you could come over?"

"I can't tonight, babe. I have to get this outline done. I'm meeting my advisor first thing."

"Okay." He must hear the disappointment in those two syllables. Or the desperation.

"What's wrong?"

I tell him about the envelope. "Do you think there's any way it could be from my mom? I mean, how many Lilys are there in the world? Well, technically I guess there are quite a few, but how many that would know Edith?"

"Why don't you wait to see what your grandma says, and we can take it from there? It could be nothing."

"But don't you think that after my dad died, Edith would have said something? I mean, if she knew anything about my mom?" The sound of the rain pinging against my roof and windshield is getting louder.

"What I think is that you're overthinking it."

He's right, but another question that has been twisting through my mind slips out in a whisper: "Why not me? Why didn't she write to me?"

I hate how pitiful the words sound.

"After you've talked to Edith, we'll psychoanalyze every single thing she says," he promises. He's teasing me, but I can't think of a comeback, so I say nothing. I lean my head against the seat and close my eyes, trying to ignore the pressure in my chest, the knife pricks dancing at the edge of my thoughts.

"I've gotta go," Trevor says. "Sorry I can't be there."

"It's all right. I'm fine."

"I wish I could, babe."

"I know. Don't worry, I get it."

I dart through the rain, fumbling with my keys before stepping inside onto the small landing that leads to my basement apartment. I want to crawl under a blanket and hide. I don't think I can face marking any papers tonight. Hell, I can't even face the dirty cereal bowl I left in the sink this morning.

I flop onto the couch and open my laptop. Before I can talk myself out of it, I Google *Lily Wilder*. It's not the first time I've searched for information about my mother, but I've never used the surname Wilder before. I tried Calsley, of course, and her maiden name, Koestra, both without any luck. As I type in *Wilder*, my heart thumps nervously.

There's a link for Lily's Wild Flower Emporium, which momentarily makes my breath catch, but I quickly realize it has nothing to do with my mother, despite the uncanny connection to flowers. I keep scrolling. Some young woman's Facebook profile; a character in a novel with the same name; a clothing store in Utah.

I snap the screen shut. Nothing. Which is exactly what I expected.

I'm too distracted to get any work done, so I don't even try. I wrap myself in a blanket and binge-watch four episodes of *Alias*. Somehow, Sydney Bristow's life as a grad student who also happens to be a double agent for the CIA seems simpler than mine at the moment. At least she still has her dad. Even if she hates him.

Later, I stand in front of my dresser and pick up one of the wooden maracas my dad brought back for me from Mexico. The shells have started to split at the seams, but I refuse to throw them out. I press the cracked wood to my cheek, then stare at myself in the mirror, at the grown-up girl with straight, brown hair who is clutching a broken souvenir as if her life depends on it.

My mind may be spinning with renewed thoughts of finding my mother, but it's my dad I miss. He's the one I want.

He always was.

DANAH 🐦

DANAH TIPTOES DOWN THE hall, sneaking past her mother in the kitchen, her six-year-old feet doing little hop-steps as she approaches her father's study. The door is partway open, and a soft, amber light spills onto the hallway floor. Inside, her father is sitting at his big, heavy desk, leaning back in his chair, staring at a stack of papers. His glasses have slipped down his nose, and when he turns toward her, he tips his head to peer over the frames.

"Shouldn't you be in bed?"

"I can't sleep."

Her father sets down the papers, takes off his glasses, and studies her for a moment. She hovers in the doorway, looking back at him with wide, solemn eyes, trying to curve her mouth into a frown.

"Come on," he says, reaching his hand toward her. "Let's go."

Together, they pad back to her bedroom, and as they pass the kitchen, Danah senses her mother's eyes watching them.

A sliver of moonlight slips between the crack in Danah's curtains, and in this shaft of pale light, Danah can make out her father's features as he sits on the edge of her bed. His hair looks dark in the shadowy room, although she knows it is the same light brown as hers. It's messy right now, as if he's been running his hands through

11

it, like he does when he's thinking. A smile tugs at the left side of his mouth, and she knows he is going to make a joke or say something to make her laugh.

"I have a very special song for you," he says.

Danah snuggles into her blankets.

"Oo-oh, my Da-a-nah, what a day I've had!" he sings. His voice is low and husky as he makes up a nonsense song about departmental meetings and sociology lectures and what he ate for lunch in the university cafeteria.

Danah closes her eyes, slowly sinking into the rhythm of her father's voice.

She wonders if, far away, in the kitchen, her mother is listening too.

EDITH 🐿

AFTER DANAH LEAVES, I lie on the couch a while longer listening to the rain lash against the windows. Each gust of wind is a fresh assault on my pounding head, feeling for all the world like thousands of tiny icicles drilling into my skull. Danah was in and out of here so fast it was hardly worth her taking off her boots. I reach for the water she left me, spilling some of it as my trembling hand brings the glass to my lips. What I want is to move from the couch to the comfort of my bed, but I can't summon the strength to sit up. Oh, what a special kind of suffering the Good Lord has seen fit to bestow upon me!

It's not just the migraines either. I've had more than my share of misery, that's for sure. My mother liked to remind anyone who would listen: "It is through our suffering that the glory of God will be revealed." Ha! I gave up on God's glory long ago. The only thing my suffering ever revealed was more suffering.

As the rain continues its relentless drum roll against my skull, I'm thankful that Danah at least had the forethought to pull the living room drapes before she waltzed out of here. I certainly don't need every Tom, Dick, and Harry peering in at me from the sidewalk.

Eventually, I manage to roll myself off the couch. I stagger to the bathroom for another migraine pill, then inch my way toward my blessed bed, where I lie down fully clothed, my head throbbing with every heartbeat. I close my eyes and wait for sleep and medication to deliver me from the pain.

These are the things I put my faith in now.

BY MORNING, MY HEADACHE is mostly gone; all that's left is a slight pain behind my left eye and a dull pulsing in my temple. It's a good thing too, because today is my shopping day with Alice. Her eyes have been getting worse over the past few years, so we do our shopping together, splitting the cost of a taxi. Ben, her husband, unloads the groceries when we return, carrying mine straight to my kitchen. I suppose it's his way of thanking me — heaven forbid he ever step foot in a grocery store. Still, the whole arrangement suits me just fine. I have to do my own shopping regardless, and I enjoy Alice's company.

I open the drapes in the living room to let in the pale morning light, then pull the chains that hang down from my Zaanse clock to return the weights to their highest position. The clock was a wedding present, shipped all the way from Holland. I have always liked it — the brass fittings, the Roman numerals on the face, the small statue of Atlas standing at the top holding up the world — but I could do without it chiming every thirty minutes when I have a migraine. I put the kettle on for a cup of tea and take out my recipe tin. Although I can still feel the lingering remnants of my headache, I am intent on being productive, on making up for yesterday's inertia.

I've been baking ever since I was a little girl. By the time I was ten years old, I was in charge of making four loaves of bread every Saturday; we never had the store-bought kind in our house. I had to get up early to start the dough — before the sun came up, most of the year — but I didn't mind. I loved those hours in the empty

14

kitchen: measuring out the flour, breathing in the heady scent of yeast. The precision of baking appealed to me, even at a young age: all those exact quantities, counting down the minutes until the loaves were just brown enough to come out of the oven.

"Give us this day our daily bread," Father prayed, even though I was clearly the one providing the bread, not God. But I would never have had such blasphemous thoughts as a child. I was a good little girl. Scared proper.

This morning, I decide to make cranberry-nut bread. It's a quick loaf, not the kind of bread I made as a child, but I don't have time today for kneading and rising and kneading again. Danah bought me an electric mixer, and while at first I didn't like to use it, this morning I'm happy for it to do the work of creaming together the butter and brown sugar. I use a wooden spoon for the rest of the ingredients, though. Overmix the batter and the texture of the bread will be all wrong. I fold in the chopped walnuts and cranberries, then pour the mixture into a loaf pan. While it's baking, I plan to sit down with a second cup of tea and the crossword puzzle. I never did get to the crossword yesterday. It's sitting on the side table in the living room, waiting for me, the newspaper page folded into a neat rectangle.

I wash up all the dishes first and wipe the counters. Danah has set my mail aside — flyers mostly, by the look of it. I can't stand all that junk. How many people do they think actually look at this stuff? I should find out if I can stop having flyers delivered altogether.

The kettle clicks off, and I make my tea. Settled comfortably in my chair by the living room window, I pick up the crossword, filling in the easy answers first. There are a few clues that have been used several times before: *poet's preposition* and ____ *vera*. I pencil in *ere* and *aloe*; you'd think whoever makes these things could at least come up with something new.

By the time I pull my finished loaf from the oven and set it on the stovetop to cool, it's almost time to meet the taxi. Working quickly, I run a dry cloth around the inside of the sink to get rid of the water spots, then crack open the window to let in a small draft of fresh air. I survey the kitchen. I still have a minute or two, so I sift through the pile of mail on the counter to see if there's anything worth saving and am brought up short by a creamy envelope addressed to me in familiar handwriting. Seeing it, my heart flutters against my chest like a moth at a window.

My Dutch clock clangs out the hour, and I set the envelope down. The taxi will be here any second. I imagine Alice is already making her unsteady way down her steps, so I have no choice but to put on my coat and slip into my boots. In my preoccupied state, I neglect to wear a hat or gloves although it's cold enough to warrant both. I am distracted as I approach the taxi, but I at least have enough sense to reply when Alice says good morning.

I don't offer her any assistance getting in the back seat. She may need help reading labels and selecting the correct items from the shelves, but she'd be quick enough to remind me that she's still quite capable of climbing into a car, thank you very much.

"Do you mind if we make a quick stop at the bank?" Alice asks once I've manoeuvred in next to her.

"No, of course not," I say, although I'm anxious for our errands to be done. The unopened letter tugs at my thoughts, pulling my mind in a million directions.

Alice's quick stop at the bank takes almost fifteen minutes, but I bite my tongue. We move slowly through Sobeys. I have a short list, but Alice's feet are dragging.

"Is this cream of mushroom? It doesn't look right." She peers closely at the can in her hand before holding it out for me to see.

"Yes, it's the mushroom. They've just changed the label."

"I don't want the celery. I don't like the cream of celery."

"It's not celery. It's mushroom."

After I've convinced Alice that she has the correct soup, we move on, lumbering down the aisles. My mind is elsewhere, though, weighted with a secret knowledge from the last time that spidery handwriting showed up.

JANE LILY ❧

THE OFFICE OF DR. PATTERSON, Psychologist, is located in Edinburgh's Old Town, directly above Essington Chocolatiers. I wonder sometimes if the people sampling the boutique chocolates at street level ever think about the pain that must be unspooling above their heads. Assuming, that is, they are even aware of Dr. Patterson's office. There is a brass name plaque outside, but why would anyone notice it unless they were looking for it, unless they needed his specialized services?

During my first few sessions, I was preoccupied by the sickly sweet scent of chocolate seeping up through the floor. Whenever I mentioned it, Dr. Patterson gently chided me for attempting to change the subject. Eventually, I was able to ignore the smell.

His office is comfortable enough, with its beige walls and dark-brown furniture, everything done in boring neutrals, no doubt intended to be soothing. When I meet with him, we sit on wide leather armchairs, facing each other. Together, we scrutinize my past. I am supposed to be learning how to face it, and also my future. Apparently, one is necessary for the other.

Weeks ago, Dr. Patterson asked me to call him by his first name: Niall. I was about to object, but then, realizing how hypocritical that would make me, I grudgingly agreed. I didn't want to give him any reason to suggest that, in the end, I wasn't really all that different from my mother.

So I call him Niall, like he wants.

I am aware, today, as I climb the steep stairs beside Essington Chocolatiers, that we don't have many sessions left. We have talked about pretty much everything there is to talk about. I wait in the small reception area for Niall to summon me. There's not much to look at here: an oil painting of a black grouse, some outdated magazines, the frosted door to Niall's inner office. I'm only there a few minutes when the door opens, and Niall waves me in.

"How are you feeling?" he asks as I settle in to one of the dark-brown armchairs.

"Pretty good. The same."

He sits down across from me, notepad in hand. He is dressed casually, a button-down shirt, no tie. He's a good-looking man, probably in his mid-forties, maybe younger, and I imagine he has a wife, a family, but he is careful to steer the conversation back to me whenever I try to dig for details. He must make his notes after I leave, because I've never seen him write much of anything on that pad during our sessions. Either that or he has an incredible memory. He sometimes surprises me by revisiting a detail from one of our prior conversations that I don't even remember sharing.

We usually exchange a few pleasantries before he gets down to business. Today we talk about the weather, how the fog won't seem to lift from the city. I wonder if he's going to use it as a metaphor for my situation: not being able to see the road ahead or something inane like that. How I've become lost in the fog of my past. Although we might be beyond all that now.

Instead, he surprises me by saying, "I never asked why you chose the name Wilder specifically."

We've talked about my name before. Right at the start, when I first began seeing him. He asked me then about my reasons for changing it at all. I thought it was fairly obvious, but Niall likes me to talk things out. It isn't for his benefit. The idea is for me to understand things better by saying them out loud.

"I didn't want to be found," I told him then, that first time he asked.

That wasn't good enough for him. "It's not hard to track someone down, even with a new name," he argued.

"I didn't expect anyone to look that hard."

He had nothing to say to that.

I can't tell, today, if he's merely curious or if he's hoping to uncover some hidden significance in the name Wilder. I'm almost sorry to disappoint him. "It's from Laura Ingalls Wilder. An American author." Then, wanting to give him something more, I add, "I loved her books when I was little."

We go through our regular dance, back and forth, back and forth. Niall prompts me to explore my feelings; I do my best to be honest.

I am so tired. Despite my earlier response, I am not feeling well at all. It takes all my energy just to sit up straight.

Our hour is almost up when Niall says, "I wonder, is Lily Wilder really all that different from Lily Calsley, or even from Jane?"

I consider what he's asking. My voice, when I answer, sounds childlike. It comes out as a whisper. "For a little while, I think she was."

"It is interesting," Niall says, rubbing his chin thoughtfully, "that you chose a name connected to your childhood, isn't it?"

JANE LILY 🐦

JANE LIKES TO SIT with her sketchbook under the branches of a sprawling honey locust behind the barn, out of sight from the house. Even though she has lived her whole life on this farm, within throwing distance of her aunts and uncles and cousins, at eleven years old, she spends most of her time alone.

She has friends, but they live in town, and during the summer months, she rarely sees them. Outside of school, they seem distant, far removed from her life. Her cousins, too, have more to do with her at school than outside of it, despite the fact that they live just across the road. Last year, she sat beside her cousin Tessa every day on the bus — they were in the same split 4/5 class — yet at home, they almost never play together.

Right now, as she relaxes against the thick trunk of the honey locust, she is concentrating on drawing a flower, a single long-stemmed rose. She can't get the petals right. It's a hot day, and if it weren't for the shade, the August air would be unbearable. Even in the shade, her T-shirt sticks to her back, and her pencil continually slips between her sweaty fingers.

It's no better in the house. Worse, actually. At least out here there's room to breathe, no one watching her every move, ready to criticize her at the drop of a hat.

The grass is dry and prickly; it makes the bare skin on her legs itch. She shifts her position, and when she looks up, she sees her three cousins making their way toward the pond on the other side of the road. They throw their towels to the ground, and Stuart, the oldest, does a running cannonball into the water. Tessa and Catherine shriek as he splashes them, their laughter ringing through the air.

Jane glances back at her drawing. The pencil lines have smudged where her damp hand was resting against the paper. She flips to a new page and starts another sketch, this time drawing a daisy. Daisies are easy.

JANE'S MOTHER IS STANDING on a wooden platform, hanging the laundry on a clothesline that stretches across the yard. Jane approaches slowly, clutching her sketchbook behind her back.

"I can finish that," she offers. She enjoys pinning up the clothes, then reeling them out over the lawn, watching them dance in the breeze — when there is one.

"I'm fine here. Perhaps you could set down your scribbling and make yourself useful some other way. There are potatoes that need peeling on the counter. Look around, see what needs to be done. I shouldn't have to tell you."

"It's not scribbling," Jane mutters, turning to go into the house.

"What did you say?"

"Nothing."

The kitchen is stifling. The windows are all open, but without a breeze it makes little difference, so Jane takes the pot of potatoes outside to peel. She sits on the back step and scrapes at the potatoes with a peeler that's so dull she may as well be using a spoon. When she's done, she sneaks upstairs to her bedroom and closes the door.

Her room is small, with a dormer window where the ceiling slopes toward the floor. This is where she likes to sit, on the window's wide, wooden sill. She can see the pond from here, and she considers asking if she can go for a quick swim, like her cousins. Then she changes her mind. Edith will only find more work for her to do. Better to stay out of sight.

It is hotter upstairs than it was in the kitchen. She strips down to her underwear and flops, spread-eagled, onto her bed. After a few minutes, she reaches for the library book on her nightstand. Edith might not approve of sketching, but she has never discouraged Jane from reading.

The quilt on her bed was her mother's when she was a girl. It's ugly. A series of green and yellow squares with raggedy tufts that make Jane think of miniature scraggly beards. She doesn't dare complain, though. She likes the idea of sharing something with her mother, with a different version of her — a younger, secret version, who Jane thinks probably hated this quilt too. Why else would her mother have given it to her?

An hour, maybe more, slips by as she lies on her bed reading. Then, suddenly, she is pulled back to the thick, heavy air of her room by her mother's shrill voice.

"Jane! Get down here!"

Quickly, she pulls on her shorts and T-shirt. Edith is standing at the bottom of the stairs holding out a pot.

"What's this?" she says, shoving the pot toward Jane's face. "You call this peeled?"

Janes takes the pot and heads back to the kitchen, Edith close on her heels.

"You rush through everything," Edith is saying. "If you'd just take the time to do things properly, you wouldn't have to do them twice."

Or if we had a peeler that actually worked, Jane thinks. She stands at the counter with her back to her mother, sweat trickling down her neck, and attacks the potatoes one more time.

DANAH ✤

SOMEONE CALLS MY NAME as I'm hurrying up the hill from the student parking lot, which is on the opposite end of campus from Kenneth Taylor Hall. It's on the opposite end of everything, really. I turn around and see Dwayne, another sociology student, jogging toward me. I slow down just long enough to let him to catch up since he's heading to the same meeting I am. Our department is hosting a visiting professor from Australia in two weeks, and we're both on the planning committee.

"I thought I was running behind," he says, "but when I saw you, I knew I must be okay. Or are you not planning on being the first one there today?"

"Shut up. I'm late too."

"Danah Calsley late? Unheard of." He's smiling as he falls into step beside me.

I walk faster, half tempted to break into a jog. It's freezing today. The sky is white, leached of colour, and what little sun there is throws a watery light over the buildings, which somehow makes everything seem colder. We pass through the archway of Gilmour Hall, with its castle-like towers, old stonework, and trailing ivy. So many of the buildings on campus have a fairy-tale kind of charm;

then there's Kenneth Taylor Hall, an ugly brick box surrounded by a sea of cement. No gardens for us. We do have some rocks, though. Great hulking stones placed in strategic clusters around the outside of the building, meant to liven the place up. Too much cement? No problem. Let's add some rocks.

Dwayne steps in front of me as we approach the entrance to Kenneth Taylor Hall, making a show of holding the door open. He bows as I breeze past him, then follows me to the elevators.

"You think Sanders is still pissed about this?" he says, pointing to a flyer taped inside the elevator.

"Probably. She hates sloppy work." The flyer, like all the others posted around campus, has a label stuck over the incorrect time that was initially printed to advertise our visiting professor's public talk. It wasn't until after our committee had plastered them all over campus that someone noticed the error. "I'm just glad it wasn't my mistake," I say as the doors slide open on the seventh floor.

"Something like that would never happen on your watch," Dwayne says. He motions for me to go first.

"True."

When we walk into the conference room, I am relieved to see that Pauline Sanders, my advisor and the committee chair, isn't here yet. The other three committee members, all students, are still taking off their coats and getting settled.

Dwayne plunks down beside me. "Look at that, plenty of time," he says, elbowing me playfully.

I pull out my notes from the last meeting. Across the table from me, Susan sets down a Tim Hortons cup, and I fight off a stab of jealousy. I'd kill for a peppermint latte right now.

Pauline arrives, dressed in a stylish sweater wrap that accentuates her height, and, without any preliminaries, launches into her agenda. She's the one who arranged for our department to host Professor Arthur Williams, and I happen to know that while he's here, the two of them are going to be discussing an idea for a joint project. I would do anything to get in on that project; it's the kind of accomplishment that, if he were here to witness it, would make my dad's eyes light up with pride. Not to mention that it could completely alter the trajectory of my career.

Williams is a big name in sociology. His book, *The Monster Next Door*, was a *New York Times* bestseller and earned him an appearance on Oprah. He's an expert on secret deviants, which ties in perfectly with my own research around university-aged women who keep their eating disorders a secret from the people closest to them, namely their family members. Pauline got me onto the topic without knowing how close to home the idea of secrets within families would hit.

I'm barely listening to Pauline right now, though. My mind keeps skipping ahead to my visit with Edith and how, exactly, I'm going to bring up the letter. Pauline suddenly stops mid-sentence and stares at me over the purple rims of her glasses. I swallow. Shit. Did she just ask me something? Her gaze moves around the table, and I let out a shaky breath.

"The timing for Arthur's visit isn't great, being so close to Christmas, so we'll need to work to fill seats," she says. "I want those talks full."

Beside me, Dwayne is nodding enthusiastically. Then I catch sight of Susan. She's chewing her lip, eyes glowing with self-importance. I would put money on it that she's dying to blurt out how many people she personally has lined up.

Pauline continues. "Getting people to the departmental talk shouldn't be much of a problem. Arthur's name alone will bring out the university crowd; even people in anthropology know who he is. It's the public talk that might be a challenge."

Susan's hand shoots into the air. "I've been promoting it on social media," she says. "Lots of people are asking me about it. I have six friends coming for sure."

Yup. Called it.

"That's great," Pauline says smoothly. "But there are a lot of seats in that room. I want each of you to invite anyone and everyone you can think of. Your parents, your neighbours, your parents' neighbours. We need bodies in there, and I'm trusting all of you to make that happen."

Her eyes settle on me again. I've never let her down, which is one of the reasons I'm hoping to have an edge when it comes to being considered for the joint project. I could ask my landlord. He and his wife don't get out much; they might enjoy coming to a university event. I invited Edith a long time ago, but I should probably remind her again. How the hell does Susan even have six friends?

"After his meeting with the grad students on Thursday, we need a place for dinner. Danah, can you arrange that? Make a reservation somewhere for about ten people?" Pauline looks up at me again.

"Sure." I jot down a quick note on my ever-expanding to-do list.

"We also need someone to get him to the restaurant. Actually, someone will need to take him back to his hotel and then pick him up again for dinner."

Dwayne immediately volunteers. What's with him this morning? I eye him suspiciously, wondering if he knows about the project too. The last thing I need is him as my competition.

AFTER THE MEETING, DWAYNE follows me out. "I thought for sure you were going to offer to drive Williams around, Danah. I'm surprised you let me beat you to it, given your little crush on him. What is it about him anyway? Don't tell me it's his irresistible Australian accent."

I stop and pretend to consider. "No, I think it's probably just the fact that he's hot." We step into the elevator. "But the accent doesn't hurt."

"I thought Susan might jump in before I did. Her and her little social media promotion. Is she trying to top Obama's re-election story or something?"

I can't help laughing out loud. This is what I like about Dwayne: he makes me feel lighter.

We part company in front of the Mills Memorial Library, where I plan to spend the hour and half before my tutorial reviewing the notes from my earliest comp readings. I take the elevator to the fourth floor, then pull out my phone to text Trevor. Partly, I want to see how his thesis meeting went, but mostly, I want a pep talk about confronting my grandmother.

My phone is dead. With a groan, I toss it back in my bag and make my way to my usual spot near the big bay window that over-looks the courtyard in front of the library. Two students have beat me to it. First-years by the look of them. They've arranged all four armchairs so they can sit with their feet propped up and giggle into each other's armpits. Annoyed, I keep walking until I find an empty seat at the end of a row of shelves. At least there aren't any other people near me. The reason I come to the fourth floor is that I can't stand listening to the sniffling and coughing and other weird noises in the busier parts of the library.

I pull out my notes and start reading, trying to keep the questions most likely to appear on my comprehensive exam at the forefront of my mind, but it's no use. I can't focus. Instead of sitting here, wasting my time, I decide to go to the Student Centre and get that peppermint latte I wanted so badly earlier. There aren't many tables available, so I end up brushing off someone else's crumbs before sitting down. The minutes tick by. I sip my latte and notice, abstractedly, that pretty much everyone around me is busy — staring at laptops, flipping through papers, scribbling in notebooks. Intently focused. Like I should be.

MY TUTORIAL IS IN the basement of Kenneth Taylor Hall. The class-rooms down here all smell musty, despite the new carpets that were put in over the summer. The rooms were painted at the same time, and for a while the fresh paint masked the smell of mildew, but it didn't last, and eventually the mustiness seeped back.

Six or seven students are already sitting as I make my way to the podium at the front of the room. The rest of the students straggle in while I take out my notes from Professor Stone's lecture and arrange them in front of me. Did Edith even hear me yesterday when I said I would check in on her? I pass around a sheet of paper to take attendance, then start talking. I stumble over my sentences. The students don't seem to notice, though. They sit in front of me with bored expressions while I ramble on about Marx's theory of alienation: how humans in a capitalistic society become estranged from their own humanity until they are no longer able to reach self-actualization. The words *alienation* and *estranged* echo in my brain, ringing with meaning that has nothing to do with Marx or his theories.

I keep checking the clock. I can't decide if I'm hoping for time to speed up or for it to slow down. In the end, I let everyone out twenty minutes early. Then I stand for a second in the musty, empty classroom gathering my thoughts and my courage.

I drive to Edith's house in a distracted daze, praying that her headache is gone. I'm still trying to figure out what I'm going to say to her, but when I turn onto Alder Street, my thoughts are interrupted by ribbons of bright yellow caution tape roping off my grandmother's entire front yard.

When I step out of the car, I am struck at once by the unmistakable and acrid smell of smoke.

EDITH 🌱

I'VE BEEN SITTING HERE for hours, staring out the Kophers' living room window. Even from in here, I can smell the smoke. I can taste it too. A scorched bitterness that clings to the back of my tongue, no matter how many cups of tea Alice serves me. I can't see my house from this vantage point, just the edge of my driveway and a corner of the front lawn, both cordoned off by that flimsy yellow tape. It's just as well. I don't want to look at the house — at the boarded-up front door and the smoky grey windows.

The fire trucks are gone now, along with all the neighbours who came outside to gawk. The street is empty and silent.

Still no sign of Danah.

I close my eyes, temporarily giving in to the fatigue that has settled in my bones. A dull pain throbs behind my left eye, but I don't want to bother Alice for Advil. She's done enough already.

The sound of a car door slamming rouses me. Danah. Finally. She sure took her sweet time. I watch as she stands by the curb, her face creased with confusion. What is she waiting for? My message was clear enough.

"Danah's here," I announce. I rap noisily on the window until Danah looks in my direction; recognition flashes across her face, and she hurries toward the Kophers' front door.

I don't know why she looks so surprised. What did she think I meant when I said there'd been a fire?

ALICE AND I RETURNED from our shopping this morning to find the entire street blocked off by fire trucks with their lights flashing.

"What's going on?" Alice asked.

Through the chaos and confusion, I spotted Ben. He was shuffling as fast as he could toward our taxi, his face grim. I strained to see past the trucks. Were they in front of my house or the Kophers'? Ben opened the back door of the taxi and poked his head inside. My stomach curled with dread.

"Been a bit of a fire at your place, Edith," he said. "Let's get you ladies off the street now."

"What do you mean 'a bit of a fire'? What are you talking about?" My voice came out harsher than I intended, but really, what on earth was he saying?

He took my hand and helped me out of the taxi. "Just a small kitchen fire. They put it out right quick."

I shook him off and marched toward my house, toward the knot of firemen on my front path. As I got closer, one of them stepped in front of me.

"This is my house," I said. I made to move around him, but he put a hand on my shoulder, stopping me.

"Chief," he called to someone behind him. "Homeowner's here."

An official-looking man in a uniform approached and introduced himself to me.

"I want to see my house," I told him.

"I'm afraid I can't let you do that just yet," he said. "But as soon as it's safe, we'll let you inside. The worst of the damage occurred in the kitchen, which is where the fire originated. Fortunately, your neighbour noticed the smoke before the fire spread too far." The chief nodded toward Ben, who had followed me to the edge of the lawn.

Had I left the oven on? No. That was impossible. "How —" I started to say, but I couldn't continue. I couldn't get the words past the scorched air in my throat, where it felt like I had swallowed a mouthful of ash.

"We think it started in your range hood. Possibly a short circuit."

"I didn't use the range hood. Are you sure it wasn't the oven? I was baking …" My voice trailed off as I tried in vain to look past him, to look into my house, into the gaping hole where my front door used to be.

The chief followed my gaze. "We had to kick the door in," he said. "It's more common than you'd think — fires like this. I've seen fridge compressors burst into flame, even dishwashers that weren't running. If a wire short-circuits, it creates a spark, and something like a range hood, which collects a lot of grease, can ignite quickly. Like I said, though, the worst damage was contained to the kitchen. We got here pretty quick."

He said something else about smoke and water damage to the rest of the house, but I was hardly listening. His words were gibberish, swimming in the air around my head.

Ben suddenly appeared at my elbow. "Come on, Edith," he said. "Come and sit down for a minute. You're white as a sheet."

"I'm fine," I snapped.

"Go with your neighbour," the chief said gently. "You'll need to call your insurance company. You'll also need to find somewhere to stay until you're able to regain access."

I didn't have the strength to argue. Or to keep standing there in the cold without so much as a hat or gloves. I called my insurance company from the Kophers' kitchen. Then I called Danah. When she didn't answer, I left a message explaining about the fire and where she could find me. Two messages, actually. I called both her home number and the one for her cellphone, which I kept written down on a little card in my purse because it was so hard to remember.

NOW THAT SHE'S FINALLY here, Danah is full of questions. I say little while Ben fills her in. I'm tired of talking. Tired of all the fuss. Let him go over the details with her; he seems to enjoy it enough.

"How bad is it?" Danah asks, turning to me, her eyes wide.

"I don't know," I answer. "They wouldn't let me see it. I can't go inside until they've finished their air quality checks."

Danah accepts a cookie from the plate Alice holds out to her, then starts in about how awful she feels for not coming earlier, but she didn't know, she didn't get my message, her phone is dead, et cetera, et cetera. I wave away her excuses.

"I'll need somewhere to stay," I point out, since that small fact doesn't seem to have registered with her.

"Oh! You're not ..." She looks around the Kophers' living room, then seems to catch herself. "Of course. You can stay with me."

"Well, that beats being thrown out on the street." I shake my head when Alice passes in front of me with her store-bought cookies. I'm done sitting here. I want to be on my way.

"I'M SO SORRY I didn't get your message," Danah says again as we're driving to her apartment. "It's a good thing you weren't home when it happened."

"Is it? If I'd been home, I could have put it out myself without destroying the rest of the house."

"Maybe," Danah says, but she doesn't sound convinced. "Well, at least your neighbour saw the smoke. Thank goodness for that!"

I wonder how long she will feel the need to be so doggedly optimistic. "He only saw anything because he had to walk halfway down his front walk to get the newspaper. They used to bring it to the door, you know. Now they just throw it from the sidewalk."

I *am* grateful that Ben noticed the smoke when he did and that the fire was small enough to be put out quickly, but I wish he'd at least had the presence of mind to give the firemen my spare key. Then maybe they wouldn't have had to break down my front door.

It seems a small thing to think of, really.

I stare out the passenger window at the wet clumps of leaves clinging to the curb. It feels like at any moment I could dissolve into a similar soggy mess.

"At least we'll get to have a nice, long visit," Danah says suddenly in that falsely cheerful voice she has adopted over the last hour.

I snort. I'm in no mood for pretences. Ever since I stepped out of the taxi this morning and breathed in the pungent smell of smoke, I have been beset by the memory of another fire. Hardly a real fire, not like this one, but its memory is charged with emotions I have no interest in revisiting.

EDITH 🐏

THE BABY IS CRYING again. Edith is in the kitchen, doing her best to ignore Jane's cries so she can get the dishes done. She focuses her attention on the calm voice of the radio broadcaster as he delivers the twelve o'clock news: Buddhists in Vietnam are protesting the absence of free elections while the number of U.S. troops in Vietnam continues to rise. Jane's cries grow louder. Edith can't very well clean the kitchen with a baby crawling around, so she'll have to stay in her playpen whether she likes it or not. Edith reaches for her heavy ceramic mixing bowl and sets it carefully in the sink. She has a loaf of bread baking in the oven and fresh eggs (just collected from the henhouse that morning) boiling gently on the stove; yet, in spite of these not-so-trifling domestic feats, she knows she's barely keeping it together. She will not fall apart today. She doesn't have time to fall apart today.

She has just finished drying the bowl when from the other room Jane unleashes a sudden and panicked wail. Sucking in her breath, Edith tosses the dish towel onto the counter and marches into the living room to see what Jane's problem is now.

Jane is standing at the edge of the playpen, gripping the wooden bars with her chubby fingers; her face is smeared with tears and snot. She lifts her arms to Edith.

"I'm not picking you up," Edith says. "You're fine."

She looks around for something to wipe Jane's face with. Then, biting back her disgust, she rubs at the snot and tears with the hem of her apron. Jane is still snivelling, staring up at Edith with wide, beseeching eyes.

It's almost enough to make Edith relent.

"Play with your bunny," she says, bending over to pick up the stuffed toy from the floor of the playpen. "I can't keep running in here every three minutes to keep you company."

As she straightens, she smells something burning.

Rushing back to the kitchen, she discovers the dish towel she threw aside only a moment earlier has caught on fire. The edge of the cloth is resting against the gas burner where her eggs continue to boil innocently. She flings the dish towel into the sink and turns on the faucet. As she watches the water splash over the ruined towel, her tears finally begin to fall. Her entire body shudders.

Why did Frank have to go and leave her all alone to deal with everything? She's not cut out for motherhood. Eventually, she lifts her head and wipes her nose with the same apron she used to clean Jane's face. Enough is enough.

Besides, she still has lunch to make.

DANAH ❧

EDITH DOESN'T WANT TO talk about the fire; in fact, she doesn't seem to want to talk at all. She sits silently on my couch watching as I carry armfuls of stuff from my bedroom to the living room, where I dump it in a pile on the floor. I've stripped and remade the bed, put my dirty sheets in the wash, and set out a clean towel for her, all while she sits there motionless, following me with her eyes. The thought crosses my mind that she's gone into shock. I think I might be about to as well. Having Edith move in with me was definitely not on my agenda for today.

"We should eat," I say after removing the last of my things from my room.

"Where are you going to sleep?"

I pat the couch. "It's a pullout."

I've only slept on it once before when Trevor and I stayed up half the night watching *The Walking Dead*, snuggled in a cocoon of blankets. I remember the mattress being lumpy and uncomfortable. I don't mention any of that to Edith, though.

I don't have much to offer in the way of dinner, so I end up microwaving some leftover stir-fry that's been sitting in my fridge for three days.

It's strange having Edith in my apartment. I've always gone to her house, never the other way around. Now that she's here, I'm embarrassed by how messy my place is. I can only imagine what's going through her mind when she follows me to the kitchen and takes in the dirty coffee mugs littering the counter and the bowl with crusted-on cereal in the sink. Especially since I've never seen her house anything short of pristine.

I divide the stir-fry onto two plates while Edith stands in the doorway, watching. I wish I had some wine. I'm guessing that right about now both of us could use a drink.

When we sit down to eat, Edith eyes her plate suspiciously. "Are these mushrooms?" she says.

"You don't like mushrooms?" I swallow a mouthful of rice and red pepper. "This isn't hot enough, is it?" I set down my fork. "Do you want something else? Should I order a pizza?"

"This is fine. There's no need to get yourself all worked up. I'm not very hungry anyway."

We definitely need wine. I make a mental note to stop at the liquor store on my way home from campus tomorrow.

AFTER DINNER, WHILE MY phone is finally charging, I check my messages. There's a text from Trevor wishing me luck with my little "talk" then another asking if I'm home yet. I send him a quick reply letting him know that Edith is staying with me and promise to call him later with the details. I can hear Edith in the kitchen, washing dishes. I go in to stop her.

"You don't have to do those. Sit down, relax."

"I've been sitting all day."

I reach past her to pick up a tea towel.

"I'm fine in here," Edith says. "I'm sure you have other things to do."

I leave her to the dishes, but I can't settle, so I end up puttering around, giving the bathroom a quick once-over and making a half-hearted attempt at tidying the living room. When Edith finally sits down to watch *Jeopardy!*, I slip outside and call Trevor from the driveway. Within minutes, my hands are aching from the cold.

"How long is she staying?" Trevor asks.

I switch the phone to my left hand, stuffing my right in my pocket. "I don't know. Two weeks, maybe?" I close my eyes. "Or longer."

"Did you ask her about the letter?"

"Not yet. It seems kind of insensitive to bring it up right now, don't you think?" As much as I want to know the truth, I'm also relieved to have a reason to put off confronting her. I need time to think.

"Don't make excuses, Danah. You're never going to find out if you don't ask."

"I'm not making excuses. She just had a fire! I'm trying to be considerate. Besides, it's not like she's going anywhere."

I clomp back down the stairs and am blowing on my frozen fingers when Edith looks up from the television. "You don't have to sneak outside to make your phone calls, you know."

I nod. What's it to her? It's not her hands that have frostbite. "I have some work to do," I say. "Do you need anything? Like a toothbrush or something?"

"Alice took care of all that. I will have a cup of tea, though." She pauses. "And it would be nice if you joined me."

I can't afford to waste another entire evening, but I go into the kitchen to boil some water, convincing myself that I'll be able to make up for the lost time later.

VERY QUICKLY, I REALIZE how misguided my hopes of catching up are. The restoration company has started work at Edith's house, and she wants me to help her sort through all the stuff they moved into her garage. Normally, the restoration company would take care of every single item affected by a fire, but Edith, being Edith, insisted on cleaning almost everything herself. "I don't want a bunch of strangers touching my things," she told me. "What if they take something?"

"Grandma, they're professionals. They're not going to steal your stuff."

"How do you know that? I prefer to deal with it myself, thank you very much."

I have about a million reasons why I don't have time to help, but I can't exactly say no, given the circumstances. I call Trevor, hoping he'll feel sorry for me and agree to come too.

"I would, babe, but I can't today. I don't have time."

"Oh, and I do." I can't keep the sarcasm out of my voice.

"Danah, I have a meeting this afternoon. I can't just —"

"I know. I know. It's fine."

But it's not fine. It's not fine at all.

By the time I drive back to my apartment to pick up Edith, she's waiting for me outside, wearing a pair of loose-fitting pants that Alice must have lent her. I still have to go inside to change, so I don't know why she's standing there, guarding the door like that. I get that she's impatient to see her house, but seriously.

"Give me two minutes," I say. I brush past her, remembering my earlier plan to stop at the LCBO. Damn. How could I forget that, of all things?

THERE'S A RESTOREALL VAN taking up Edith's entire driveway, so I park on the street. The house doesn't look much different from the outside. The caution tape is gone, but the front door is still boarded up, and the windows are coated with a layer of smoke residue so thick they're a dark grey. Steve, the owner of the restoration company, meets us outside and leads us around to the side door by the kitchen.

"We've removed all the charred debris, essentially gutting your kitchen," Steve says. "We do that right away to help with the odour."

He's not kidding about the gutting part. The cupboards and the backsplash have been ripped out, leaving the drywall jagged and torn. The walls in the rest of the kitchen are stained a sickly black. Sections of the vinyl flooring have buckled — from the water damage, Steve explains — giving the floor a rippled appearance. I steal a glance at Edith's face, but if she's as shocked as I am, she doesn't show it.

"How long did you say it would take to fix everything?" I ask.

"Between two and three weeks. Depending on when the new cabinetry comes in. That sometimes holds us up."

Three weeks. Oh, God.

We move to the living room next. Like the kitchen, it's completely empty except for an air scrubber and a deodorization machine humming loudly in the middle of the floor. Steve is explaining the purpose of each piece of equipment, but Edith barely acknowledges him, so I try to look interested on her behalf.

The walls, the floor, the windows: everything is coated in a greasy grey film. I don't know what I was expecting, exactly, but it wasn't this. I mean, I knew the smoke and heat did damage throughout the house, but seeing Edith's normally spotless living room layered in grime is unnerving. Edith's expression never falters. She takes it all in with a steely indifference, although I know it must be horrifying, seeing her house like this, one ruined room after another.

"Since the door to the second bedroom was shut, that room was mostly spared," Steve says. "We'll still scrub the walls and repaint, but you'll notice the stuff you had in there was less affected by the smoke. It might have a bit of an odour to it, though."

Edith still hasn't said a word. We take a cursory look into the empty bedrooms, then follow Steve back through the remnants of the kitchen.

"Before you get started in the garage," he says, "I need to warn you that some things might not be salvageable. Any items that were damaged by heat won't respond to cleaning, and depending on the material, smoke residue can be impossible to remove." He takes us back outside, and we cross the few steps to the garage. "We've left out some dry sponges and a degreaser. Set aside anything that needs replacing, and we'll add it to the schedule of loss for your insurance adjuster."

I glance at Edith. I hope she's up for this. While I would never use the word *sentimental* to describe her, I also know how certain feelings can become confused with objects, until it's impossible to separate one from the other. Until the object becomes the emotion itself. Like the maracas on my dresser that I'll probably never throw out, even when the cracks get so wide, the seeds fall out.

Somehow, I doubt Edith will have the same problem.

WE WORK IN SILENCE. It's cold in the garage, and although the sun is shining, only a tiny sliver of light penetrates the narrow window in the back wall. It's depressing work, picking through boxes of smoke-smudged dishes, knick-knacks, and books, deciding what's worth the effort of cleaning and what should be tossed. I try to make my voice cheerful, but I give up on that when I start to sound annoying even to myself.

Although Edith doesn't have a lot of stuff — her small house has never seen clutter — the number of items spread out in her garage is overwhelming. In addition to all the boxes, there are pieces of furniture, a spoon collection, and a clock with intricate brass carvings that I don't know how Edith will ever get clean. Within five minutes, our clothes are filthy, and the ashy smell of smoke is making me sick.

Edith tells me to leave the few items from the spare bedroom: a wooden chest, a nightstand, a lamp. As Steve said, they appear mostly untouched by the smoke. They'll still need to be cleaned, but they aren't coated, like everything else, in an oily black residue.

"Start with one of the boxes," Edith says. "We might as well get through the worst of it now."

As I'm sifting through the contents of my second cardboard box, I come across a silver frame engraved with tiny roses. It's small enough to fit in the palm of my hand and has a photo in it of a young girl sitting on the same pink chair Edith still has now. I remember my dad lowering himself onto that chair the first time we met Edith after moving to Ontario. He looked so uncomfortable that day, sitting ramrod straight. The girl in this photo doesn't look too impressed either. She is poised on the brink of the chair, hands folded in her lap, unsmiling. Defiant.

"Who's this?" I ask, turning the picture toward Edith, who is scrubbing the cover of one of her *Reader's Digest* condensed books.

She pauses. She looks at the picture as if she's trying to remember who it could be. Then, turning back to the book in her hands, she says, "That's your mother." Her words are flat, but they tear right through my ribcage and into my heart.

First the letter. Now this. Although it's not really the picture that shocks me: it's the way Edith so casually mentions my mother.

I study the little girl on the chair. She doesn't bear any resemblance to the mother I remember. This girl's hair is pulled back tightly into two braids, whereas Mom's hair was always a tumble of loose brown curls. Then again, I have reconstructed her image so many times I'm not sure that anything I remember about her is real.

"I didn't realize you had — I've never seen this before," I say.

"It was in my bedroom."

What? Does she have other pictures? From when I knew my mother? From after she left us? I hesitate, wanting to say more, wanting Edith to say more. The air around me is charged, humming with a high, thin note of expectancy. Now that Edith has said the words *your mother* out loud, my mind spirals around the letter and the name Lily Wilder. I have to ask. This is the perfect moment to ask.

But I don't know how. I'm jarred by the realization that my mother exists outside of my own small world of memories. She has a whole history that Edith is part of, and it's not inconceivable — a thought I would have dismissed outright a week ago — that they're still in contact. That they have been all along.

"Do you —" I fumble. "Are you still in touch with her?"

"With your mother? No." Edith seems to weigh her next words, and I wonder if she's about to finally reveal an intimate detail, something about my mother I can grab hold of.

I lean toward her.

Edith rests the book she's holding in her lap. She looks straight into my eyes. "I haven't heard from her in a long, long time, Danah."

I take a deep breath. So, I'm wrong about the letter then. Lily Wilder, whoever she is, has nothing to do with my mother.

I look down at the photo, at the challenging set of the little girl's chin, and try to imagine that determined young face growing into my mother's tired one. And I wonder why Edith kept this particular photo squirrelled away in her bedroom, never once sharing it with me, the one person she must have known would be dying to see it.

I don't say anything else, but as I watch Edith return to cleaning the book in her lap, I want to scream, "What else are you hiding?"

JANE LILY 🐦

I AM MUCH MORE open with Niall now than I was at the beginning. He must have thought I was a pain in the butt those first few times we met when I sat across from him and refused to cooperate.

"I don't really see the point in this," I told him during our very first meeting. He leaned back in his chair and waited. I wanted a justification for his exercise, so I waited too.

He tried a different approach. "You said your mother tolerated you. What did you mean by that?"

"I don't have much interest in rehashing my childhood. Trust me, it's not going to help." I considered standing up and just walking out. What would he make of that? Nobody would blame me if I decided these sessions were a waste of time. I could go to the shop downstairs and treat myself to an obnoxiously expensive box of dark chocolates.

"Facing the past can give you the strength to face the future," Niall said, and I fought the urge to roll my eyes. "Tell me about your mother."

"She suffered many disappointments. I was one of them."

Already I could feel the first flickers of a headache approaching. A sort of strumming at the base of my skull.

Finally, resigned, or maybe just bored with my recalcitrance, he said, "Okay, then tell me about the letters."

EDITH ✒

WHILE I AM GRATEFUL for Danah's help, this whole sorry process of sifting through my belongings is not something I particularly want to share with anyone else. Not even Danah. Having the entirety of my private life spilled across the garage floor is like wandering around in public wearing my nightgown. Worse, as we work, Danah asks one question after another. Every time she picks up something she doesn't recognize, she wants to discuss it.

"Who's this?" she asks, holding up a photo for me to see.

I answer as levelly as possible, unwilling to attach much significance to the photograph itself or to the unspoken past it represents. "That's your mother," I tell her flatly. But when Danah's voice falters afterward, I can hear how much that simple acknowledgement has shaken her.

She doesn't stop there. She wants to know if we're still in touch. What good would it do for her to know? I brush off her question, but seeing that photo in Danah's hands, admitting the fact of Jane's existence out loud — that has shaken me too. I am surprised at the clarity with which I can remember the day that photo was taken. I do not normally make it a habit to dwell on the past, so for it to exist somewhere in my mind in such vivid detail seems an unnecessary waste. But there it is, all the same, and behind that memory are a thousand more, all jostling for a spot at the front of the line.

JANE LILY 🦚

JANE'S DIRTY FACE IS pressed up against the wire mesh of the chicken coop; her little fists clench and unclench. Inside the coop, the hens are running in crazed circles, clucking madly. The rooster is chasing them, and they can't get away. Feathers fly through the air, and Jane's heart beats wildly with every frantic flap of their wings. *They need to get out*, she thinks, beginning to panic herself.

She moves to the little hinged door near the ground and unfastens the latch. She swings the door open. At first, the hens rush unseeing right past their chance at freedom. Then, one hen pauses long enough to stick her head out. She runs free, and the others follow.

Jane steps back and watches them escape. She did this. She saved them. She claps her hands and twirls in the yard.

Mid-spin, she hears a door banging shut. She looks toward the house and sees her mother flying across the grass toward her. Jane's joy vanishes as she watches her mother's angry face come closer. Even the chickens begin to scuttle away.

"What are you doing?" her mother shrieks. "You can't let them out! What's wrong with you?"

Tears sting Jane's eyes. She was only trying to help.

THE CHICKENS ARE BACK where they belong, and Jane is upstairs, lying face down on her bed. She has been sent to her room without dinner. The unfairness of her punishment burns.

There is a knock on her bedroom door. Jane doesn't answer, but her mother walks in anyway. "You may have some dinner now, Jane. If you're sorry for what you did."

Jane's stomach growls. "I don't want dinner." She turns her back to her mother. "And I'm not sorry."

She hears her mother's footsteps stomp away. Lifting her head, she peeks toward the hall to make sure she's alone. Then, carefully, trying not to make any noise, she climbs down from the bed and pushes her bedroom door closed again. Maybe she'll stay in here forever. Then her mom will be sorry.

IN THE MORNING, HER mother calls up the stairs, "Jane, come down and have your breakfast. Mr. Cressman will be here soon."

Jane wants to protest. She's not coming out. Ever. But the smell of food is enough to lure her to the kitchen table, where her plate is already set out with two strips of bacon, scrambled eggs, and a thick slice of homemade bread.

"I imagine you're hungry," her mother says.

Jane doesn't answer.

"When you're done, I want you to put on the dress I laid out. Then, bring me the comb so I can braid your hair."

"Why do we have to get our pictures taken anyway?"

"You know why. Uncle Pieter wants a family portrait. Mr. Cressman will come here to do our photos, then when he's done the other families, we'll join the rest of them for a group picture."

Jane sulks as her mother tugs at her hair. She doesn't want her picture taken. She wants to hide in her room and pretend she's someone else. A girl with two parents who love her. When Mr. Cressman asks her to smile after positioning her to his liking in the pink chair, she shakes her head.

"I'm too sad to smile," she says. She looks pointedly at her mother.

Edith ignores her. "Just take the photo," she tells Mr. Cressman.

DANAH ✀

EDITH AND I CONTINUE to work in uncomfortable silence. Neither of us mentions what just happened. Me, because I don't know what to say, or because I'm scared, or maybe because I'm still trying to process the fact that we have finally acknowledged the reality of my missing mother. I can only guess why Edith is so quiet. Is she as surprised as I am by the words that slipped out of her mouth?

Eventually, I suggest we stop and save the rest of the sorting and cleaning for tomorrow. I'm too wound up to keep sitting on the cold floor pretending nothing out of the ordinary has just passed between us.

I bring Edith back to my apartment, along with a box of books she wants to finish going through. I don't stick around. I stay long enough to shower, scrubbing the grime off my skin and out of my hair. My clothes are likely ruined, smeared with black stains that I doubt will ever come out. Even though my mind is swirling with questions, I leave Edith by herself and head back to campus.

My office on the sixth floor of Kenneth Taylor Hall is mercifully empty. There are four of us who share this room, but apart from our mandatory office hours, no one really spends much time here, other than Taryn, although she hardly counts as normal. Her desk is decorated with mini Christmas lights, for Christ's sake. Year-round. That alone says something.

I pull out the student papers I've neglected for the past two days. Norms of reciprocity, functionalist perspectives, intersubjectivity. The words float before my eyes, but all I can think of is that somehow, in some weird way, my grandmother is still connected to my mother. The photo of her as a little girl obviously has nothing to do with the letter I saw, but it's strange that after years of nothing, not a word, suddenly the name Lily and a photo of my mother both crop up within days of each other. It's as if my mother's presence has been lurking all this time, undetected, right under my nose. And something isn't right. Edith made it sound like she hadn't heard from my mother in years, but I'm not convinced I believe her.

There's no way I'm going to be able to concentrate, especially on the incoherent arguments of undergrads trying to make sense of social theory, so I give up on marking and text Trevor to see what he's doing.

He doesn't reply, which means he's probably turned off his phone. He has the annoying habit of doing that when he's working. I consider popping up to the seventh floor to see if he's in his office, but before I make up my mind, Navi floats into the room.

She's the only person I actually like in our shared office, although I haven't seen much of her lately. It's as if all the second-year Ph.D. candidates have gone into hiding these last few weeks. Navi's convinced she's going to be kicked out of the program after her first comp. I'd never admit it, but I'm nervous too. Not about getting kicked out, but about not living up to people's expectations.

"Well, well, well. Fancy meeting you here," Navi says, dropping her bag onto a chair. "I haven't seen you in ages. What's new, girl?"

Where do I start? I decide to keep things simple. "My grandmother's house almost burned down yesterday, so now she's staying with me. Which is just awesome."

Navi makes a face. "Ugh. Like that's what you need right now. I basically told my family to fuck off until after my comps. Then they can talk to me again. And feed me comfort food while I drown my sorrows in a bottle of vodka."

I consider telling Navi about the photo and the letter, but then I'd have to explain my whole life story to her, and, as much as I like her, we're not that close. What I really want is for Trevor to turn on his damn phone.

Navi keeps talking. "So, you must be excited about the Arthur Williams thing. I can't believe you're going to get to hang out with him! I should've joined the committee."

"No, you shouldn't have. It's a crap-load of extra work. You would hate it."

I start packing up my things, as if I can trick myself into believing I'm being productive by giving in to the urge to move. That and I can't make small talk right now. I'm too confused.

I pull the hood of my coat tightly around my face as I make my way across campus. It's not even five o'clock, but already it's dark. I step carefully around the puddles that line the path and consider how much I'm dreading hanging out with Edith. I can predict how the evening is going to unfold, weighted with more stubborn silence as we both grapple with the aftermath of the stupid fucking fire.

EDITH MAKES US OMELETS for dinner, and, surprise, surprise, we actually manage to have a somewhat normal conversation while we eat. She asks how the rest of my afternoon went, and I pretend that I got a lot done. I ask what she did, and she says she read a book that Alice lent her. We're both enjoying a glass of red wine with our omelets since I made damn sure to stop on my way home this time. I grabbed a bottle of rye too for good measure.

When we're done eating, she waves away my offer to help clean up. While she's in the kitchen, I pull out my study notes. I skim through them, trying to find the spot where I left off in the library, strangely comforted by the sound of someone else washing my dishes. And by the full glass of wine on the table beside me.

Edith rejoins me in the living room and picks up her book. We sit for a while, both of us reading, until she retreats to the bedroom. I have no idea what she's doing in there, but I'm happy enough to be alone. So far, just as I predicted, we've managed to neatly side-step the elephant in the room: the grown-up version of a little girl sulking in a pink chair.

I LIE AWAKE FOR a long time on the lumpy pullout trying to recon-cile the grandmother who keeps a picture of her daughter in her bedroom with the grandmother who has never once mentioned her daughter to me. The living room is cold, and something in the kitchen — the fridge? — is making a constant humming and click-ing noise. Has it always made that sound? I try to distract myself by picturing Edith's bedroom in her bungalow and imagining where the photo was. I've only ever been in her bedroom once, so it's hard to summon up the specifics. All I remember is that it was unnaturally neat. The bedspread was pulled perfectly flat, and her slippers were lined up with military precision. I go over each piece of furniture in my mind, trying to recall any picture frames at all. Was it on her dresser? It had to have been on display or it wouldn't have been gathered up with the rest of the stuff to clean. No matter how hard I try, I can't place that silver frame anywhere.

It's strange to think of my mother as a kid, living with Edith. What was it like for her, having Edith as a mother? When I finally drift to sleep, my thoughts return to my own childhood, where they circle around the memory of another little girl, fervently praying for her mom to come home.

DANAH 🐑

DANAH AND HER BEST friend, Penny, are singing as they skip down the sidewalk. *Step on a crack, break your mother's back.* When Penny's foot accidentally lands on a gap between the squares, they both laugh, although the thought of hurting her mother makes Danah nervous. She avoids even the tiniest cracks, just in case.

She promises Penny as they turn onto their street that she'll come right back out if she's allowed. And it is this thought that consumes her as she climbs the steps to her front porch.

The door is locked, which is strange. Danah knocks, then stands with her hands dangling at her sides. She feels funny standing there, as if she is visiting someone else's house. After a few minutes, she rings the doorbell. Still nothing. Finally, she heads to the back of the house and tries the door there, which, thank goodness, isn't locked. She lets herself in, but right away she is aware of a strange stillness, as if the house is holding its breath.

"Hello?" she calls out. "Mom?" She takes off her shoes and carries them in her hand. "Mom? Where are you?"

As Danah slips through the empty rooms, her heart begins to pound. The air around her is thick and still. The house feels unfamiliar, the rooms bigger, everything a distorted version of itself. She doesn't trust the walls, as if they might reach out and touch her when she's not looking.

"Mom?"

Danah steps into her shoes, flattening the backs of them under her heels. Her mom hates when she does that. She unlocks the front door and runs down the porch steps, letting the screen door slam behind her. Penny and her brother, Ryan, are already outside, playing with sidewalk chalk. Danah walks toward them, her panic melting with each step.

"I can't go biking," she tells Penny. "My mom's not home."

"Let's do hopscotch then."

Ryan draws a chalk circle around an ant. Every time the ant leaves the circle, he draws a new one.

"You can't play with us," Penny says to him, but he doesn't even look up.

"Come on," Danah says. "Let's go over here." She takes Penny's arm and leads her further away from Ryan, further away from her own strange and silent house.

A little more than an hour later, just as Penny and Ryan are being called inside, Danah's father pulls up in his dark blue sedan. Danah runs to meet him as he climbs out of the car.

"Hey, Squirt! What have you been you up to? Look at you, you're filthy!"

Danah follows him to the front door, and immediately her uneasiness returns. It's as though the house has swallowed her mother. She thinks back to her game of jumping over cracks on her way home from school. Did she miss one? Is *she* the reason her mother is gone? Something hot and wobbly settles in the bottom of her stomach.

"Any idea what Mom's making for dinner tonight?" her dad asks as he reaches for the door handle.

"She's not home," Danah says. She can't look at him when she says it.

"Not home? Where did she go?"

The windows on the house are watching Danah, like eyes. "I don't know," she whispers.

"That's strange," her father says, more to himself than to her. "Let's go inside and see what's going on."

Later, after he's ordered pizza and made countless phone calls, he takes her in his arms and hugs her tightly. "Well, sweetie, it looks like it's just you and me tonight."

"How come? Where did Mommy go?" Danah asks, snuggling against her father's warm body.

"She's gone away for a bit."

AS DANAH LIES IN bed that night, pressing her stuffed monkey to her cheek, some of the house's earlier strangeness creeps into her room. She focuses on the thin strip of light from the hall and the sound of her father's voice, a low murmur drifting to her from the kitchen. She buries her face into the monkey's soft body. Her lips barely move as she pleads again and again: "Mommy, please come home."

JANE LILY 🌱

I HAVE TRIED, MORE than once, to explain to Niall my need for escape. He always listens patiently, one eyebrow raised slightly, as I ramble on. When I apologize for not making any sense, he reassures me that this is exactly the sort of thing he wants me to talk about.

"The more you say, Lily, the more we'll both understand," he reminds me, over and over.

I imagine that the whole business of us meeting to talk about my life must seem rather futile to him. It certainly does to me.

"Have you ever felt what it is to shed a skin?" I asked him once. "To crawl out from under yourself? There's a certain thrill to starting over." He nodded at me to continue — he knew better than to interrupt anything that had the potential to turn into a revelation. But that was all I had to say. Every time I tried to explain the unrelenting urge to run away, the *why* of it, I came up short. I sounded pathetic.

I never talked to him about what came after that thrill. I didn't mention the uncomfortable knowledge that all the resulting lightness of starting over was, at least for me, temporary. That I had known all along how the weight of life would return, pushing me back into the mud, where I would struggle and gasp until finally all I could think about, all I could concentrate on, was that sweet feeling of escape.

I AM GOOD AT leaving. I know how to disappear. Like water through a sieve of silk, I slip away. Surely those around me must see it coming? Must sense its inevitability as my presence grows fainter. Before I am gone.

EDITH 🐦

EDITH DIDN'T SEE IT coming. She never for a minute imagined Jane would up and leave the way she did. No explanation. No goodbye. At seventeen, Jane is as headstrong as they come, but still Edith is as shocked as everyone else in Missionville by her daughter's nerve.

On the heels of her disbelief comes annoyance. Whenever Jane decides to come slinking back, Edith plans to drill some sense into her. But as days go by, Edith's irritation cools to resignation. After a full week, the women in her church set up a prayer chain. The minister visits. Everyone is praying for Jane, Reverend Thompson assures her, and for Edith too. She is reminded to rely on God and to trust in His infinite wisdom. She has been reminded of that before, when Frank died, and she doesn't remember it helping much. A different minister sat across from her then, in this same kitchen, offering the same empty platitudes about God and His plan and learning to accept His will.

She's had enough of His will, thank you very much.

Now, as she sits with her back straight and listens politely to Reverend Thompson droning on about lost sheep, she can't help but notice how his left eye twitches. He expounds on what lengths a shepherd will go to in order to return even one sheep to the fold.

He pauses. His eye twitches. Edith isn't interested in parables right now. She always thought that shepherd was a fool anyway. She has no intention of going looking for Jane, but if God wants to abandon the rest of His flock to bring her home, she will leave Him to it. And when Jane does come back, it had better be with her tail between her legs.

After two weeks with no word — Jane could be dead in a ditch for all Edith knows — she finally receives a letter. She opens the envelope with determined fingers. She knows who it's from, even though there's no return address; she recognizes Jane's lazy handwriting.

The message is short. Jane's fine. She has no plans to return. She won't say where she is, but after years of working at the post office, Edith knows how to read a postmark. The letter was mailed in Vancouver.

So. All the way across the county, then. Jane may as well be on the other side of the moon.

Edith takes the broom down from its peg behind the kitchen door. She sweeps the floor with hard, angry strokes. Then, still dissatisfied, she fills a bucket with bleach and hot water, pulls on a pair of yellow rubber gloves, and gets down on her hands and knees to scrub. The kitchen floor slopes slightly to one side, a fact that has bothered Edith since the day she moved in to this farmhouse. As she scours the worn wood, she curses Frank, then Jane, and God too, for good measure. What did she do to deserve any of this?

EDITH IS SITTING AT the kitchen table while the minister's wife stares at her with wide, concerned eyes.

"Are you well, Edith? I noticed you weren't at church this morning." Evelyn Thompson's brow is creased, and drops of perspiration are forming at her hairline. "I brought you some blueberries." She points to the small bowl of berries sitting on the table in front of them, as if Edith might not have noticed them otherwise.

"Thank you," Edith replies. What does she want with blueberries? Perhaps she'll bake them into some muffins for Lucy Knaverly, who just delivered twin boys not too long ago. Edith can imagine how tired that poor woman must be. Can remember, actually, the exhaustion that seeps into your bones after a birth like that.

The minister's wife is still studying her, no doubt preparing a report for her husband. If Edith doesn't start attending church services again, she supposes Reverend Thompson will consider *her* a lost sheep, and the thought almost makes her laugh out loud.

"You make sure you take care of yourself, Edith," Evelyn is saying. "Let us know if there's anything we can do. Anything at all."

Her daughter has run away, has cut off ties, but she's not dead. Edith doesn't understand why everyone feels the need to act as if this one thing, her daughter disappearing, must be nearly unendurable. But still, she must face facts: Jane is gone. And ever since she left, the empty rooms in the farmhouse have echoed with her absence.

THE FORMERLY NEAT ROWS of the garden are overgrown and choked with weeds. Sugar snap peas poke their way through the middle of the tomato plants, wrapping themselves around the vines as they climb toward the sun. The spinach has wilted and is turning a sickly brown. Edith sees it but can't bring herself to care.

Frank's brother Case mentions it to her once, casually, but she supposes the state of her garden isn't really what he's concerned about.

"It's a cryin' shame," he says. "All that produce going to waste."

She shrugs. "You're welcome to it." Her carelessness in the garden probably offends his sensibilities as a farmer. Or maybe his gentle reproach is designed to stir her into action, summon some life back into her limbs.

"Margaret was wondering if you planned on doing any baking this week. She wouldn't mind making some of those puff pastry things with you. Says she can't get them right on her own." Case is looking at her expectantly, waiting for a reply he can take back to his wife.

Margaret was probably the one who mentioned the garden to Case, wondering if he had noticed how Edith had let it go. Told him to check in on her, like a good brother-in-law. "I'll let her know," Edith finally answers.

Case seems satisfied and turns to go. Then, swinging around to face Edith again, he says, "If you need something, just ask. You know that."

Jane has been gone for almost a month. The grey farmhouse, with its worn floorboards and leaning walls, swells with a heavy silence that bores into Edith's skull. She could no more make puff pastries than get on a table and do the Twist. She can hardly get out of bed, for Pete's sake. She knows Margaret means well, but she isn't up for baking. Or gardening. Or talking, for that matter, to people who want to know how she's doing. She just wants to be left alone.

It's ridiculous, this despair over her daughter. She has scoffed at other people's solicitous attention, chiding them for acting as if Jane is dead. But isn't she herself acting like this is one more death to mourn? Sitting down to another solitary meal after her conversation with Case, Edith thinks back to the all the silent meals she shared with her daughter. All those wasted moments when Jane was sitting right across from her. Now the empty chair on the other side of the table mocks her. It was like this after Frank died too. The aching sense of emptiness in all the spaces he used to occupy.

EDITH SITS IN HER wooden pew, her eyes dutifully closed while Reverend Thompson beseeches the Lord once again to bless the

Knaverly family and their beautiful twins that were such an unexpected gift from God. She gives an involuntary snort. By the time Reverend Thompson is done praying, she has made up her mind that this Sunday will be her last at Missionville Baptist. If God suddenly decides to start answering her prayers, He can jolly well come and find her, but until then, she's sure He has enough other sad people to keep Him busy.

After church, she shakes hands with the minister and his wife, already contemplating what ingredients she has on hand for baking. She *will* make something this afternoon. Nothing so frivolous as pastry puffs; something more substantial. Oatmeal raisin cookies, perhaps.

"How *are* you?" Evelyn Thompson says, pressing Edith's hand firmly between hers. Her eyes are wide and sincere, but they flicker ever so slightly to the next person in line, and Edith understands the question is all part of an act: the caring, concerned minister's wife.

"Fine, thank you," she replies. "A lovely sermon," she says, turning to the minister, who bows his thanks and squeezes her hand gently before shifting his attention to the next parishioner.

Edith makes her way to the parking lot without talking to anyone else and considers how easy it would be to leave Missionville. Frank's brothers would happily see her out of the farmhouse — Case's oldest, Stuart, is ready for a place of his own — and there's really no reason for her to stay now. In fact, the more she thinks about leaving, the more she is convinced that that's what she's going to do. She will talk to Case and Pieter about it tonight, and then she will begin looking for somewhere else to live.

She is done with wallowing. She will shake off the farm and all its ghosts, and in doing so, she will shake off the loneliness that has crept into her bones. She takes a long breath, pulling the heavy air deep into her lungs, feeling her spine straighten with purposeful resolve.

First, she will make cookies. Then, she will start making plans.

EDITH REARRANGES THE SUPPLIES on her small section of counter at the post office. She has worked here since she was seventeen, the same age Jane is now.

"Are you sure you want to do this?" Mary Tuttle asks.

"I'll hardly be able to drive in from Hamilton," Edith responds. "Besides, I'm not taking the truck. It's staying with the farm."

"We'll miss you here." Mary's eyes fill with sympathy. It's exactly that look that made Edith so anxious to leave Missionville in the first place. She's just given her notice at the post office, and in less than a month, she will pull herself up by the roots completely and transplant herself in Hamilton. There's nothing here for her anymore.

Her brother Ephraim left years ago. The rest of her family lives scattered in and around Kingston or else on the other side of the world — her youngest sister moved all the way to Australia after meeting her husband on a mission trip to Ecuador. Apart from Frank's family, she has no ties to Missionville. And now that Jane's gone, she has no reason to stay.

PACKING UP THE FARMHOUSE is harder than she expected. She didn't realize how many memories would be disturbed as she emptied drawers and sorted through the closets and cupboards. They fly up like dust, these memories, and by the end of the day she is exhausted — not from the physical exertion of packing but from keeping her emotions at bay.

Frank's nightstand drawer still holds his watch. Why on earth did she leave it there? Picking it up now, feeling the thin leather strap brush against the skin of her palm, she remembers setting it aside the day she boxed up every other reminder of her husband. For a while, she kept it on her own nightstand when she slept. Sometimes she would reach for it in the night, hold it near her ear, listen to its steady ticking.

Edith doesn't linger over the watch. She wraps it in newspaper and places it in the wooden chest along with the other memories she has buried in there. She does the same with Jane's school photos, the books from her bedroom, even some of her clothes. Into the wooden chest they go. If Jane changes her mind and comes back, at least a few of her things will be waiting for her. But there's no need for any of that stuff to be on display. She won't unpack this chest once it's moved either. Some things are better left undisturbed.

She keeps out just one photo: Jane as a young girl, only six, sitting in the pink chair with her chin up, defying the world. There's something in Jane's expression she wants to remember. She tucks that photo, in its little silver frame, into one of the boxes destined for her new bedroom.

DANAH ◆

I WAKE UP TO the sound of cupboards slamming and dishes rattling in the kitchen. Edith is up and apparently not too concerned about the fact that I might actually be trying to sleep.

I sit up slowly and rub my neck. I shouldn't have given Edith my good pillow. I spend a few seconds daydreaming about Trevor's soft bed and his quiet apartment. What I wouldn't give to be waking up there right now.

Edith must hear me moving because while I'm still rubbing my neck, she pokes her head into the living room. "Oh good, you're awake. Where do you keep that herbal tea we had the other night? I can't find it anywhere."

"It's on top of the microwave."

"I don't see it."

I exhale slowly. "It's in a blue box. Beside the sugar."

I head to the bathroom and splash cold water on my face, trying to suppress the annoyance already simmering beneath my skin.

As soon as I step out of the bathroom, Edith is on me. "If you'd fold up your blankets and put the bed back to a couch, we'd have somewhere to sit. We don't have to keep this set up all day, do we?"

"Grandma, I just got up."

"Well, you left it like this all day yesterday too."

Jaw clenched, I gather the blankets and carry them to my bedroom, where Edith has, of course, already made her bed. I return to the living room and obediently fold up the pullout while my grandmother watches from the kitchen doorway. Forget herbal tea, I'm going to need coffee. Preferably with a shot of vodka and some Kahlua mixed in.

"There, that's better, isn't it?" Edith asks as I replace the final cushions. "What are we having for breakfast, then?"

"Honestly, I usually just have cereal," I reply. Then, when she doesn't say anything, I add, "But you can have whatever you want." I drag the coffee table across the floor and back into place in front of the couch. That should keep her happy.

"I thought I might make pancakes for us."

"I have to be on campus early, so I'm just going to eat something quick. But you can make pancakes. For you. If you want."

Edith sighs. "I'll have toast, then."

I don't actually need to be on campus until this afternoon, but I figure that what Edith doesn't know won't hurt her.

"WHAT MAKES YOU THINK she's lying?" Trevor asks. We've just finished grabbing a quick lunch in the Student Centre, and we're walking back to Kenneth Taylor Hall, both of us clutching a hot cup of coffee.

"I don't know. It's stupid. Something in her face when I asked about my mom, like there was more she wanted to say but then decided not to."

We arrive at the sociology building, and Trevor goes in ahead of me. He doesn't bow theatrically or hold the door open. Not that I'd want him to. But still.

He heads to the elevators while I turn toward the stairs to the basement. "We can talk more after your tutorial," he says.

"I have office hours," I remind him. "You know where to find me."

Today's tutorial group is even more lethargic than Tuesday's. There's one girl in the front who doesn't even try to hide the fact that she's yawning. I consider targeting her with a question to see if it will make her sit up and pay attention, then decide to ignore her. Looking around, I'm fairly certain no one wants to be here, including me.

I wrap up my summary of alienated labour — a theme that runs through all of Karl Marx's contributions to sociology — then say, "Unless anyone has any questions, we're pretty much done here."

The bored girl in the front actually raises her hand. "Is there such a thing as alienated education? Like where what people have to learn is imposed on them by others?"

It's an interesting question, but I know what she's trying to do, and I'm not in the mood for a debate. "Marx never extended his theory to education; however, I'm sure you could draw that parallel. It sounds like you already have."

She raises her eyebrows, but as the people around her close their notebooks, it's clear the tutorial is over. I gather my own things, and when the last person has left, I turn off the lights and leave the musty room behind.

No one shows up during my office hours. They hardly ever do unless it's to complain. Usually about something I've marked. Then they come, sometimes full of indignation, other times teary with disbelief or confusion, aiming, I assume, to make me feel sorry for them.

Taryn's stupid Christmas lights are on, so I know she must be somewhere in the building. I hope she doesn't come back while I'm still here.

I'm about to text Trevor when suddenly he appears at the door, poking his head in with a smile.

"You alone?" he asks.

I gesture to the empty office. "Just me and the Christmas ghost of Taryn."

He walks in and shuts the door. He plops down in Taryn's chair and swivels toward me. "So, I've been thinking. If you really believe that your grandmother is keeping something from you, and you want to know what it is, you need to be more direct. Ask her straight-up what she's not telling you."

He leans back, clearly pleased with himself. For a smart guy, his advice strikes me as pretty dumb. "It's not that easy," I say.

"Why not?"

"It's just not."

Trevor gives me a look, but before I can explain, the office door swings open.

"Sorry, am I interrupting?" Taryn asks.

Trevor stands up. "Nope. I was just on my way out."

I offer Taryn a fake smile and pretend to be preoccupied with the Oxford edition of *Social Problems*, which is propped open in front of me. After fifteen minutes of mock reading, I stuff my things in my bag. Taryn barely glances up as I make my exit.

In the hall, I pass Professor Stone. He nods to acknowledge me, and as I return the greeting, I think about all those papers I still have to mark.

Shit.

Shit shit shit.

EDITH ❧

I'M DOING MY BEST to ignore the mess in Danah's apartment. She has piles scattered all over the place. When she cleared out her bedroom for me, she dropped everything in the living room, where it looks for all intents and purposes like she plans to leave it. A pile of clothing draped over a chair, two pairs of shoes next to the TV, odds and ends from her dresser carelessly dropped onto an end table. I don't know how she can stand it: the disorder, the confusion.

It's not just her apartment that's chaotic. Over the past two days, she's practically made me dizzy with all her comings and goings. Always in a hurry. When she comes in, she tosses her coat on the back of the couch, never mind the perfectly good closet right beside the door. I had no idea she lived like this. When she came to my house, she always hung up her coat.

Watching her, it's as if time is bending, looping me back to the farmhouse in Missionville. To Jane — just before she ran away. All those hurried entrances and exits. That last summer, Jane was forever taking off for one thing or another, throwing an explanation at me over her shoulder. I could put it down to age, but I am quite sure I never flitted about like that when I was younger.

My mother never would have tolerated such reckless energy. Jane. Jane. Jane. Over the past few days, I have been beset by disturbing flashes of memory. Just this morning, I experienced a blinding sense of déjà vu when Danah gulped down her cereal at the table while I stood in the kitchen, five feet away, yet altogether separate. I felt, in that moment, the same emotional impotence of so many other meals fraught with a tension I never understood, staring at a daughter I didn't know at all.

Jane had a way of making eating look painful, as if the very act of swallowing was an ordeal. It got to the point where we rarely had meals together, which was something else my own mother never would have allowed. But then, she was cut out for the business of mothering. She raised the six of us without batting an eye. If she had lived long enough to see the mess I made out of raising just one, she would have snorted in disgust, her eyebrows knitted in disapproval. And if she saw, in turn, what kind of mother Jane turned out to be, I'm quite sure she would have rolled her eyes in my direction as if to say, "See what you've done?"

No doubt she would have had a Bible verse for me to contemplate. Or to hang above my bed.

But it's not my fault — how can it be? — that Jane failed her own daughter so miserably. So why is my mind suddenly preoccupied with memories that serve no purpose other than to inflict pain? Hasn't there been enough of that?

EVER SINCE DANAH HIGHTAILED it out of here the minute her cereal bowl was empty, I've been sitting in her dark apartment itching with nerves. I have to do something, so I start with the kitchen. I pull everything out of the cupboards and stack it on the table in the living room. When I run out of room there, I begin piling things on the floor. Then I attack the bare shelves with a pot of hot, soapy water. I scrub the inside of the microwave too, until every dried-on splatter is obliterated.

When the cupboards are dry, I restock them carefully, lining up the boxes of cereal and crackers and Kraft Dinner. (How can Danah stomach that stuff?) I arrange the canned goods with all the labels facing outward, so you can see them. I relocate the tea and the sugar to the cupboard directly above the kettle, and I place Danah's collection of mismatched mugs in the cupboard beside that, handles to the left. What is it about being practical that people find so difficult?

When every surface in the kitchen has been scoured and every last item neatly put in its place, I breathe a sigh of satisfaction. I'll hit the bathroom next, with a bottle a vinegar and some baking soda. It's too bad about the rest of the apartment, although I do make an attempt to tidy some of the piles and to at least line up the stacks of books on her coffee table. I'd love to clear it all away, to empty her living room of all that clutter. Then maybe I could relax.

Instead, I settle for straightening the pillows on the couch. My mind is restless, and if I don't keep busy, I'm afraid of where my thoughts might go. I should bake something. Yes, that's what I'll do. Especially now that the kitchen has been put to rights.

I know just the thing to make too: lemon-ginger muffins. I remember Aunt Sybiel telling me, "Edith, my dear, lemon-ginger muffins are the staple of a happy home. I've never met a man who had room for anger after filling his stomach on them." I'm pretty sure she gave the recipe out with that piece of marriage advice to every woman she knew. By the time I was thirteen, I could make those muffins better than Aunt Sybiel, and she promised me that that fact boded well for a long and happy marriage. Ha! As it turned out, even perfectly executed lemon-ginger muffins were no match for God's will.

My aunt may have been dead wrong about me having a long and happy marriage, but there is no denying that with a hot cup of tea, lemon and ginger can calm even the most anxious stomach.

I do know that much for a fact. And sitting here, trapped in this dark and cluttered apartment, I want calming.

What I really want, if I'm honest about it, is for Danah to come home so we can finish dealing with the rest of my stuff. It's all well and good for me to spend my time scrubbing her apartment, but at the same time, I'm acutely aware of the dishes and lamps and other bits and pieces still sitting on my garage floor. Does Danah think those things are going to clean themselves?

I don't need to wait for Danah, though, to find a grocery store. There must be something within walking distance.

The temperature outside has dropped since Tuesday, and the sharp wind makes my eyes water. I should have worn a scarf, but the hat and gloves I found in Danah's front closet will have to do. I tuck my chin into the collar of my coat and set off down Danah's street at a brisk pace. The houses here are crowded close together with narrow driveways and small front yards. It's a quiet street, at least, with lots of trees, their empty winter branches arching like skeletons over the sidewalk. There are a few half-hearted attempts at Christmas decorations, but it's not like some of the neighbourhoods I've passed through where the houses are decked out to kingdom come with lights and candy canes and giant inflatable snowmen. In my opinion, a simple wreath ought to be sufficient.

At the end of Danah's street, I turn right. This road has a steady stream of traffic, and I can see a set of lights a few blocks ahead. I make my way toward that intersection, and as I approach, I note with satisfaction that there's a Foodland on the corner opposite to me. I just hope it has a decent produce section with serviceable ginger.

While I wait for the light to change, I glance around. I'm standing beside a weed-filled lot that is littered with plastic bags and Styrofoam cups. A chain-link fence separates the empty parcel of land from the parking lot of a pharmacy. Why does the city let things like this go? It wouldn't take much, surely, to clean up this small patch of garbage and dirt and weeds.

Two figures huddle against the chain-link fence. They're not wearing coats, just those hooded sweatshirts kids always have on these days. I highly doubt they're up to anything good. Something to do with drugs, probably. What kind of neighbourhood is this? Whatever it is they're doing, I have no desire to be caught witnessing it.

As I'm turning away, I see a middle-aged man in a navy peacoat leave the pharmacy. He looks in my direction, and I want to point toward the fence, to draw his attention to the teenaged criminals lurking there, but the light changes, and I simply cross the street. I no longer want to be out and about, but I've made it this far, so there's no sense going back empty-handed.

I make my purchases quickly, then march down the sidewalk, on the opposite side of the road this time, keeping a lookout for those two hoodlums the whole time.

ONCE I'M SAFELY BACK in Danah's apartment, I peel the knobby ginger root, then mince it finely. The kitchen fills with the sharp, sweet scent of fresh-cut ginger. I inhale deeply. As I measure out careful quantities of flour and baking soda, my mind finally begins to relax.

Soon there will be a dozen sweet-smelling muffins cooling in neat rows on the counter. And perhaps having the oven on will do something to help heat up the place. It's freezing down here, and no amount of toying with the thermostat seems to make any difference. I plan to speak to Danah's landlord about that. And about a deadbolt for the outside door while I'm at it.

The afternoon wears on. I sit in the living room with a blanket tucked around my feet, but even so, my toes feel like they are encased in ice. It's four-thirty when Danah finally returns, and whether it's from sitting around shivering all afternoon or from the irritation that has been steadily building in my gut, a familiar and steady throbbing has started behind my eyes. I've been trying and trying to get the TV to work, but the stupid thing won't turn on no matter how many buttons I press.

"Oh good, you're home," I say, as Danah lets her bag fall to the floor. I flinch as she tosses her coat on top of it. "You didn't say when you'd be back. I've been sitting here wondering all day."

"Sorry. I had office hours until four. I thought I mentioned that."

"Oh. Well. I went for a walk and found the Foodland. But now I can't get the TV to work. How come it won't work for me?"

Danah picks up the remote and effortlessly turns on the TV. Obviously there is some trick to it, but I guess she doesn't feel the need to explain it to me.

She turns toward the kitchen. "It smells good in here. Were you baking?"

"I made muffins." I untangle my feet from the blanket and fold it into a square. I've lost interest in watching TV. I've been waiting for Danah to come home all day, but now that she's here, I only want to be left alone. I carry the blanket to the bedroom. "I have a bit of a headache," I say. "I'm going to lie down."

I take one of my migraine pills and stretch out under the heavy comforter, closing my eyes against the scrapes and thuds of Danah moving around on the other side of the door. It's too late now to go back to my house to do more work, but I certainly have no intention of sitting around all day again tomorrow waiting for Danah. If she can't take me, I'll simply order a taxi and go on my own. I would have done that today if I'd known Danah was going to be gone for as long as she was.

I'm not helpless. I've never been helpless.

EDITH ❧

FRANK IS NOT ON his knees, but he's staring at Edith earnestly enough while he waits for her answer. They are sitting side by side on the stiff blue chesterfield in the good living room, a room reserved for special company and therefore only used a few times a year. Edith's mother must have known Frank's intentions, otherwise she never would have let the two of them sit in here.

Edith stares at the ring Frank is holding out to her. Just yesterday she was listening to the Beatles' new song, "Please Please Me," and thinking about Frank. Her mother caught her, though, and made her turn off the radio, telling her those kinds of songs were inspired by the devil. Edith put on a Pat Boone record instead and went back to mooning over Frank, as her mother called it. Really, what she was thinking about was whether or not Frank was ever going to ask her to marry him. She had half a mind to ask him herself if he didn't get around to it soon, and now here he is, hand outstretched with a thin gold band pinched between his thumb and index finger.

She breathes out a quiet *yes*. Then, reaching for the ring, she says, louder, "Yes, Frank. I will. Of course I'll marry you."

He smiles then and pats her knee somewhat awkwardly. She

slides the ring onto her finger and holds up her hand to get a better look. The small diamond glints in the afternoon light. Frank leans forward and kisses her fingers. The feel of his lips on her skin makes her entire body tingle.

He pulls her toward him, and she permits a quick embrace, glancing toward the door to the hall in case her mother is watching. "We should have the wedding soon," Frank says. "Before your family leaves."

Edith nods. This room, with its blue chesterfield, coffee table, and wooden hi-fi, is otherwise oddly empty. The collection of Delft Blue figurines she has spent countless Saturdays dusting is already wrapped and packed away. Even the formal family portrait has been removed from the wall, leaving behind a shadowy rectangle in its place. Her family isn't moving for months, but Edith's mother began setting things aside and packing them weeks ago, as soon as the plans were finalized, which is why Edith was so anxious for Frank to make up his mind already.

While her father talked endlessly about the particulars of the farm he had purchased just outside of Kingston, and her mother fretted over the practicalities of enrolling the younger children in a new school, Edith's future hung in the balance. She is twenty-two, the oldest of all the children, and has been seeing Frank for over a year, but without an engagement, she wasn't sure whether she would be moving with her family to the new farm, almost six hours away, or staying behind in Missionville with Frank to start her own life. Now she knows. She will become Frank's wife and set up house. She will become Mrs. Frank Koestra. And none too soon, if her brother Ephraim's teasing has any merit. "You should find out if the post office in Kingston is hiring any spinsters," he has taken to joking. Ephraim is staying too. He's going to take over the existing farm and presumably marry Hildy, a rather homely girl from church whom he's been seeing for the better part of five months.

Edith's mother is suddenly standing at the entrance to the living room, looking at Edith with her eyebrows raised. Edith holds up her hand and says, "We're getting married. Frank just proposed."

"Well, isn't that lovely," says her mother.

THE CEREMONY IS SMALL and simple. There wasn't time to plan anything extravagant. Edith doesn't have a wedding gown, at least not a proper one, although the cream-coloured linen dress she chose is new. Her parents splurged on a clutch hat with a small bit of netting at the front — not exactly a veil, but Edith feels quite smart in it. She's not bothered by the simplicity of her wedding; she didn't want a lot of fuss anyway.

Afterward, there is tea and cake on the church lawn, and as Edith's younger brothers and sisters wander off to sit with their friends, Edith feels a pang of loneliness. Soon they will all be gone — except Ephraim, who barely speaks to her when he's not making fun of her — and while Edith often longed for a quieter house while living in the midst of her noisy family, it crosses her mind now that she might miss them.

Frank walks over to where she is standing and puts an arm around her shoulders. "Hello, wife," he says.

She glances up at him. "I hope you're not going to start calling me that."

"Only once in a while," he promises.

EDITH'S FAMILY IS GONE. They left for Kingston two weeks after the wedding, and Edith has settled into the little farmhouse on Frank's family's property. His older brothers, Case and Pieter, each have houses across the road. His parents used to live in this farmhouse when they first married, and it's beginning to show signs of age. The clapboard siding has been painted several times, and those layers are peeling, so Frank plans to apply a fresh coat before winter. The kitchen, tacked on to the back of the house, lists to one side, and Edith mentions the slant in the floor to Frank almost daily.

"I'll fix it," Frank assures her. "But it'll have to wait until after the harvest."

Edith busies herself with the rest of the house: arranging their few belongings, sweeping and dusting the rooms, polishing the hardwood floors, tending the flower garden beside the front door.

Before the wedding, her mother gave her two items for her new house: a spoon collection and a framed cross-stitch of a pair of praying hands. Underneath the hands are the words *The family that prays together stays together.* The spoon collection, twenty-four teaspoons dangling on a wooden rack, used to hang in their dining room, and when Edith was younger it was her job to polish each and every one of those tiny spoons. Later, that task fell to her younger sisters. There is no dining room in this farmhouse, though, so Edith hangs the spoon rack in the living room, near the stairs. She's looking forward to having to polish the spoons again. She always liked that job. The cross-stitch she puts in the kitchen. She has no plans, however, to fill her home with the same quantity of Bible verses that surrounded her growing up. She doesn't want to be preached at around every corner.

Her real wedding present, though, was a Zaanse clock with weighted chains and beautiful brass work. She knew as soon as she opened it that the Dutch clock would become the focal point of her new home.

Frank gave her a wooden chest lined with cedar. He made it himself. The part he's most proud of is the carving on the lid: a collection of overlapping evergreen trees. The chest sits at the foot of their bed, and Edith is using it to store their winter blankets. She's not sure yet what she'll put in it when it's time to pull out the afghans and the heavy floral-print bedspread. The bedspread was also a gift — from Frank's brothers, or, more accurately, from his brothers' wives. The repeating pattern of petals and stems and leaves is far too busy for Edith's taste. She would have preferred a simpler design or even plain white for that matter. But beggars can't be choosers: she knows that much.

Franks spends a lot of time in the fields. When he's in the house, Edith finds herself constantly having to put whatever room he's been in back to rights, straightening the *Farmers' Almanac* on the side table in the living room or realigning the canisters on the counter in the kitchen. She prefers to have him out of the way so she can go about her business in the house unimpeded.

"WHEN ARE YOU GOING to fix the floor in here? I feel like I'm tipping over every time I do the dishes."

Frank laughs. "Oh, come on. It's barely noticeable."

"Until you drop something and watch it roll away! You promised you'd fix it."

"I will. But it's a bigger job than I thought. It'll have to wait for a bit, I'm afraid. Can you survive the winter without falling over at the sink?" Frank steps behind Edith and wraps his arms around her. "Leave the dishes," he says. "Come and watch TV."

They've started watching the *Ed Sullivan Show* on Sunday nights, but Edith won't sit down until she's done in the kitchen. "I'll be there in a minute," she says, wiggling free from his grasp.

He lets her go and wanders into the living room alone. She can hear the TV clicking on and the muted sounds of laughter.

IN THE TRACTOR SHED across the road, on Case's property, Frank and his brothers have created a little woodshop. It's where Frank made the chest for Edith. Over the winter months, Frank spends a lot time in the woodshop, working on projects for their house. He wants to rebuild the banister for the stairs; the current one is rickety, a fact that Edith has pointed out more than once.

All three brothers use the shop. They've started making furniture. Simple things: straightforward tables, almost boxy in their design, no ornamentation. Chairs to match. Frank plans to be more ambitious with the stair railing; he wants the newel posts to be ornate, or at least more interesting than the rectangular sticks he's using for spindles.

Frank also spends a lot of time watching the news. More than he used to. He's become fixated on the JFK assassination. Edith watches some of the coverage, but it's so much of the same: speculation and the reiteration of details that feel too personal to be broadcast publicly. Jackie Kennedy's muted exclamation, "Oh no," for example, seconds after her husband slumped into her lap, bleeding from his head. Edith doesn't want to hear about it. She doesn't want to imagine it.

The new banister for the stairs, fancy newel posts included, is finally installed a few weeks after Christmas. Edith likes the look of it, sturdy and smooth, but mostly she is grateful that the handrail no longer wobbles.

"What do you think?" Frank asks.

"I think we're less likely to kill ourselves on the stairs."

Edith's just finished making a tray of brownies, and as she offers one to Frank, she stands on tiptoe to kiss him on the cheek. Then she turns back to the kitchen to get the broom because he's left sawdust all over the floor.

DANAH 🐟

EDITH HAS DISAPPEARED INTO my bedroom again. Another head-ache, or so she claims. Apparently, it came on the minute I got home. She did make muffins, though, and she cleaned my whole kitchen, so I guess I should be grateful for that.

I'm staring into the fridge trying to figure out what to have for dinner when there's a knock at my door. For a second, I think it might be Trevor, and I'm worried he's come to make sure I'm actually going to talk to Edith or, worse, to do it himself. But it's not Trevor; it's my landlord, Bertie, holding a space heater in his hands.

"Your grandmother — I guess she's staying with you? — she said the thermostat wasn't working down here. I'll get it checked, but this should help in the meantime. The heat's fine upstairs, so I don't think it's the furnace."

"Oh my gosh, I'm sorry, Bertie. When did she talk to you?"

"This afternoon."

"She had a fire, so she's staying with me for a bit. Sorry, Bertie, I didn't know —"

"It's okay. Let me know if this makes any difference."

Bertie and his wife have been nothing but accommodating since I moved in. The last thing I need is Edith charging upstairs to complain about my apartment. I thank Bertie for the heater and hope at least my grandmother wasn't rude when she asked for it.

I END UP EATING a peanut butter sandwich for dinner, along with two of Edith's muffins. I spend the rest of my evening alternating between marking papers and inventing hypothetical conversations to have with my grandmother. I plan to follow Trevor's advice and ask her outright about that letter I saw, although obviously that won't be happening tonight. And now, on top of everything else, I also need to bring up the whole talking-to-my-landlord-behind-my-back thing.

I just don't understand why Edith would lie to me about being in contact with my mother. If they were exchanging letters, why would she keep that a secret? I wish I could convince myself that I misread the name on the envelope, that it wasn't from someone named Lily at all. That would certainly simplify things. And it's not like it's impossible to believe I was imagining things.

It wouldn't be the first time.

Shortly after my mother disappeared, after I understood that she wasn't coming back, I started seeing her pop up all over the place: in crowds, on the opposite side of a busy street, and once sitting on a bus that drove past me while I stood on the sidewalk trying helplessly to signal to her. None of it was real, obviously. Still, her face continued to float through my imagination and manifest itself on complete strangers. I didn't tell anyone about these phantom sightings. I was embarrassed by them. Embarrassed that I still missed her when it was so obvious that she didn't miss me.

When I was eleven, and she'd been gone for two years, my class went on a field trip to the butterfly conservatory. I was standing beside one of the feeding stations — a tray holding a rotting banana and some chunks of kiwi and melon — when I saw her up ahead on the path. She was heading toward the waterfall at the far end of the conservatory, where the path cut into the fake rock so that you could walk behind the curtain of falling water.

I was too shocked to call out, but I followed her, my heart skipping like a jackrabbit in my chest. As I passed behind the waterfall, the rush of water filled my ears like the roar of an approaching storm. When I emerged on the other side, practically bursting with hope and expectation, there was no one there except for a woman bending toward her toddler, directing his attention to a butterfly with bright blue markings on its wings.

That woman's hair fell past her shoulders in loose curls, and as I walked past her, I pretended to stare into the leaves of the exotic plants that lined the path as if it were only a butterfly I was searching for.

But I *did* see the name Lily on that envelope. I didn't imagine that. And as much as I have outgrown the childish fantasies of that desperate little girl who wanted her mother back so badly that she tried to dream her into reality, I want to know the truth. I want, finally, to understand.

Edith is my only hope. I have no one else to ask.

BY MORNING, EDITH SEEMS fine. She offers me one of her muffins.

"I had some last night," I tell her. "Thanks for cleaning the kitchen. You didn't have to do that."

"Well, it needed to be done." She nods in the direction of the space heater. "Did your landlord drop that off? I hope it's big enough to make a difference down here."

"About that. Grandma, you can't just complain to my landlord without talking to me first. He didn't even know who you were."

"What do you mean, he didn't know who I was? I introduced myself. What did you think? I just went up there like some lunatic off the street? He knew exactly who I was."

"Next time, talk to me first. I don't want to make trouble for him; he's a good landlord. I could have bought a space heater myself if I'd known you were cold."

"It's your landlord's job to make sure your apartment has adequate heat. You better make sure he gets the furnace checked too. This heater isn't a long-term solution, you know."

I take a bite of the muffin Edith set in front of me. I concentrate on the tangy taste of lemon and try to ignore the coil of irritation twisting in my gut.

After a few beats of silence, Edith says, "I don't suppose you have time to help me at my house today?"

I make my voice agreeable and lie. "Actually, I do. We can go this morning, if you want." Maybe I'll uncover some other crazy relic from my mom's past that I can use to launch into the bigger conversation I seem to be having so much trouble initiating.

WE TAKE A QUICK peek inside Edith's house before going to the garage. I am secretly disappointed by the lack of progress. The windows have been cleaned, but other than that, it doesn't look like much has happened. The walls are still coated in a grey film; the kitchen remains a gutted shell.

"Steve told me they would be starting the repairs this weekend," Edith informs me as we stare at the mess. "Replacing the drywall, the countertops, putting in new flooring. Once the drying process is done, things will start to move quickly."

I nod. "I guess they know what they're doing. By next weekend, you could be restocking your brand-new cupboards." The thought is reassuring to me on many levels.

Back in the dimly lit garage, I try to gauge how much stuff is left to clean. We got through a lot of it the other day, so I'm hoping that today we can actually finish. Thank goodness Edith's bungalow is small and she didn't have much stuff in it to begin with.

Someone has left out a bag for Edith with her clothes that were taken away to be dry-cleaned. That should make her happy — at least now she'll have pants that fit.

As we work, I keep trying and failing to find a way to approach the subject of the letter. No matter how many different ways I frame the question in my mind, it reeks of accusation.

Trevor said to be specific, to ask about the actual letter I saw instead of coming at it vaguely. I watch as Edith determinedly wipes down a glass vase. Her brow is creased in concentration, her baggy pants already smudged with black where the vase has touched them. The smell of smoke permeates my nostrils, and finally, perhaps in desperation, I spit out what I want to say.

"The day before the fire, when I stopped by, I saw a letter. It looked like it was from —" I falter but then steel myself and continue. "— it was from a Lily Wilder. That's why I asked if you were still in touch with my mom."

Edith's hands become suddenly still. She looks at me, eyebrows raised. I can't read her expression, so I don't even try. Instead, I turn away from her gaze and focus on the ceramic bowl in my lap. I hold on to that bowl as if it's the only thing anchoring me to reality. I almost don't want Edith to say anything. If I could, I would take back my words and swallow their ugly implication. I'm holding my breath, waiting for the earth to shift beneath me, to pull me helpless and unresisting toward a truth that has the power to turn me inside out.

Edith is still staring at me. I shift uncomfortably. Her voice is tired when she finally speaks. "I don't have anything to tell you, Danah. If I thought ..." She leaves the rest of her sentence unsaid.

The air is heavy. Disappointment swells into the space around me. I swallow, but my throat is dry, and frustration trips my tongue. "It's just that letter — the name Lily — it seemed like maybe it was from her."

Edith looks at me and shakes her head. "There's no point imagining things, Danah."

I set the ceramic bowl down a little too heavily, and it clunks against the cement floor, an angry thud resounding for an instant in the silence between us.

Isn't Edith at least curious about the letter I saw? Is it really so impossible to believe it could have been from my mother? What makes Edith so quick to dismiss the idea? My grandmother's absolute certainty, coupled with her quick denial, raises a yellow flag of warning in my mind. I want to believe her. But I also don't want to.

I STAND UNDER THE stream of hot water in the shower for a long time, trying to decide what to do. I shampoo my hair twice. If Edith doesn't think that letter was from my mother, then who the hell is Lily Wilder? Edith can claim all she wants that she doesn't know, but I'm not buying it. Did she see the letter before it was destroyed in the fire? Did she read it? I wrap myself in a towel and stand, dripping, on the bath mat. I twist my hair into a messy bun and stare at my face in the mirror. "You have your mom's eyes," Dad used to say, back when Mom was still around. After she was gone, he never mentioned my eyes or Mom's again.

Do I have her eyes? I don't even know anymore.

I thought the reason he didn't want to talk about her, the reason no one ever mentioned her, was because it was too painful. Now I wonder if there was something else all along. Something Edith is hiding from me.

When I step out of the bathroom, Edith is sitting in front of the space heater. Good. She can sit in front of it and warm her toes all afternoon for all I care. I'm not hanging around. I have shit to get done. I may not have been enough for my mother to love, but I sure as hell intend to live up to my father's expectations. Even if I do have *her* eyes, it's him I take after in all the ways that matter.

I'M THE ONLY ONE in the office, which is how I like it. A few days ago, Pauline sent me an email to check on my progress, but I've been reluctant to answer. My careful plan for these last weeks of comp prep is disintegrating like wet Kleenex. I need to make a new schedule for what little time I have left, but I also have to finish marking Stone's students' papers.

I'll mark five papers, then redo my schedule. I still have time to get everything done: Stone's work, getting ready for Arthur Williams, preparing for my comps. Taking a long, slow breath through my nose, I pull out an essay discussing Charles Horton Cooley's interpretation of the looking-glass self: how we use other people's opinions of us to define ourselves. The premise of Cooley's theory dredges up uncomfortable memories of my mother. When I look at myself through her eyes, I see someone who was easy to walk away from. Someone unlovable.

I slam down my pen and lean back in my chair. I can't keep letting these ridiculous emotions hijack my brain. Enough already. I clench my jaw and will myself to focus. Just then, the door to the office opens, and Taryn prances in. Awesome. Absolutely fucking awesome.

I don't care. I'm not going anywhere. I'm going to sit here and ignore her and get shit done. Navi and I joke that Taryn probably sleeps in Kenneth Taylor Hall since she spends so much time here, but at the moment, the thought of sleeping here actually appeals to me. Almost anything would be better than returning home to Edith and all the unspoken words between us.

If I can outlast Taryn, I tell myself, that will be my one coup for the day. My one small victory. I turn back to the paper in front of me and continue reading. I scribble a few comments in the margin, assign a grade, and move on to the next one. I get through three more papers. It's been over an hour, and Taryn shows no signs of leaving.

I am contemplating how late I am willing to stay when Trevor calls. His voice is cajoling. "Hey, we've hardly spent any time together the last few days. Let's go out for dinner. I want to take you on a date."

I glance at Taryn. Seriously, is this how she spends her Friday nights? "That sounds perfect. I'm still on campus, but I'm leaving soon. What time were you thinking?"

"Pick you up at six?"

"Sure. Love you." I hang up and take a deep breath. Sometimes Trevor knows what I need even before I do.

Taryn pushes back her chair and stretches. "Busy, eh?" she says, turning toward me. She stands up and starts packing her bag while I check the time on my phone: 5:32.

I need to get moving too, but I want her to leave so I can claim my one small success of the day. Then I'll have to boot it home before Trevor shows up at my apartment and is forced to make small talk with Edith.

Halfway home, I realize I can't remember whether or not I locked the office door. I can't imagine I didn't — we lock the door just to go down the hall to the bathroom for Pete's sake. Still, I can't remember actually doing it. I don't have time to worry about it now, though. Trevor is probably on his way, if he's not at my apartment already.

Edith is eating when I walk in, and I can see from the look she gives me that she's not impressed.

"I waited," she says, "but then I decided to go ahead without you since, once again, I had no idea when you'd be back." She motions toward the kitchen. "There's more if you want to heat it up."

I bite my bottom lip. "Actually, Trevor's picking me up. We're going out for dinner."

"Oh. I see."

"Sorry."

Am I, though? It's not like Edith isn't used to eating alone.

TREVOR TAKES ME TO Pass Da Pasta. We've been here before, and while I don't remember disliking it, I'm not thrilled with his choice. The dining room is noisy and too bright. It's impossible to have a conversation without raising your voice. When he said he wanted to take me on a date, I had something more intimate in mind.

"Edith is driving me crazy," I tell him while we wait for our drinks to arrive.

"Why?"

"I don't know. She criticizes everything I do and makes these snide little comments like 'You could try hanging up your coat once in a while.' I feel like I'm eight years old and always in trouble."

Trevor laughs.

"It's not funny. I seriously don't know how much longer I can take living with her! I hardly get anything done."

The family beside us has two young children, and the toddler keeps dropping her fork. The mom bends over to retrieve it, then gives it right back to the kid, who, of course, drops it again. The jangling sound of her fork hitting the floor again and again sets my teeth on edge. Why the hell did Trevor choose this place?

"Yeah, but you also said she bakes and cleans for you. That doesn't sound so bad," Trevor says.

Our waitress appears with my wine and Trevor's beer, then scurries off without asking whether or not we're ready to order, which is just as well since I haven't even looked at the menu yet.

"She complained to my landlord behind my back. He had to buy a space heater because of her."

Trevor raises his eyebrows. Encouraged, I go on. "Oh, and for the record, I asked her about the letter this morning. She flat-out denied being in contact with my mother."

"Maybe she's telling the truth."

Our waitress returns, so I scan the menu quickly, deciding to play it safe with cheese cappelletti. Trevor orders a burger, which makes me more annoyed that he chose an Italian restaurant since obviously he never planned to order an Italian dish.

While we wait for our food, I listen as he describes the latest revisions to his thesis chapter. It's hard to hear him over the noise of clanging plates and the voices from tables squished too close to ours. The kid beside us, the same one who was dropping her fork, doesn't want to eat her pasta. "I no like it!" she screeches, turning her head away from the spoon her mom is waving in her face.

Why are we talking about Trevor's thesis? Shouldn't he be asking me more about finally confronting my grandmother? Then helping me come up with a plan for what to do next? He was the one pushing me to stop pussyfooting around in the first place.

"Do you think she's lying?" I ask. "Do you think there's a chance my grandmother has been in touch with my mother all along and for some reason just doesn't want me to know?"

Trevor sighs. "I think you should probably be having dinner with your grandmother tonight." He looks at me pointedly, and I consider for a moment how satisfying it would be to throw my glass of cheap wine in his face. However, before I have a chance to fully contemplate it, our food arrives.

"Forget it," I mumble. "You obviously don't understand."

"Danah, you know I understand. But you have to talk to your grandmother. All this speculating is going to drive you crazy. It's going to drive *me* crazy."

I focus on my pasta. When I finally speak again, I try to keep my voice measured and calm. "I told you, I did talk to her. She said she hadn't heard from my mom in a very long time. When I mentioned the actual letter I saw, she said I was imagining things." I stare at Trevor. "What do you want me to do? Hook her up to a lie detector?"

He doesn't answer. He doesn't have to, because our waitress chooses that moment to sidle over to us. "How was everything?" she asks, clearing our plates, all bright smiles despite the obvious tension emanating from our table. "Can I get you anything else? The dessert menu?"

Trevor glances at me as if I might suddenly decide to order some tiramisu and a cup of espresso.

"No thanks," I say as politely as I can manage. "I think we're done here."

On the silent drive back to my apartment, my eyes begin to sting. Trevor has no idea how difficult any of this is for me. He can't even be bothered to try to understand the situation from my perspective. Why is it so hard for him to see that bringing up something that's been buried this long isn't exactly a cakewalk? There are a lot of difficult feelings suppressed under all the silence around my mother, and every time I mention her, I uncover more of them. He can stick to worrying about his thesis chapter. Fine by me. I can take care of myself.

Still, as he backs out of the driveway after I deliberately climbed out of the car before he could lean over and kiss me, I can't stop the tears from falling. I stand there in the dark and digest the fact that the one person I thought I could trust to understand what I'm feeling has completely disappointed me.

JANE LILY 🐦

WHEN I FIRST ARRIVED in Europe, disillusioned and discouraged, I ran around for a while, chasing my tail like a dog. I'd landed in Amsterdam, but at some point during the long, lonely flight there, I'd changed my mind about staying in the Netherlands. I hopped around from one country to the next, experimenting with languages, cultures, and men.

Every time I slept with someone new, I was cementing the fact that I could never return to my old life. I wanted to draw a firm line between my previous life and this one. No, not draw a line: build a barrier. One that I couldn't cross, not even if I wanted to.

For a while, I felt liberated and alive. Carefree. The last time I'd felt like that was when I ran away when Danah was just a baby. I simply took off one Saturday morning. After a two-hour bus ride, I ended up at a nudist resort, where I spent fourteen days pretending to be somebody else, all while Andrew did his best to hold things together at home. I went back, though, that time. I knew all along I wasn't going to stay away for good. But the next time, even before I left, I knew Andrew wouldn't take me back again so easily. I had no doubt he would learn about my flight to Schiphol, but I didn't think he would bother following my trail from there. By that point, I wasn't worth chasing.

I moved around aimlessly the first few years, never allowing myself to become too involved with any one person or too connected to any one place. When I got tired of that, and when I had become someone I hardly recognized anymore, someone with no resemblance to the woman who'd left behind her daughter and husband, I finally stopped running. I was in Edinburgh. I had climbed Arthur's Seat, my hair whipping around my face in a mad frenzy, my body straining against the wind. As I sat at the top of that cliff, looking down at the New Town rubbing up against the Old Town, I realized I could stop here, in this city with its strange juxtaposition of past and present, with two versions of itself fighting to coexist.

THAT WAS ALMOST FIFTEEN years ago. I got a job at Pulp and Pen, a cozy used bookstore tucked away on a narrow close in the Old Town section of Edinburgh, and I drifted through the days, the months, the years in mostly peaceful solitude. The shop itself was quiet, although it was connected through a side door to a noisier café, and people, including the staff, wandered freely between the two, allowing occasional bursts of sound to penetrate the stillness.

A few months ago, when I was still working, Hamish came over from the café to ask me a question. He's young, maybe twenty-six, and handsome in a boyish kind of way. Long eyelashes, permanently flushed cheeks.

"Lily," he said that day, slapping his hand against the dark wood of the bookstore's front counter, "do you reckon there's such a thing as a second chance?"

His question caught me off guard. I found myself unable to speak. Finally, I nodded, and he moved on, satisfied. How could I begin to explain to Hamish the force of conviction behind my seemingly meek agreement? How I had spent a good part of my life chasing new beginnings so that not only did I believe in second chances but also third and even fourth chances. That if I didn't, I wouldn't be standing here at all, behind this counter where he knew me only as a middle-aged salesclerk with a Canadian accent.

I wanted to chase after him, to put a hand on his shoulder to stop him from walking through the bookstore and back into the clatter of the café. I wanted to warn him. For all of the new beginnings, for all those times I started over, I left behind pieces of myself. So yes, I believed in second chances, but not in surviving them whole. I didn't chase after him or even call out. It seemed like a waste of energy.

After work that day, still unsettled by Hamish's odd question, I walked through the Princes Street Gardens, which sprawl across the ancient loch dividing the Old Town from the New Town. The flower beds were pale, their usually bright colours muted as the sky slowly changed from a subdued purple to a sombre grey. I wandered along the pathways beside the shadowy blossoms and, not for the first time, faced what I'd left behind.

I had come here, to these gardens, when I first I arrived in Edinburgh, and I had discovered that I could confront my ghosts here with an equanimity I had not been able to muster elsewhere. These paths, set against the backdrop of Edinburgh Castle, are infused with a peace and a calmness I find comforting; I walk them often and am always awed by the castle towering on the hill, looming against the horizon.

That day, as I drifted through the park, I thought about my mother and how easy it had been for me to pull away from her, from the farmhouse where I had grown up, from Missionville itself. She had made my life miserable in so many ways, but still I must have loved her even as I fled her suffocating grip. She was my mother: love was inevitable, if also, in our case, invisible.

With Andrew and Danah, it was different. I did not go so easily. Even the tranquillity of the gardens could not counter the battle of indecision I continued to fight years after I left. I loved my daughter, and I loved my husband. No, there had never been a question of love — just the inequality of it. Andrew was an easy person to love, and Danah had loved him with a fierceness I couldn't match. In the face of that kind of devotion, I couldn't compete. Couldn't even come close. If I had, would it have been enough to tether me in place?

These are the questions Niall wants me to contemplate. "You must understand your past if you ever hope to make peace with it," he's forever reminding me.

And I suppose it is peace I am seeking now. What else is there?

THE FIRST LETTERS I wrote were on plain stationery. Cheap white paper I bought from Tesco. I had to be careful with my money, but after a few months of working at Pulp and Pen, I splurged on a block of thick, textured paper. It had a richness to it that gave my words more weight. I developed a partiality for high-end paper — velvety smooth and scented with importance. We carried lots of it in the shop, so it was easy enough to get my hands on.

Lately, I've been using a set called Crisp Linen. The pages are small, half the size of regular writing paper, but each sheet is covered with an almost imperceptible pattern of crosshatched lines, which lends it an incredibly pleasing texture. I didn't get this set at Pulp and Pen: it was a more recent and extravagant purchase from a boutique I came across while following the twisting route for one of Edinburgh's Old Town Ghost Tours.

·I've never gone on an official Ghost Tour, but during the day, I like to wander along the different paths laid out in their pamphlets. The routes weave through the side streets that veer off the Royal Mile and always end near a graveyard. The paying customers must crave an eerie brush with the dead in cobblestone courtyards where beheadings once took place or in the excavated cellars beneath buildings that were razed after the Plague. I don't want the spiel. I can imagine the details well enough. I just like to follow the routes, the morbid paths of all those ghosts who have gone before. Ever since I stopped working, I struggle to fill my days. Hence, the long walks. I sleep a lot too. And even then, in the haziness of my dreams, I can't stop myself from revisiting the past. I am watching my life on rewind, and I can't figure out how to make it move forward again.

I am a ghost myself. Or, at the very least, a ghost of my former self.

NIALL HAS ALL KINDS of theories about this backward-moving momentum and what my mind is unconsciously trying to do. Sometimes, when I am watching him nod as I talk, his body leaning toward me, all that intense attentiveness makes me want to say something to jolt him out of his professional posture. I want to see him suck in his breath or narrow his eyes in disgust or even recoil from me. I want to see him fumble with how to proceed because sometimes I can't stand his calm demeanor, his careful accent, his attitude that everything I am experiencing is completely understandable and that nothing about me surprises him in the least.

Once, I almost mentioned the tooth. I thought I might finally catch him off guard, but at the last minute I changed my mind, afraid of being disappointed.

"What was that there?" he asked. "You were about to say something."

"It was nothing," I replied. "I forget."

He raised his eyebrows and waited. We both knew I was lying, but his expectant expression didn't faze me. I'd changed my mind about saying anything, and no amount of pressure would make me reconsider, as he well knew.

He knows about the letters. He encourages them. According to him, it is a healthy coping mechanism. So, I felt quite justified in spending £20 on the small box of Crisp Linen stationery and another £12 for the matching envelopes.

I am, after all, supposed to indulge myself now. It's part of my therapy.

DANAH 🐟

I GET UP EARLY and head straight for campus. I don't even want to look at my grandmother; I don't trust myself to be civil. Trevor should try having a conversation with her if he thinks it's so easy. But first he can listen to her lecture him about making the bed and keeping the cushions straight — "Is that really so hard?" she whines — and wiping out the sink every single goddamn time he turns the tap on because water marks are a sign of laziness. The list goes on and on. She's free with her little tips and her not-so-gentle criticisms, but when it comes to answering questions about my mother, she has nothing to say.

The sixth floor of Kenneth Taylor Hall is eerily quiet. I step out of the elevator and glance toward the empty administrative offices. I really hope I'm the only one here because I don't want to talk to anyone. Not even Navi, although the chances of her coming in on a weekend are next to nil.

As soon as I turn down the hall, I can tell my office door is open. Fuck. And of course, of all people, it's Taryn, diligently scribbling away at eight o'clock on a Saturday morning. She doesn't look up when I walk in, and in response to my greeting, she starts tapping her pen on her desk like some sort of manic metronome.

"Everything okay?"

She turns to face me. "The office wasn't locked this morning." *Tap. Tap. Tap.* "I keep a lot of important things in here —"

I smack my forehead, more theatrically than necessary. "Ohhh, I couldn't remember if I locked it last night. But then I figured I probably had. Out of habit, you know? Sorry."

"You *knew* you hadn't locked it?"

"I *thought* maybe I hadn't. Nothing happened though, right? You're not missing anything?"

"No, but still. You share this space with other people."

"I'm aware of that. I said I was sorry."

Taryn goes back to whatever it was she was doing, but I can hear her sucking in air through her nose. Seriously? I am not in the mood to deal with her little temper tantrum. She's just as bad as Edith, with her disapproving snorts and angry silence.

I lower my head into my hands. I need Dad. He would know what to say right now to soothe the fraying edges of my mind. I have no one to talk to. Not even Trevor, not after last night. He'd probably side with Taryn about the stupid door anyway.

WHEN I WAS IN high school, I had to do a project for my grade eleven history class. I can't remember the details now, but it had to do with the Treaty of Versailles, and I was all worked up about it, stressing over having to design a costume or something dumb like that.

I remember stomping around the house, slamming my bedroom door, and yelling at Dad that I was probably going to fail the whole course.

He gave me time to cool down, then came into my room, where I was lying face down on my bed, sulking, and he told me to change into a pair of shorts.

"Shorts?" I said, incredulous. "Dad, it's snowing."

"I'm going to teach you to play squash. Come on. Let's go."

He took me to the campus Athletic Centre, where we shut ourselves into one of the courts. The walls were scuffed with black marks, and the room smelled like rubber and sweat.

"It stinks in here."

"You'll get used to it. Here, put your goggles on."

Dad was always introducing me to activities. His motto was: a healthy body for a healthy mind. We'd gone canoeing, played tennis, tried rock climbing. Now this.

As it turned out, I liked squash. There was something immensely satisfying about thwacking that little rubber ball against the wall. By the end of our game, I was breathing hard and sweating. I was also smiling.

"When you feel yourself getting stressed, Danah, look for a physical outlet. Something to get your blood pumping. It will help."

I don't remember what happened with the project. Obviously, I must have finished it, and I probably got a good mark. I would remember if I didn't because the few bad marks I did get in high school stand out in my memory like sharp sticks.

"I'm heading out," I say suddenly to Taryn. I know what I need to do, and at the thought, a weight lifts from my shoulders. At the door, I turn back and say, "Don't forget to lock up when you leave." I don't wait around for the dirty look I'm sure Taryn shoots in my direction.

I warm up at a slow jog on the treadmill, then continually increase my speed until the rhythm of my feet hitting the belt and my breathing become the only two things I am aware of. As the kilometres click past on the display, I enjoy a satisfying burn of accomplishment. I always forget how good it feels to run until I am back in the gym or out on the pavement actually doing it.

I become much more forgiving of Edith as I run. For all her nitpicking and her refusal to discuss my mother, she was there for me when I needed her most. I have to give her credit for that. After Dad died, she was the one who guided me through the blur of days that followed, offering a steadying hand while I wandered around in a grey swirl of grief and confusion. I was grateful then for her stubbornness and strength; I relied on it.

She came with me to the funeral home to make arrangements. Sitting across the desk from the funeral director in his dark suit, I could barely swallow past the ball of grief in my throat. He was going on and on about the placement of flowers, visitation hours, and music selections. I watched his lips move, the bottom one too shiny, wondering if he had licked it or was wearing too much Chapstick. It was Edith who answered his questions and agreed to the various details.

She also helped me pick out a headstone.

"We don't want anything too ornate," she told the guy at the monument place. "Something simple and solid."

Had I told her that?

I followed her around the showroom, thankful she was doing all the talking because every time I opened my mouth, I found myself choking on air.

Aunt Georgina, Dad's only sister, flew to Ontario for the funeral. I had no energy for her. I avoided her, convinced that, given the chance, she would point her spindly finger at me and rain down blame and censure, just like she had when I was a child still stunned by my mother's disappearance.

Because she came then too. She stayed with us in Vancouver for a few days to help around the house: doing laundry, making my lunches, cleaning. One afternoon, I went outside and found her on the porch, scrubbing the living room window with a handful of newspapers. I must have asked her what she was doing because I remember her turning around to explain.

"The paper doesn't leave streaks," she said. "I guess your mom got tired of cleaning your grubby fingerprints off the windows."

Her words knocked the breath out of me. I fled to my room and threw myself face down on the bed. I spent a lot of time like that while she was with us — hiding in my room, my face buried in blankets.

Dad seemed grateful to have her there, though. I don't think he had any idea how she talked to me when he wasn't in the room. She was nice enough in front of him. But every time she trundled me off to bed, she would hiss at me to get down on my knees to pray.

"You need to ask for forgiveness for what you did." Her voice was only a whisper, but it had an edge to it that scared me.

I didn't know what I had done, but I knew it must have something to do with my mother leaving, so I knelt beside my bed, and I prayed. I'd never liked my aunt, but in those awful days right after my mother disappeared, I despised her.

So, at Dad's funeral, I kept my distance from Aunt Georgina. I didn't want anything to do with her. And Edith, intentionally or not, continually ran interference for me. I remember Aunt Georgina cornering me at one point to ask something about the sandwiches for the reception, and before I could open my mouth, Edith appeared and swiftly answered on my behalf. I slipped away, silently thanking my grandmother. If anyone knew anything about the sandwiches, it was Edith anyway.

At the very end of the church service, when Dad's coffin was being wheeled down the aisle to the waiting hearse, Aunt Georgina collapsed beside me. We had both stood up to follow behind the coffin. Suddenly, grabbing my arm, she let out a heart-wrenching wail and fell to the floor. I stood there, frozen, looking down at her, while people rushed to help.

Edith nudged me forward. "She'll be fine," she said. "You keep going."

I stepped into the aisle and walked behind the coffin like a zombie. Aunt Georgina must have recovered because she made it to the gravesite, where she stood sniffling loudly beside the minister.

"I've never seen anyone so vulgar at a funeral," Edith said later. "I hope she doesn't stick around long."

I'm sure I must have smiled, despite the pain that was swallowing my heart.

"Me too," I said.

THAT NIGHT, STILL SORE from running, I dream about my father. I dream about him a lot, and sometimes my dreams are so real it feels like I am actually seeing him again. In my dreams, wherever we are or whatever we're doing together, I seem to know we only have a bit of time or that he shouldn't be there at all, but I never know if *he* knows that. I'm afraid to tell him. I try to make the most of those stolen moments, try to attach meaning to every word, every look, every touch. We usually end up doing totally mundane things, like playing mini golf or going for a walk, but each moment is tinged with this extraordinary specialness for me, as well as with longing. Even though he is right beside me, it's during these dream encounters that I miss him the most.

Strangely, his arrival in my dreams often seems like the most natural thing in the world. "Hey, Squirt," he'll say, walking into my office or meeting me on the path to the parking lot, and while I'm always happy to see him, I'm never surprised. Never shocked, like I should be. Usually, I feel in those dreams the way I did as a child when he'd been away on a trip and finally came home. Like his absence was only ever temporary.

DANAH ✥

DANAH HAS BEEN EXCITED all day. Her dad is returning from his trip to Mexico, and she can't wait to see him. Being alone with her mother was fun at first, but her dad is better at playing and doesn't get mad all the time like her mom does.

"When will he be here?" she asks, although she already knows it won't be until after dinner. "I mean, what time exactly?" She wants something more specific than "after dinner."

"I don't know, Danah. Sometime around seven. Maybe a bit later."

"But what if I'm in bed?" Danah can't miss his arrival. She loves the way he scoops her up and hugs her so tightly that she knows he's missed her too.

"You can stay up until he gets here," her mother promises, and Danah is so relieved she does a little dance before hugging her mom. They are both smiling when Danah runs down the hall to finish her special Welcome Home card.

By the time their dinner dishes are being cleared, Danah is so jittery her mother sends her away. "Go play," she orders. "I don't want to keep tripping over you."

Danah doesn't want to be alone; she wants to wait with her

mother. She likes this feeling of what she assumes is their shared excitement. Still, she marches off obediently to her room, where she entertains herself fretfully for about fifteen minutes. Then, just as she is about to ask if she can come out again, she hears a car door outside. She pauses in her doorway until she is certain that someone is walking up the front steps. Sure enough, the front door opens just as she careens around the corner and into the front hall, where her father is already grinning.

"Hey there, Squirt," he calls out, dropping his bags to the floor. "Did you miss me?"

Danah is in his arms in an instant. Her mother stands off to the side, waiting patiently for her own hug.

LATER, WHEN DANAH IS sitting on her dad's lap in her pajamas, he tells her he has a present for her. She's been waiting for this. He always brings her back a souvenir when he goes away. He lifts her gently from his lap and rummages in his suitcase for a few minutes.

"Where did it go? It has to be in here somewhere. Hmmm … I wonder if I packed it?"

"Daddy!" Danah squeals. Even though he goes through this same routine each time he presents her with a gift, she can't help but feel a little bit worried. Did he really forget to bring her something?

"Ah, here it is." He produces a paper bag and hands it to her with a flourish. Then, turning to her mom, he adds, "And I have a little something for you too."

Her mother's present is in a small cloth bag tied with a blue ribbon. She nods at Danah to open hers first, so Danah peeks into her paper bag and pulls out a pair of intricately carved wooden maracas. As she begins to shake them experimentally, her mother opens her own bag. Inside is a colourful beaded bracelet. Danah would have liked a bracelet too, but she's happy with her maracas.

Especially when her father leans down and whispers in her ear, "I wanted something special for my favourite girl."

Danah glances quickly, almost guiltily, at her mother before relaxing into the warmth of his words. He is her favourite too.

JANE LILY ❧

I CANCELLED MY APPOINTMENT with Niall today. My headaches are getting worse, and this morning I didn't have the energy to go out. Instead, I moped around my flat feeling a little bit sorry for myself. There wasn't even anything interesting on TV. I did notice, however, that the sun was back after two days of rain, and I found its warmth mildly cheering.

By the afternoon, I am feeling much better, and I think about calling Wanda, from the bookstore, to see if she wants to stop by, but then I change my mind because I really don't want to hear her go on and on about how the new salesclerk is awful and how everybody misses me.

I end up going outside to putter in my little garden, which has been sadly neglected the past few weeks. Most of the flowers are dead or almost dead, like the Scottish bluebells and delphinium, but the forget-me-nots and winter pansies are still bravely holding on. The base of their bed is layered with leaves, which I meant to scoop out ages ago. Quite a few weeds have sprung up too. I begin pulling them out one by one, ripping their deep roots from the soil. I find it soothing.

As I dig through my garden, the heady scent of soil and the gentle fragrance of the pansies makes me nostalgic. I think briefly about planting some tulip bulbs. Why have I never planted tulips? Growing up, the front of our farmhouse was edged with tulips four rows deep. Every year, Uncle Case brought us more bulbs, sometimes shipped directly from Holland, always encouraging my mother to add more and more varieties.

"With your tulips," he told us, "you want to create a symphony of colour. It is like music for the eyes, no?"

My little garden is actually quite pitiful, even when it hasn't been neglected for months on end. I inherited it from the previous owner of my flat, and I've done nothing to enhance it. I maintain it only, tending to the shrubs and perennials that were here when I moved in. Still, it gives me pleasure. Flowers have always given me pleasure. The garden, unprepossessing as it is, takes up a good chunk of my tiny lawn, and for much of the year a wild array of flowers wave their heads in greeting as I approach my front door. Often, in the summer, I keep a vase of fresh-cut flowers in the kitchen — just a simple arrangement, nothing like the elaborate bouquets I used to put together when I worked at Noble's Florist. My mother often had jars of fresh flowers scattered around the farmhouse in Missionville too. Remembering those splashes of colour and fragrance makes me think there must have been some tenderness in her after all, under all that armour.

I grab hold of a thick dandelion stem and tug. I'd expected a reply by now. Niall keeps telling me to be patient, but surely that advice rings hollow even to him. What would he think, I wonder, if he saw me out here preparing my pathetic garden for winter, cleaning out the beds, weeding — would it seem as pointless to him as it suddenly seems to me? And what about the ridiculous impulse to plant bulbs that won't poke through the soil until spring? That won't bloom for months and months and months? What would Niall think about that? Planting flowers for next year — surely he would find something significant in that fleeting notion.

THE HOUSE I SHARED with Andrew in Vancouver had beautiful gardens, although I never had much to do with them. They were kept weeded and mulched and tightly pruned by a landscaping company. In keeping with my job as a florist's assistant, my only responsibility with the gardens was to choose which cuttings to display in the heavy crystal vase we'd received as a wedding present from Andrew's sister. That vase was one of the only good things to come from Georgina. She never liked me. I don't think she thought I was good enough for her little brother.

In the end, she was right. I *wasn't* good enough for Andrew, was I? I wasn't good enough for Danah either. In fact, when it comes right down to it, I haven't been good enough for anybody.

Ever.

JANE LILY ✍

LILY IS STUDYING HER husband's face as he reads a book in the Victorian wingback chair in the corner of their bedroom. Pale afternoon sunlight spills through the blinds, bathing Andrew's features in a soft light. Originally, this was meant to be her spot, a quiet place to read or relax —Andrew has his study, after all — but he prefers the light in here. His brow is furrowed: either he's concentrating on whatever's in front of him or he disagrees with some part of it. She hesitates before finally interrupting him, although he must have seen her standing there, watching him.

"Andrew," she says slowly, "can I talk to you?"

Andrew murmurs something that sounds like assent, but he doesn't stop reading. She waits.

"Andrew," she says again, her voice sharp.

He sighs and looks up. "What is it?"

Why does he have to act like listening to her is such a chore? She wanted to talk to him now, while Danah is busy with her friend outside, so they could have a few minutes alone. But this is all wrong. He's looking at her expectantly, impatiently, so she ends up blurting out the news she intended to offer up like a carefully wrapped package.

"I'm pregnant."

He says nothing. Eventually, he sets his book down. He gets out of the chair and moves toward her. He hesitates slightly. "And ... are you happy?" He is standing so close. She could easily tip forward, let herself fall into him.

She nods. "You?"

"Of course!" he says with too much energy.

He reaches for her then, but she is already turning away. And in that split second of confusion, it occurs to her that she's always the one putting space between them.

EDITH ❧

DANAH IS ALREADY GONE when I get up, so it looks like I am going to be left on my own again today. Last night she wasn't home for more than five minutes before she ran out the door with her boyfriend. Never mind that I'd made a tuna casserole for us.

Well, I'm not going to sit around her cold apartment all day twiddling my thumbs. I've already decided to go back to my house to check on the restoration crew. Someone needs to keep an eye on them. While I'm at it, I'll pop over to see Alice. I want to ask Ben to keep tabs on the house during the week. Although Steve promised to meet with me to explain everything that's being done — "We'll keep you in the loop" were his exact words — from where I sit, that's hardly reassuring.

Maybe I should bring a little treat for the workers, something to keep them motivated. Cookies. They can eat those quickly before getting back to work. I used to give Frank a tin of oatmeal raisin cookies to keep in the tractor during the long afternoons of harvesting. I made them with extra oatmeal and a generous dollop of corn syrup so they would be more filling. I sent them out with him after lunch, sometimes still warm from the oven.

"You're a keeper," he would tell me as he tucked the tin under his arm. Then he'd pull me into an embrace and kiss my forehead.

I did try. With Frank, I really tried.

Right, well, if I'm going to make cookies, I'll have to buy oatmeal and raisins. I already know from reorganizing the cupboards that Danah doesn't have any. So that means back to the Foodland. I'm not thrilled at the prospect, but I'm also not about to show up at my house empty-handed now that I've made up my mind to bring something.

Besides, the Foodland isn't far. What is it I'm worried about anyway? Running into more criminals? There was a time, I am sure of it, when I would have marched right up to those hooligans I saw by the fence and pulled them away by their ears without giving it a second thought. I would have rained the very wrath of God upon their heads and sent them skittering off with their tails between their legs. But times are different now, and I am so much more fragile than the person I used to be.

Criminals or not, there's no sense being crippled by indecision. I need ingredients, and I know where to get them, so I bundle up in borrowed layers and head out. I grab Danah's umbrella from a hook by the door and carry it purposefully up the stairs with me. As I approach the intersection by the empty lot, a young man comes bustling down the sidewalk. I grip the umbrella like a club, prepared to swing if need be. He passes by me without so much as glancing in my direction. Not even a polite nod or a hello. Today's youth have no manners. It's no wonder they end up doing drugs in public, out where anybody can see.

I purchase the things I need without incident, unless you count the young girl with a hoop through her bottom lip who rings up my total. It crosses my mind that she's probably in cahoots with the young men I saw the other day. As soon as I get back to Danah's apartment, I'm going to remind her landlord about that deadbolt.

I ORDER A TAXI while the cookies are cooling on the counter. When it drops me off on Alder Street, I notice right away that my front door is still boarded up. Why on earth is that taking so long to be fixed? It looks awful, nothing but a flimsy sheet of plywood tacked to the front of the house. There's a RestoreAll truck in the driveway, so at least somebody must be working. That's a relief. I walk around to the side entrance and let myself in.

"Hello?" I call out.

A man in dusty coveralls appears in the doorway to the kitchen and looks at me skeptically. "Can I help you?"

"Oh, I'm just checking on things," I say, trying to peer past him. "Are you the only one here today?"

"Sorry, but you are ...?"

"I live here."

"Do you need something? Steve never said nothing about —"

"I don't need permission to check on my own house, surely? Steve told me I was welcome to look in anytime."

The man steps aside and motions me past him. "There's not much to see. We're just putting up the drywall now."

There's a second man in the kitchen holding a measuring tape in one hand and a utility knife in the other. He stares at me warily before returning his attention to the large slab of drywall behind him.

"Doreen's here too. She's cleaning the walls, getting them ready to paint." The man who let me in suddenly sticks out his hand. "Name's Chris," he says. "And this is Ricky. Doesn't look like much yet, I'm afraid, but it'll come."

I shake his hand, then look around for somewhere to set the cookies. "I made these for you," I say, and, failing to find anywhere better, I set them on a bright orange cooler sitting against the frame of my former wall. "Well, I guess I'd better leave you to it." I don't want to see any more of the house. I just want to get out of here, away from the mess and the smell of drywall dust and the sight of complete strangers wandering through my home.

I shouldn't have come. I tramp next door to Alice and Ben's, but they must be out because no one answers. I turn around, and since I have nowhere else to go, I let myself into my cold garage, where I survey the neat rows of boxes lined up against the wall. Everything has been sorted and cleaned, and now it sits waiting, like me, for the rest of my house to be ready.

My eyes fall on the wooden chest along the far wall. Thank goodness it was in the spare bedroom, away from the smoke. Imagine if Danah had dug through it while we were working in here! It's bad enough she saw the letter. Besides, I've already told her as much as she needs to know.

It was the name Lily on the envelope that Danah noticed. And while I know full well that Jane goes by Lily now, it still strikes me as strange to think of her by her middle name. I never did understand all that nonsense about changing her name.

"I'm not going to call you Lily," I told her. "Your name is Jane, and I'll call you Jane."

We argued about everything near the end.

I run my hand over the surface of the wooden chest, over the raised edges of the pine trees Frank carved into its lid. Then, without warning, I sink to my knees on the cold cement floor and give in to the wave of grief that seemingly comes out of nowhere.

EDITH ❧

IT IS ALREADY A hot morning, although the sun has only been up for an hour at most. Edith is busy in the kitchen making strawberry jam, so as Frank leaves the house to begin the first cut of hay on the far western field, Edith takes no notice of him. She clears away his breakfast things then turns her attention back to her pot of boiling sugar and strawberries, giving the bubbling red mess a slow stir. When the sugar has dissolved, she mixes in a spoonful of lemon juice. The air grows thick with the warm and sugary scent of cooking berries, and the morning passes in unremarkable increments, measured by the steady growth of bright-red mason jars lined up neatly on the counter, ready to be sealed with a thin layer of paraffin.

When Frank doesn't come in from the field at noon, Edith is annoyed. She has a hot meal waiting for him and resents the wasted effort of making it if he can't be bothered to show up on time. Later, she will imagine that she felt a prickle of worry, that she was concerned by this uncharacteristic break in routine. But at that moment, consumed only by selfish anger, she assumes that he has lost track of time. As the potatoes and thick slab of ham she has prepared for his lunch begin to cool, she silently curses his carelessness.

He'll have to eat his lunch cold. She's not going to bend over backwards to keep it warm. If he wants hot food, he should bloody well come in when he says he will.

Even months later, knowing the awful truth of that morning's events, Edith's final memories of Frank remain tinged with resentment. Not because he missed lunch but because that small grievance was replaced by one so much larger: because of everything that followed.

Somewhere close to one-thirty — she glances at the clock over and over while she waits for him — Edith hears footsteps approaching the back door. She is about to give Frank a piece of her mind, but it's not Frank, it's Alex Rumsden from the farm next door, gesturing frantically as he spews out a series of incoherent words and fragments. Something about an accident. The tractor. Frank.

"It was too late, Edith," Alex says. "It was too late when I found him. I don't know how long he was pinned —"

Edith's head fills with white noise. She stops listening, or she tries to. But the words have already penetrated her brain. The understanding that Frank is dead, that he missed lunch because he is dead, slams into her like a brick. "Where is he?"

"Still in the field ..." Alex Rumsden's sentence trails off, its conclusion left unuttered.

WHAT EDITH CAN'T STAND to think about later is how long Frank lay out there in the field, pinned under the heavy tractor, and whether or not he'd been conscious, all while she stood at the counter, spooning her jam into jars. He was driving the Farmall along the steep slope at the edge of the field, at the border of the Rumsdens' property, it was explained to her later. The narrow front tires on that tractor would have made it unstable, especially on the sloped embankment.

"He must've been rushing," Pieter says.

Edith says nothing. When the tractor rolled, crushing Frank, did he cry out for help? All they know is that by the time Alex Rumsden noticed the capsized tractor, Frank was already dead.

Edith passes through the next few weeks in a fever of disbelief. Her actions have the force of routine to guide them, but she often finds herself stopping mid-task, staring ahead, unsure of where she is or what she is doing. The one thing she is constantly and acutely aware of is her anger. She is angry with Frank for leaving her. She knows this is irrational; she knows he didn't leave her, really, but she can't escape the feelings of abandonment that pummel her day and night. And then her inner fury is silently and dangerously refueled when she discovers, to her dismay, that she is pregnant.

She thought she'd been careful; she paid close attention to her cycle. Yet now she is going to have a baby even though she's not ready. Even though Frank is dead.

The Koestras rally around her. She is not to worry, his brothers assure her. She can stay in the farmhouse as long as she wants. Case and Pieter will take over Frank's fields. They have always farmed as a unit anyway. Their wives, Margaret and Isobel, promise to help Edith, while Frank's mother clasps her hands and thanks the Lord for the miracle of this pregnancy.

And so begin the lies. Because Edith doesn't see the miracle — to her mind, this pregnancy is nothing short of an encore to an already hellish nightmare. But she doesn't dare admit that out loud.

DANAH 🐦

I HAVE NEVER MISSED a deadline before, so when I email Professor Stone asking him for more time to finish marking his students' papers, exaggerating the circumstances around Edith's fire just a bit, I am ashamed of both needing an extension in the first place and lying about the reason. As I'm contemplating how low my request will sink me in Professor Stone's opinion, Edith pokes her head around the corner of the kitchen. "I'm making scones," she says. "Assuming you're not planning on rushing out somewhere, I thought we might have breakfast together for once."

"I actually don't have anywhere to be today, but I do have a lot of work to do."

"Not so much that you can't eat, surely?"

"No, I have time to eat. It's just, I'm getting behind. But thank you, scones sound delicious."

As Edith putters around in the kitchen, I turn my attention to the student paper in front of me. Although, now that I've asked for more time, I've lost all motivation to keep marking. I check my messages on the off chance that Professor Stone has already replied. No luck.

Soon, the scent of fresh baking wafts into the living room.

Standing up to stretch, I peek into the kitchen and watch as Edith slices a knife through two steaming scones and smears them with butter.

"I'll make tea for us to have with those," I say.

"It's already in the pot."

We sit down at the table together, our scones and tea placed neatly in front of us.

"I'm meeting with Steve tomorrow," Edith says. "They've started the drywall in the kitchen, and I need to pick my paint colours. Will you be able to drive me?"

If they're getting ready to paint already, does that mean her house might be ready early? I feel a small thrill of hope at the prospect. "It depends what time you're meeting him. I have a class at ten, but I can be back by noon."

"Oh, I'm not waiting that long. I'll just take a taxi. While I'm there, I'll stop by Alice's again. No one was home yesterday."

"You were there yesterday?"

Before Edith can answer, there's a soft knock at my apartment door. It's my landlord. Again.

"Hi, Danah. Wanted to let you know I have a deadbolt for your door, and my son-in-law can install it later this afternoon if that's okay."

I glance at Edith, but she quickly disappears into the kitchen. I turn back to Bertie. "Sure, that's fine. Did my grandmother talk to you about this? I really don't need a deadbolt."

"It's no problem. Like I said, David can put it in this afternoon. Is everything else okay?"

"Everything is fine. I'm sorry. I don't have any complaints, Bertie. I'd let you know if I really needed something."

He nods. "Okay then. I'll send him down later."

I shut the door and lean against it, closing my eyes. "Grandma?"

Edith returns to the living room. "Well, he's certainly quick about things, isn't he?"

WHILE EDITH SITS AT the table doing a crossword puzzle, I flip blindly through my research notes. I am accomplishing absolutely nothing. Trevor's advice is still bouncing around in my brain, but I don't know how to get Edith to talk. I clear my throat, intending to broach the subject of my mother again, but at the last minute I chicken out and instead rather lamely remind her about Arthur Williams' visit.

"I'm not exactly one for all that academic mumbo jumbo," she said back when I first told her about it.

Maybe now that she's trapped in my apartment, her opinion will have changed.

"You could ask your neighbour friends to come too. They might like it. I'm supposed to get as many people as possible to attend."

Edith looks over at me. "Oh, I don't know," she says. "When is it again?"

"Next Thursday. He'll speak for about an hour, and then there'll be a Q and A. People usually love his talks. He was on Oprah."

"I guess I could ask Alice. She likes that Oprah woman."

Edith resumes her crossword, and I lean back on the couch, wondering why it's so hard for us to have a conversation like normal people. Every time I steel myself to push back about the letter, to ask her why she's so sure it wasn't from my mother, I hear her clipped voice saying, *There's no point imagining things*, and my mouth clamps shut.

I need to talk to Trevor. We haven't spoken since our stupid dinner at Pass Da Pasta, which is not like us at all, but when I finally cave in and dial his number, my call goes straight to voice mail. I don't bother leaving a message.

If it wasn't for Edith, I'd slink into my bedroom and burrow under my blankets. Maybe have a good cry. But since I have nowhere to hide, I put on a brave face and snap open my laptop to check my email. Professor Stone has replied: he hopes I will endeavour to get the papers done, but if that isn't possible, then he agrees there isn't much to be done but hand them back late. Oh, and he'd like to talk to me after tomorrow's lecture. My stomach clenches uncomfortably. Maybe I can still get the papers done.

Who am I kidding? Even if I stay up half the night, I'll never finish.

Dad used to spend hours poring over papers and journals in his study, sometimes missing meals because he was so immersed in his work. Why didn't I inherit his mental stamina? I doubt he ever had to make up excuses. How did he do it? Because while it's true that he spent a lot of time shut in his study working, he also always had time for me.

I REMEMBER WAKING UP from a nightmare once, practically hyperventilating, and when Dad came into my room, he sat on the edge of my bed and rubbed my back until I calmed down. Then he took me outside, in my pajamas, for a night walk. We made our way down the sidewalk, hand in hand, stepping across the large shadows cast by trees. I should have been scared, but the strangeness of our street — the looming shadows, the dark houses — was not frightening as long as my hand was tucked securely into my father's.

We went all the way to the park by the river.

"Can you hear the water moving, Squirt?"

I strained my ears to listen. There were other sounds, too. A breeze rustling through the branches of the trees, a car somewhere in the distance on a street that seemed, at that moment, far away. Dad led me to the swings, and in the near-quiet darkness we sat for a long time, swaying back and forth. In tandem.

I HAVE HUNDREDS OF memories like that one — moments shared with my father, just the two of us, long before my mother left. Where was she when he took me camping in the Okanagan or when he taught me to fish on the banks of the river or when he carried me on his shoulders through the zoo because my legs were tired? What possible reason could she have had for not being there with us?

JANE LILY ✒

LILY IS TEN WEEKS pregnant. Andrew said he was excited when she told him, but it's hard for Lily to read him lately. Sometimes she gets the sense that he's acting when he's around her, that his gestures are a charade; then she wonders if anything about them is real anymore. She knows for a fact that *she* feels like a fraud.

They weren't planning on having any more kids, so this pregnancy caught them both off guard. Danah is already seven. The thought of starting over with a baby again — the crying, the nursing, the diapers — fills Lily with a kind of dread she would never admit to Andrew. But there is also a thin thread of hope growing inside her, taking shape alongside the tiny fetus.

She has had some light spotting the past few days. The same thing happened when she was pregnant with Danah, so she's not too worried, but still, she has decided to wait until after her next checkup to tell Danah about the baby, when she can be sure everything is okay. She needs to take it easy, that's all. Which is why she's staying home this weekend while Andrew and Danah go camping with friends. She is looking forward to being alone.

Danah is so excited about the trip that she was up early this morning, way earlier than she needed to be, and she hasn't stopped moving since.

"When are we leaving?" Danah asks Andrew for the umpteenth time.

"Right after breakfast, Squirt. You all packed?"

"Dad!" Danah shrieks. "You know I'm packed!"

When their friends finally pull up in their motorhome, Danah runs out the door without even saying goodbye. Then, just as Lily is about to call out, Danah suddenly swings around and runs back.

"Bye, Mom!" she says breathlessly, squeezing her arms around Lily's waist. "See you tomorrow!"

Andrew tells Lily to enjoy herself and kisses her on the forehead. He used to kiss her on the lips. Then they are both gone, and Lily stands in the hall measuring the house's silence with long, even breaths.

SHE SETTLES HERSELF ON the couch with a book. Time stretches before her in luxurious waves. After a few chapters, she gives in to the urge to close her eyes, and the book slips from her fingers. She can't remember the last time she had a nap before lunch.

She wakes to a dull ache in her abdomen. Shifting her position doesn't help; no matter how she arranges herself, she can't get comfortable. In the bathroom, she discovers she is spotting again, only this time it's heavier. There's more blood, a thick stream of it. The same thing happened with Danah, she reminds herself. But she knows this is different. Affixing a thick overnight pad to her underwear, she walks carefully to the bedroom and lies down, keeping herself as flat and still as possible.

She stares at the ceiling. She tells herself everything will be fine, she just needs to stay still, but the cramping only gets worse. The pad, when she checks it, is soaked with blood. *Okay, okay, okay,* she repeats as she looks up her doctor's number with shaking fingers. He instructs her to get herself to the hospital. She has no way of contacting Andrew, and there's no one else she wants to call, so she lines her underwear with more pads and drives herself to the hospital. She sits in one of the plastic chairs in the waiting room while more and more blood seeps out of her.

Finally, she is led to an examination room, where she is given a gown and told to wait once more.

The doctor is brisk, almost unfriendly, when he comes in to examine her. "You're having a miscarriage. The bleeding and cramping will ease once the fetus is expelled."

She already knew. She knew it in the bathroom at home.

"Is there anyone you can call?" the doctor asks. His tone has softened.

"No," she says. When he's gone, she climbs off the examination table and fumbles for her clothes, her purse, her shoes. Behind the flimsy curtain that separates her from the rest of the world, she pulls off the bloodstained gown and sticks two fresh pads to her underwear.

Once she is dressed again, she has to sit on the bed briefly to steady herself. She feels a sudden, fierce flash of anger with Andrew and, however unfairly, with Danah too.

DANAH ✎

DANAH IS DRAGGING HER feet. They have been walking up and down the streets on Granville Island forever. Her mom pulls her into one store after another, where she spends an eternity examining pieces of hand-blown glass or wooden sculptures or paintings. She especially likes looking at the paintings.

"I used to draw all the time when I was young," her mother says. "I had a sketchbook that I took with me everywhere."

"You don't draw now."

"No, I don't."

"Are we going back soon? I'm hungry."

"One more stop," her mother says. She pushes open the door to a souvenir shop filled with hats and mugs and stuffed bears in T-shirts. Danah wanders over to a rack of keychains. She twirls a miniature wooden totem pole in her fingers.

"Can I get one?" she calls over to her mom.

But her mom doesn't reply because she is flipping through a binder of pictures in plastic sleeves. "DeWeir," she says out loud. "This is him. Morian DeWeir." She looks up then, and because of the strange expression on her face, Danah thinks something must be wrong.

"Mom?"

Her mom turns her head suddenly as if she had forgotten Danah was even there.

"Come on. Let's go."

THEY TAKE THE BUS home, and all afternoon Danah's mom is distracted. She has trouble unlocking the front door, and as soon as they're inside, she tells Danah to go play.

"Can I watch TV?" Danah asks, sensing in her mom a kind of confusion that she hopes will yield an automatic yes.

"For a bit. Not too long, though."

Danah skips off to the living room and settles happily on the couch to watch *Rugrats*. She can hear her mom rattling around in the kitchen. A loud crash jolts Danah's attention from the screen, and she runs to see what happened.

"I dropped a lid," her mom says, holding up an empty pot. "Did that scare you?"

"I thought you fell."

"No, no, I'm fine." But she doesn't look fine. Her hands are shaking.

WHEN HER DAD COMES home, Danah rushes to greet him. He doesn't usually work on Saturdays, but he had a special meeting today at the university.

"Hey, Squirt. How was your day?"

"Good. We went shopping."

Her mom comes to stand behind her, and Danah decides not to say how boring it was. Or how weird Mom got at the souvenir store.

"I wanted a totem pole," she says instead. "But Mom wouldn't let me get it."

"You don't need a totem pole," her dad says. "What would you do with a totem pole? Where would we even put it?"

"Dad! It was a keychain. Not a real one!"

He winks at her, and when Danah turns to see her mom's reaction, Lily is studying both of them, biting her bottom lip. Something in her mom's eyes bothers Danah, but she doesn't have time to think about it because her dad reaches out to tickle her, and she has to run down the hall, screaming, to get away from his long arms.

EDITH ✎

"I DON'T HAVE GOOD news, I'm afraid," Steve says. "When we pulled up the linoleum in the kitchen, we noticed that some of the floorboards underneath were rotting. Turns out a few of the joists holding up the floor were starting to go as well."

"What does that mean?"

"We have to tear the whole floor out. We can't continue with the other stuff until the floor is fixed. It could take us an extra week to get everything done. You're still staying with your granddaughter, right?"

"Yes, but I can't stay with her forever."

"Yeah, we'd hoped to finish doing the drywall today and maybe even start getting the cabinets installed, but we can't do any of that now until the floor is dealt with."

"Is someone starting on the floor today, then? It doesn't seem like anyone is doing much of anything." I look pointedly at the empty rooms around us, where I expected to see people busy at work.

"We're waiting to hear back from your insurance since this will alter the quote we provided. That should happen quickly, though. Everyone wants you back home as soon as possible." Steve smiles, but I am hard-pressed to return the favour. "We'll keep working in the other rooms," he assures me. "The walls have been cleaned. As soon as your colours are picked, the painters will get started."

The setback with the kitchen floor is discouraging, but there is nothing to gain by dwelling on it, so I bite back my frustration and flip through the paint samples Steve hands me. It doesn't take long to select the shade of beige I prefer. The one I choose is called Sand-castle, although I can't see how it's any different from Desert Tan or Mushroom. Who comes up with these names anyway? They're nothing short of ridiculous.

I trudge next door since Alice and I have arranged to have lunch, and because I'm not in a hurry to return to Danah's empty apartment, I take Alice up on her offer to stay afterward and crochet. We sit in the living room, which is bright and comfortable, warmed by the afternoon sun, and we lapse into companionable silence, each of us, I presume, lost in our thoughts.

We are crocheting lap blankets for a nursing home. I have not attended a church service in years, but soon after moving to Hamilton, Alice recruited me to join Gospel Light's Caring Hands Committee, where no one seems to mind that I'm not a member of the church. We knit and crochet all kinds of things: lap blankets, baby blankets, hats for the homeless, even tea cozies that the women sell at bazaars. I have no intention of reacquainting myself with God, but I do enjoy the sense of purpose the various projects give me.

We do other things besides crocheting. The church runs a program called The Cupboard, which operates like a food bank, and the Caring Hands staff it once a month. In just a few days they're putting on a community breakfast, which I've pressed Danah into helping out with, although to be honest I'm surprised she has the time for it. I am drawn to these women's desire to do some good. To make themselves useful. Whatever other sins may be levelled against me, I can at the very least lay claim to these acts of compassion. Although, perhaps I put more stock in them than I should.

As I sit in the sunlight in Alice's living room, I fight off a growing despair at the thought of prolonging my stay in Danah's apartment. I doubt she'll be thrilled at the prospect either. Not that it should make any difference to her given how little time she spends there.

"How are things going at Danah's?" Alice asks, and I look up sharply, wondering if I have said something out loud. "It must be nice spending time with her," Alice continues, "even if the circumstances aren't all that ideal."

"I don't see all that much of her. She has some sort of exams coming up, and she's getting ready for a guest speaker. A professor from Australia. Which reminds me, she wanted me to ask if you'd be interested in coming to hear him talk. Apparently, he's been on Oprah. Ben is welcome too, of course."

Alice shakes her head. "It's a shame she's so busy. And right before Christmas, too. I'll talk to Ben. She must find having you around helpful, though?"

Does she? Not as far as I can tell. "I do my best," I say. I don't mention the strain between us, the constant tension that brings me back to the farm in Missionville and everything I endured in that lonely place.

"I'm not sure I'll be making many more of these," Alice laments softly, holding up a slightly misshapen blanket for me to examine. "I can't keep the rows straight."

"Your blankets are as good as they ever were. Besides, the people using them don't care if they're square. All they want is something to keep their legs warm."

"Still," Alice persists, "I can't make them like I used to."

I don't respond. I'm caught up in my thoughts of the farm, of Jane's long-ago betrayal and the string of damaged moments leading up to it. One thing has become increasingly clear to me as my mind dips in and out of the past: my daughter didn't disappear all at once.

She left in pieces.

JANE LILY ✒

JANE IS NOT SPEAKING to her mother. She has nothing to say to her, and even if she did, her mother wouldn't hear her, not really. She hears what she wants to hear, sees what she wants to see, and refuses to accept that there are other ways to experience the world. Jane doesn't know how her mother can stand it: living as if everything is so absolutely black and white.

Jane sits at the dinner table, silently chewing her food, staring at a spot on the wall just past her mother's head. She can hardly swallow for all the angry words blocking her throat. She wants to spit those words right in her mother's face, but even with the cold courage of indignation, she doesn't dare. Instead, she swallows them with her gummy potatoes and then washes them down with milk.

"Rebecca isn't going to the dance either," her mother says, as if that settles it. As if that fact alone proves her point, and Jane should nod in meek acceptance — concede, like she always does.

She picks up another forkful of overcooked pork and forces it down. She imagines endless nights like this one. Silence. Simmering anger. Her mother deliberately unaware. So confident in her *rightness* that she can't conceive of disagreement.

The piece of stringy meat in Jane's mouth won't go down. She can't swallow it. She chews methodically, moving the pulpy mass from one side of her mouth to the other. Then she coughs into her napkin to spit it out. And as she's closing the napkin over the disgusting chunk of chewed-up meat, she makes a decision. She *will* go to the dance. She will sneak out and walk all the way to town if she has to.

IT TAKES JANE ALMOST an hour to get there, and as she tramps along the dark road, she can feel her heart pounding with an exhilarating mix of fear and excitement. When she walks into the soft glow of the lamps lining Main Street, some of her anxiety dissipates. She can see the bowling alley on the corner, and as she approaches, she can hear music drifting through its thin wood walls. The dance will be upstairs. The door to the bowling alley swings open, and a small group of teenagers tumbles out. They walk down the street together, a tight-knit, laughing bunch. Jane watches them go, standing by herself on the sidewalk.

She has friends too, and some of them will be inside. She can hardly wait to see their expressions when she walks in. Light-headed with anticipation, she walks up the narrow stairs inside Mission Lanes, her Sunday shoes click-clacking on the wood.

She is not dressed right at all. She sees that at once. Most of the girls are wearing pants with jean jackets, their wrists layered with bracelets. Her knee-length pleated skirt looks ridiculously old-fashioned. There are other girls in skirts, but theirs are plaid, and they hang differently; they don't flare out like hers. Still, she is here, and she is determined to have fun. She looks around for Sarah and Jenny, the closest thing she has to real friends. She spots them sitting at the side of the hall, their faces softly lit by a glowing lantern on the table in front of them. There are people with them that Jane doesn't recognize, but she makes her way over anyway.

"Jane? Holy cow, guys, it's Jane! How did you get here?" Jenny sounds shocked to see her, and in that moment Jane is shocked too at her own daring.

"I walked," she says.

There are several exclamations, and Jane beams with pleasure, momentarily forgetting about her ugly skirt. It was worth every panic-stricken minute on the dark road to be here now, in this brightly lit room, with the music pulsing behind her and the energy in the room spinning through her veins.

"Sit, sit," Sarah says. "You must be exhausted. Stanley, get this girl a drink!"

Quick introductions are made as Jane is offered a seat at the little round table. Once she's had enough time to recover, one of the boys she's just been introduced to asks her to dance. Still giddy with exhilaration, she agrees.

As the sandy-haired boy takes her hand and leads her to the dance floor, she admits that she can't remember his name.

"Morian," he says.

"Morian," Jane repeats, and they are pulled into the crowd of swirling bodies.

DANAH ᴥ

PROFESSOR STONE IS AN imposing figure. He is tall with a crop of white hair and heavy-framed glasses, and he carries himself with an imperious air that demands respect. As a rule, I try to stay on his good side. Everyone does. Now, as the last of the students file out of the lecture hall, he motions for me to join him at the front of the room.

"I'm so sorry," I start, "I thought I'd given myself enough time, but then my grandmother had a fire and —"

"Sit down, Danah." He gestures to one of the seats in the front row, then sits beside me. He turns toward me, and my hands begin to sweat. "This isn't just about the papers," he says. "I'm disappointed that you didn't get them done — I hate not following through on deadlines, and we promised to have those back in a week. It's irresponsible, and I think someone like you recognizes that. But on top of that, there have been complaints about one of your tutorials. Specifically, that you ended it early, and some of the students felt shortchanged."

He's waiting for me to reply, but I am so caught off guard I don't know what to say. Someone complained about being let out early? "I ... uh ... I wasn't feeling well, so I wrapped up a few minutes early. I didn't realize anyone would mind."

There is a pause while Professor Stone looks at me long and hard. "Is there anything I need to know, Danah?"

I shake my head. "No. Everything is fine, really. Again, I'm so sorry about the delay with the papers. I'll have them done in a day or two, I promise. And I apologize about the tutorial. I should have used the full time."

"Take care of yourself, Danah. If you need help, just ask. I've seen students buckle under pressure, and it usually starts out small and snowballs from there."

AFTER MY LITTLE MEETING with Professor Stone, I'm too embarrassed to return to Kenneth Taylor Hall. That and I don't want to run into my advisor, who for all I know is preparing a similar speech for me. I consider calling Trevor to tell him what happened, but since things are weird between us right now, I text Navi instead to see if she wants to grab a bite to eat.

I'm not on campus, she replies.

I try Dwayne. While I wait for an answer, I sit at one of the tables in the Student Centre, but when he doesn't reply after ten minutes, I decide to just get something for myself. Professor Stone is worried that I'm struggling, that I might buckle under pressure. Me. Danah Calsley. The daughter of Andrew Calsley, one of the most respected sociologists in the country. The worst part is, Stone might be right. My comps are creeping closer and closer, yet when I think back on all the work I've done — all the readings, all the notes on different arguments, explanations, and rationalizations — it blurs together into one indistinguishable clump. I fight off a flare of panic. I'm fine. I'm totally fine. I'm just a bit distracted at the moment.

If I hadn't seen that letter, if Edith wasn't living with me, I wouldn't be having these problems. Whenever I look at my grandmother, my frustration morphs into anger. If she would just open her mouth and tell me the goddamn truth, maybe profs wouldn't have to pull me aside to express their concern. Maybe I could get on with my life.

I throw my half-eaten bagel in the garbage and step outside. A few lazy snowflakes are swirling around, and as I breathe in a lungful of sharp, wintry air, I'm close to crying. I wish I could run away. But I was never any good at that either.

AUNT GEORGINA USED TO take the ferry from Vancouver Island to visit us at least twice a year when we lived in B.C. She came more often after Mom left. Dad didn't know how much I hated her, but I like to believe that if he knew half of what she said to me in the weeks right after my mom disappeared, he'd have been attending her funeral instead of the other way around. I was just little, though, and I didn't know how to tell him, so I never said anything. Maybe I was trying to protect him. Or maybe I was trying to protect myself. In any case, I believed her; I believed all the horrible things she said.

"Could've seen this coming," she muttered. "I knew from the start there'd be trouble with that one. She showed her true colours after you came along."

I didn't know what Aunt Georgina meant, but I knew it had something to do with me being born and Mom somehow turning into a bad person.

The worst was at bedtime, when she forced me to pray, because I understood that what I was praying for was forgiveness. I knew my aunt blamed me for my mother leaving. So, trembling with guilt and a sadness I doubt she could begin to comprehend, I absorbed the unspoken accusations behind her words and accepted them as truth. I already believed in my heart that I was responsible for what had happened. I didn't need Aunt Georgina pointing her spindly finger at me to know that much.

A FEW WEEKS BEFORE Mom disappeared, or maybe it was only a few days, we had a fight over a sandwich. In hindsight, the argument seems so stupid, so trivial, but when it happened, the room was charged with emotion. I remember Mom standing beside me, hands on her hips, insisting I eat the crusts that I had intentionally left on my plate. Arms crossed, I glared at her and refused.

"Daddy never makes me eat them! He even cuts them off for me."

Mom took a big, shuddery breath and stalked out of the kitchen. As she left, I made a nasty face behind her back and stuck out my tongue. She turned around just in time to see me doing it, and I caught the defeated expression in her eyes even as I started to say I was sorry. And I *was* sorry.

Later, when she was gone, I replayed that scene over and over in my mind, wishing with all my heart that I could take it back. The look on her face when she caught me sticking out my tongue was easy enough to read, even for a nine-year-old.

So for that and all my other sins, in those first weeks after she left, I got down on my knees and I prayed. For forgiveness. For my mother to come back. For Aunt Georgina to return to Victoria.

For someone to tell me it wasn't my fault.

DANAH 🐦

DANAH IS RUNNING AWAY. She has packed a bag, taken a few slices of bread and some crackers from the kitchen, and is about to sneak out the back door. Her heart thuds loudly under her thin T-shirt. A few weeks ago, on her eleventh birthday, Aunt Georgina called to sing to her, and she promised Danah she would bring something for her when she next came to visit.

She's supposed to arrive this afternoon, and Danah doesn't want to see her. Not even if she's bringing a present. Her presents are never good anyway — last year she gave Danah a doll, which was a stupid thing to give a ten-year-old. So today, Danah has decided to run away and only come back after her aunt is gone. It has crossed her mind that her aunt might not leave when she finds out that Danah is missing — like how she stayed and stayed right after Danah's mom disappeared — so she left her father a note explaining. That way, he'll make sure Aunt Georgina goes back to Victoria so that Danah can come home.

So far, everything is working perfectly. She plans to slip out the back door and run through the yard to the side gate. She glances behind her before opening the door slowly, trying not to make too much noise. As she steps into the yard, her father's voice stops her in her tracks.

"Where do you think you're going, young lady?"

"Um ..." Danah stares at her father, sitting calmly in a lawn chair, reading the newspaper. "I was just —"

"Your aunt will be here soon. Let's go inside and clean up. You can help me decide what to make for dinner tonight. I doubt she wants grilled cheese." He winks at her as they head back into the house.

Danah's shoulders sag when she sees her aunt's grey car pull up in front of the house. She still plans to get away. Maybe not right away, but once her dad is busy talking to his sister, she can try again to sneak out.

Aunt Georgina has an annoying habit of shaking her head and sighing every few minutes, as if Danah and her father are the most pitiable people on earth. It won't be long before she corners Danah and reminds her that she is responsible for the empty chair at the table, shaking her ugly head and making her annoying tsk tsk noises in Danah's face.

Danah hasn't decided yet where she's going to sleep when she runs away. Penny has a fort in her backyard, but if Danah's going to stay that close to her house, she might as well stay in her own bed. Maybe she should wait until morning. Get up before anybody else and sneak away while they're still sleeping. Yes, that's what she'll do. The bag that she packed is in her room, ready to go.

As she gets ready for bed, she finalizes her plan. She's brushing her teeth, trying to decide whether or not she should pack her toothbrush, when there's a knock on the bathroom door.

"Hey, Squirt, can I talk to you?"

"Sure." She rinses her toothbrush and follows her dad down the hall to her bedroom. He must have left Aunt Georgina all by herself in the living room. Good.

"I found this in my room," he says, holding up the note she left him this morning.

And just like that, her plans crumble around her.

JANE LILY 🐿

I COULD ALWAYS PICK up the phone and call, but what would I say? I still don't know what it is that I want. I do know that I watch for the mail every day. And every time I sort through the advertisements and bills that are slipped through my door, I pretend to myself that I'm not looking for anything in particular.

Wanda, from the bookstore, comes to see me one day after work. She tells me how good I look, then busies herself in the kitchen putting some cookies on a plate and making us both a cup of tea.

"I hope you like Fig Newtons," she says. "I was going to get something with a wee bit of chocolate, but then I ran out of time, so I asked Mark to pick something up, and this is what he got. They're not bad, actually. I quite like them myself, but not everyone is keen on them."

She sets the plate on the coffee table and sits next to me on the sofa. I reach for one of the Fig Newtons, noting in that instant how skeletal my hand looks. I have lost so much weight these last few weeks. "These are fine," I say. "Thank you."

"You've been doing some work in your garden then? Paula said she saw you outside digging up a storm. She would've stopped to say hello only she was with her boys, and they were already running late. My own garden is a disaster. Mark is next to useless when it comes to anything outside, so it's a bit overrun I'm afraid. Some days I want to tip the whole lot of it in the bin and be done with it!" Wanda laughs without conviction. "Have you talked to Paula or anyone else from the café? She's been meaning to catch up. Everyone misses you, they really do."

"I saw Hamish the other day at the shops. He said he had proposed to his girlfriend." I take a sip of my tea and wait for Wanda's version of events to spill out.

She shakes her head. "Either that girl's an idiot or there's something about Hamish we don't know. You know he cheated on her, right? She caught him red-handed. But somehow he wooed her back, and next thing you know he's telling everyone he wants to marry her. 'Almost losing her was the best thing that could have happened to me,' he says. What a bunch of malarkey."

I think back to the day Hamish asked me about second chances. Apparently, his girlfriend believes in them, too, but I doubt either of them understands the repercussions that will reverberate through their marriage as a result of that one mistake. Assuming, of course, that it was only once.

"Maybe it's true," I say. "Maybe almost losing her made him realize how much he really loved her."

"She'll hold it against him forever, she will. I bet sure as sugar she uses it every chance she gets. And in the end, all she'll do is drive him to cheat again! They're both idiots, if you ask me."

AFTER WANDA LEAVES, I consider the implications of starting a marriage that other people already consider to be doomed. How do Hamish and his fiancée stand a chance? God forbid either of them have any family members who will visit after they're married and sit in their living room passing silent judgment. Or worse, voice their disapproval in so many different ways that it becomes a presence in the room, lurking behind every word and gesture.

JANE LILY ✐

GEORGINA SIPS HER TEA gingerly, and Lily waits for her to comment that it's too hot or too strong or too sweet. Andrew's sister doesn't visit often, but every time she does, Lily feels like she is walking on eggshells. Georgina has a way about her, a habit of commenting on everything that is both annoying and exhausting. For whatever reason, Andrew either doesn't mind or chooses not to notice.

"What's the story with your neighbour?" Georgina asks, setting her teacup on the coffee table. "Do they not have time to take care of their lawn, or do they just not care?"

Lily follows Georgina's gaze to the house across the street. There are a few dandelions on the grass, but otherwise their lawn looks fine to her. What does it even matter to Georgina? Why is she so bent on seeing the worst in people? Hell, even Lily's hair bothers Georgina, which would be funny if it weren't so damn infuriating.

"How can you stand having all that loose hair in your face?" Georgina asked her earlier. "Don't you just want to pull it back and out of the way?"

"I like wearing it down," Lily said. *What about you*, she wanted to add, *how do you stand that stick up your ass? Doesn't it ever get uncomfortable?*

RIGHT NOW, GEORGINA IS washing the dishes, no doubt judging Lily for build-up of soap scum on the plastic drying rack or the crumbs that have accumulated in the cutlery drawer. Lily herself is down the hall, giving Danah a bath. Danah is six and doesn't need much help, but Lily is grateful for the brief reprieve bathing her daughter provides. When she left the kitchen, Andrew was sitting at the table, basking in the attention of his sister, enjoying the steaming mug of decaf coffee she had just placed in front of him. It should be Andrew doing the dishes, really. His sister is the guest. But Georgina would never agree to that. To putting her precious brother to work. So Lily left her sister-in-law to the dishes in order to get Danah ready for bed, biting back the urge to point out to Georgina her strict adherence to routine, to the structure she, Lily, provides for her daughter — ideals that she assumes Georgina must place near to godliness.

"Why can't I stay up?" Danah is asking, her head a halo of bubbles. "I'm not tired."

"Aunt Georgina wants some time alone with your dad. She doesn't see him very much, so they need a chance to visit."

"But they won't be alone! You'll be there." Danah splashes her hands into the water. "It's not fair!"

"Put your head back." Lily pours warm water over Danah's scalp, using one hand to block the soap from falling into Danah's eyes. "If you get ready for bed nicely, I'll read you an extra story. Maybe even two."

"How come Aunt Georgina doesn't have any kids?"

"Not everybody has kids."

"I don't think she likes them."

"What makes you say that?" Lily asks.

"She doesn't like me."

"Of course she likes you. She loves you."

Danah makes a face, and in that moment, Lily feels a kinship with her daughter that makes her heart ache. Somewhere deep inside her blooms a sense of longing so intense it brings her close to tears.

"Sit up now. You're all done. Pull the plug, and then I want you to get right into your pajamas. No complaining." Lily helps Danah clamber over the side of the tub, then wraps her daughter's skinny body in a towel.

This shivering, slightly bewildered child standing in front of her is so innocent. Lily is torn between the simultaneous desires to pull Danah's towel-wrapped body against her and to push her away.

Perhaps Georgina is right to judge.

Danah stumbles toward her bedroom, clutching the towel around her body, leaving a trail of small, wet footprints on the hardwood in the hall. Lily follows a few paces behind as the sound of Andrew's laughter ricochets down the hall, thrumming against her skin like a drum roll of accusations.

DANAH 🐦

"LET ME GET THIS straight. You need my help?" Dwayne is leaning back in his chair, his feet up on the study carrel in his office, looking at me with his eyebrows raised in comic disbelief.

I tracked him down after a quick meeting with my advisor, where I lied about the dinner reservations I forgot to make. "I'm serious, Dwayne," I say. "I don't know any other good restaurants to try. Sanders will freak if she finds out we have nowhere to go."

"I'm just surprised. This so isn't like you." Dwayne lowers his feet back to the floor and leans toward me. "Everything okay?" he finally asks.

"Yes! Why does everyone keep asking me that? I'm fine, just a little preoccupied. Who isn't?" Then, sinking into an empty chair beside Dwayne, I tell him about my conversation with Professor Stone.

"So, I'm just curious, why did you let your tutorial out early? I mean, normally you're such a stickler."

I let out a long sigh from somewhere deep inside. "Because the day before, I saw this letter that I was anxious to ask my grandmother about. I was done the tutorial anyway, and I just needed to get out of there." I keep talking. Dwayne doesn't interrupt me once as I go on about my mother and how I think my grandmother is hiding something. "She brushes me off every time I mention my mother. But who else could that letter have been from?" I shake my head. "I'm becoming obsessed with it. I can't concentrate on anything. I'm worried about my comps, and now apparently I can't even manage to make a simple dinner reservation!" I wait for Dwayne's reaction, for him to tell me to pull myself together.

When he speaks, though, there's no trace of judgment. "Well, the good news, Danah, is that you were so hyper-organized before all this that you probably don't *need* to do anything for your comps. Besides, you still have plenty of time before you need to panic. You could probably write your exam today and do fine. As for the restaurant, that's easily remedied now that you've left it in my capable hands. By next week you'll be drooling over Williams, and all of this crap will be a distant memory."

I can't help but smile. "Thanks. I guess I needed to vent." I want to believe that Dwayne is right. That despite how off-balance I feel right now, everything will eventually return to normal.

"I never knew all that stuff about your mom," Dwayne says, studying my face. "I get why you want to know about that letter. That would drive anyone crazy. But since you're in this propitious situation where you happen to be living with your grandmother —"

"Propitious?" I interrupt. "Who *talks* like that?"

"Intelligent people. Like me."

"Right. But please don't tell me all I need to do is ask her about it, because if you recall, I already have, and it didn't get me very far."

"You asked her about the letter, yes. She said she knew nothing about it, and maybe she's being honest. Maybe she's not. I don't know the woman. But if she *is* completely estranged from your mom like she says, and let's pretend we believe her, you still each have these separate histories that you could share with each other, which would be something. Maybe not quite what you were hoping for, but ..."

"We don't talk about her. We don't 'share' like that."

Dwayne reaches over and pats my arm. It's a strangely gentle gesture. "Be brave," he says. Then he moves past me, into the hall, and I am left sitting in his empty office with his words echoing in my mind. *Be brave.*

PENNY AND I USED to spend a lot of time in her basement, playing in a crawl space behind the closet in one of the spare bedrooms down there. It was our clubhouse. We filled it with blankets, games, and stuffed animals, and we held secret meetings in it. The only way to get to it was through a half-sized door at the back of the closet.

On one particular day, Penny dared me to go into the crawl space alone, without a flashlight, and to stay in there, in the complete dark, until she came back for me.

"Okay," I said. It sounded easy enough. I crawled inside on my hands and knees and sat cross-legged in the middle of the small room while Penny closed the door, encasing me in total darkness. I couldn't see anything, not even my own hands. I assumed Penny was sitting on the other side of the door in the closet.

"Penny?" I called out. "How long do I have to sit here?"

Silence.

"I'm not even scared," I said. I waited for what seemed an impossibly long time. I was growing bored and uncomfortable. The black space around me seemed to solidify, pressing against me. I started to worry about running out of air. I tried shifting my position, straightening one leg to relieve a cramp in my knee, but when my foot hit something soft, I quickly pulled it back.

I drew my knees up to my chest, hugging them to myself. Where was Penny? The house above me was strangely quiet. Had Penny left? Gone somewhere with her mom, forgetting all about me?

"Penny, this isn't funny," I said into the silence. "I'm coming out now."

I thought the air really was running out because my head felt light. My arm, when I reached out for the door, was shaking. I leaned forward and touched the wall. Where was the door? Which way was I even facing? Something shifted in the dark space to my left, and I choked back a scream. I was on my knees now, fumbling blindly for the small metal door handle. I was crying, but I didn't care. I just wanted out. Finally, my fingers closed around the smooth knob, and I pushed the miniature door open, scrambling onto the floor of the closet.

Penny had closed the closet doors, and when I burst through them, the spare bedroom was empty. Wiping my nose on my sleeve, I made my way up the carpeted stairs. Penny's mom was in the kitchen, humming, blissfully unaware that her monster of a daughter had just left me alone in a basement crawl space, huddled in terror.

I crept past her and down the hall, toward Penny's bedroom.

"Hey!" Penny said, looking up from the book she was reading. "You weren't supposed to come out till I said!"

"You took too long. I got bored."

"You mean you got scared. Are you crying?" She snapped her book shut and laughed. "That wasn't even fifteen minutes. I was going to get you after fifteen minutes. I can't believe I'm friends with such a baby!" Then, her face turning serious, she shook her head sadly and said, "It's official. You're a coward."

Her accusation surprised me. The word *coward* hovered in the air between us. I couldn't believe that she, of all people, would call me that. I had worked so hard to be brave during the long, empty stretches of time right after my mother left, and she knew it. During the last few months, I'd I fought the urge to cry over and over even though my heart was breaking, so hearing my best friend in the world call me a coward when I was fighting tooth and nail to be strong was a slap in the face.

Now, after listening to Dwayne tell me to be brave, I feel the sting of that slap all over again. When did I become so weak?

I END MY AFTERNOON tutorial exactly on time, spending a good portion of it looking around the room wondering who complained about me. Afterward, as I cut through the Student Centre, I am forced to weave through a display of pre-Christmas vendor tables piled with stuff like sweaters, jewellery, and knitted hats. Christmas shopping is the last thing on my mind, but I stop in front of a table selling jigsaw puzzles anyway. As I browse through the selection, I think about how many times I've seen Edith working on a puzzle in her living room, sitting at a card table she sets up expressly for that purpose.

When Dad and I first moved to Ontario, back when he still quarterbacked my visits with Edith, he would drop me off for some bonding time or whatever it was supposed to be, and Edith and I would often work on a puzzle together. Sitting at that card table provided us with a comfortable way to pass the time. In fact, even visiting Edith as an adult, I enjoy the ease of small talk with her when our frequent silences are sanctioned by the kind of concentration a difficult puzzle demands.

I look through the selection and choose a puzzle with a colourful and complicated pattern of hot air balloons, imagining Edith's pleased expression when she sees it. As I pay, I feel a sudden flush of goodwill. Dad would be proud.

EDITH SEEMS GENUINELY HAPPY with the puzzle when I present it to her. We sit down at the table together and rummage through the box for the edge pieces. Edith has a rule about doing the border first. I asked her once, a long time ago, why she had to do it that way, and her answer was: "I just do. Are you going to help me or argue with me?"

Sitting across from Edith at my kitchen table, with the puzzle between us, I can practically taste the words I want to say, but as soon as I open my mouth, they dissolve on my tongue.

These unarticulated utterances and the yearnings they represent remind me of the long-ago hope I held out when I first realized I was going to meet Edith. Dad was the one who arranged it, soon after we moved, and I was reluctant at first — I didn't want to meet my grandmother at all — but I was foolish enough, or naive enough, to think maybe she would have answers for us when we showed up on her doorstep. I thought that when she saw me, the truth might just come spilling out.

DANAH ✌

DANAH IS SITTING WITH her father in his study, curled up on a brown leather recliner, reading, while he works at his desk. There is only one small window in the room, but Danah likes the closeness of the air, a pungent mix of sweat and paper and ink.

"Danah," her father says, swivelling around to face her, "how do you feel about the fact that we're moving?"

Danah looks up from her book. "How do I feel?" she repeats, buying time while she decides whether he is looking for honesty or assurances. Her father recently accepted a position at the University of Guelph, and they're moving in July, right after she finishes grade eight. "I'm excited, I guess," she finally ventures, although that's about as far from the truth as possible. "I mean, I'll miss my friends," she adds. She doesn't tell him that Penny suggested she stay behind and move in with her family, and that, however briefly, she considered it as an option. She also doesn't admit that leaving this house makes her nervous. It's been five years since her mother left, but if they move, how will she know where to find them?

"I think the change will be good for us," her father says. "You'll make new friends. Who wouldn't want to be friends with someone like you?"

Danah rolls her eyes, but she's smiling when she turns back to the book in her lap.

THE MOVE ITSELF IS uneventful. While they're packing, Danah realizes how even after all these years, traces of her mother linger around the house: the piano she bought at an auction but never learned to play; the drapes she painstakingly selected after months of deliberation; the books she added to Danah's father's collection but then signed on the inside cover to mark them as irrevocably hers.

The drapes stay with the house, but Danah insists on taking the piano with them. She still hopes that one day she might learn to play something more advanced than "Mary Had a Little Lamb" on those ivory keys. As for the books, she cannot say what compels her to pack all of her mother's copies when she so ruthlessly clears out her own. Her mother's name, maybe, scrawled in blue ballpoint pen on the inside covers — proof that she existed once, in this house, in Danah's life.

Eventually, all their possessions are loaded onto the TransCanada truck to begin the long trek across the provinces. Danah and her father follow a few days later in a plane. Their new house is located on a quiet street close to the university's campus. Danah's bedroom has a cushioned window seat that looks right into the branches of a giant maple tree. When it's windy, the leaves brush against her window, tapping out a gentle greeting.

Their first few days are spent in languid companionship, with lazy mornings followed by hot and humid afternoons working side by side to unpack and set up their new home. They buy four fans, but even with every fan on high speed, the air in the house remains heavy and damp. Danah makes jug after jug of lemonade while her father assures her that eventually they'll get used to the heat.

Danah doesn't mind the heat; she is content in their stifling little cocoon, just the two of them, temporarily isolated from the rest of the world. She knows, however, that soon her father will start work again, and not long after that, she'll begin her first year of high school in an unfamiliar building where she will be a complete stranger to everyone she sees. She won't know where the bathrooms are, and she'll have nobody to talk to about her first day. Well, nobody other than her father, and Penny, of course, who will be waiting for her to call with all the details.

Before she left Vancouver, she and Penny spent as much time together as possible — lying on Penny's trampoline in the evenings, staring at the stars, listening to the Red Hot Chili Peppers while they talked about how different life would be for both of them in a few weeks.

"Promise you'll stay in touch," Penny instructed. "I want to know everything about your new school, especially the boys. My mom said they'll all be farmers. You could end up marrying a farmer from Guelph!" She stared at Danah in mock horror, and then they both started laughing because moments earlier they'd been close to crying, and they needed some way to release all the emotion of those final summer days together.

"My dad said we might come back to B.C. at Christmas. To visit my aunt. Ugh. But maybe I'd get to see everyone again then."

"You'll probably have a new best friend by then," Penny said. "And you won't want to come back at all."

It's hard to imagine having any friends, let alone a new best friend, as Danah and her dad acclimatize to their new home and to the heavy humidity that weighs the air down like a wet and solid presence. Danah spends many hours on her window seat, staring at the maple tree, wishing she was back in Vancouver.

"I have a surprise for you," her father says one day. "Tomorrow we're going to meet your grandmother. We're finally going to see her in person."

Danah stares at him. "I don't want to go," she says.

Her father gives her his look, the one he uses when she's about to disappoint him, and she knows then that she's going to drive with him to Hamilton to meet this Edith person whether she likes it or not.

EDITH ❧

EDITH SHIFTS FROM FOOT to foot as she stands staring out the living room window. Her granddaughter is on the way to her house at this very moment. She's seen pictures, of course, but after years of polite thank-you notes and Christmas cards, she's actually going to see Danah in the flesh. Andrew too. She spoke to him for the first time years ago, right after Lily disappeared, when he called her hoping she might know something they didn't.

It was strange, hearing him talk about Lily and Danah. He described how he'd come home to find Danah alone outside the empty house. How Lily was just gone. As he spoke, Edith couldn't reconcile the person he was describing — his wife, Danah's mom — with her daughter. Except, of course, for the fact that she had run off.

Before that call, Edith had never spoken to Andrew. She only knew about his existence at all, and Danah's too, because their names had been thrown at her in those first few curt letters from Jane. By then, Jane had relented enough to at least include a return address. Edith almost didn't get the letter about her being married to Andrew at all; she had already moved to Hamilton and had no way of letting Jane know. Her in-laws forwarded it to Edith's new address, and Edith was able, finally, to write back and explain that she was living in Hamilton now. She wanted to arrange a visit, despite the vast distance between them, but it was clear that Jane had no real interest in actually connecting. She must have wanted her mother to know she was married, but that was all, because she didn't reply to any of the letters Edith sent. Then, when Danah was born, Edith received another envelope. It contained the birth announcement from the newspaper, as if that particular piece of news was no more interesting than a recipe or a sale on eggs at the local IGA. Edith sent a gift, again suggesting some kind of visit, a chance to see each other, to meet the baby, but Jane didn't acknowledge the gift or the request to arrange a visit. So Edith was left waiting for whenever the next letter might come.

She waited a long time. When it came, almost a decade later, it was just as short and impersonal as the ones before it. It had no helpful information that she could share with Andrew. In it, Jane admitted to Edith that she'd left her husband and daughter. She didn't want anyone to look for her. She was telling Edith as a courtesy, nothing more.

Andrew got his own note around the same time, confirming what everyone had known all along: Jane or Lily or whoever she thought she was had no intention of coming back. And Edith knew full well what that meant.

BY THE TIME THE white Acura pulls up in front of her house, Edith has smoothed her slacks and adjusted her hair at least a hundred times. Her fingers feel numb with cold, although it is easily over thirty degrees outside. She watches as a tall, solidly built man emerges from the driver's seat. Then, from the passenger door, an uncanny echo of Jane climbs out: the same long limbs, oval face, watchful eyes. The girl's hair is lighter in colour, and straight, but there's no denying who her mother is. Edith stands on the small porch, wondering what on earth she is expected to say.

Thankfully, Andrew speaks first. "You must be Edith," he says, reaching out his hand. "I'm Andrew, and this is Danah. We've been looking forward to meeting you."

Edith shakes both of their hands, then ushers them inside. The house is filled with the aroma of cinnamon from the spiced coffee cake she made that morning. She quickly busies herself in the kitchen preparing tea and slicing the cake, which she serves on her best china. When she returns to the living room, every glance at Danah causes her heart to squeeze with a long-forgotten pain.

She listens as Andrew describes his current position and also the one he left behind in British Columbia. They speak politely about what Danah will be taking in high school and her favourite subjects. Edith briefly mentions the farm in Missionville where she lived before moving to the city. No one mentions Jane, but her absence weighs heavily in the room. Although the words never brush past her lips, Edith is brimming with questions. She imagines that Andrew and Danah have questions to ask of her too, but no one, it seems, has the courage to approach the gaping hole caused by her daughter's desertion.

Instead, all of their unspoken memories collide in the heavy air around them, then collapse wearily as the afternoon wears on.

JANE LILY ✎

THE HEADACHES ARE GETTING worse. I knew this was going to happen. I've known it for weeks. Back in October, which feels like a lifetime ago, I left the bookstore early because I wasn't feeling well. I hadn't been feeling well all week, but that day, in addition to being tired and having a persistent ache at the back of my skull, I also felt sick to my stomach. If I moved too quickly, I got dizzy. Things hadn't improved by the next morning, so I stayed home again. I started throwing up during the night. I was used to headaches, but this was different. I made a doctor's appointment and called the bookstore. Wanda was concerned — whether about me or how many more shifts she would have to cover, I couldn't tell.

"You sound terrible," she told me. "Get some rest. Don't worry about coming in until you feel better."

I grunted some form of reply and hung up the phone.

My doctor didn't seem too concerned. She was attentive, polite, and thorough. Just in case, she told me, she was sending me for an MRI. But it was nothing to worry about, nothing at all. Simply routine procedure.

Except that when she asked to see me again to discuss the results, I knew immediately that if it was nothing, like she'd promised, she wouldn't have insisted on telling me in person. I returned to her office and sat across from her with my heart pounding in my ears and my clammy hands pressed against my pants.

A voice inside my head, caught in a frantic loop, whispered, *I don't want to know. I don't want to know. I don't want to know.*

"Lily," my doctor said, and the voice in my head grew louder. *No. No. No.*

But her next words somehow made it through the barrier of sound that was now roaring in my ears — not even an intelligible phrase anymore but a sound like waves crashing on shore, white, blank, filled with fury — as her soft voice penetrated all that noise to tell me: I had a tumour in my brain.

A high-pitched wail began to build somewhere deep inside me, but I sat there silent and stone-faced, refusing to absorb this piece of information.

My doctor continued, undeterred. "It's inoperable, Lily. We can't take it out. We have other treatments we can try, but I don't want to be falsely optimistic."

I nodded. Was I supposed to say something? An inoperable tumour. She had to be mistaken. I remember thinking that she must have been confusing me with someone else. I hadn't thrown up in days. I was getting better. There couldn't be anything seriously wrong with me. Surely ...

"I'm going to refer you to Dr. Lawson. He's an oncologist and will be able to explain more about your options." My doctor looked so serious. Her voice, her manner, they emanated concern and understanding and something very like pity. I needed to get out of her office. But when I stood, I was shaking so badly my legs wouldn't support me.

"I don't think I can walk right now," I said.

I was taken in a wheelchair down the hall to an elevator and up to the oncologist's office. A few of his words made it through my haze of disbelief. Radiation. Small chance. Months. Maybe weeks. Pain relief.

My life narrowed to a pinprick of meaning: I had a brain tumour, and I was dying. Very likely sooner rather than later. I had to tell Wanda I wouldn't be back to work in a few days. I wouldn't be back at all. My days became an unfulfilling cycle of hospital visits, rest, and cardboard meals. And thinking. So much thinking. In those first few days, although my mind was free to travel wherever it pleased, and though I tried to control its path, it found its way into the cracks and tiny trails that led, always, to Danah. Would she sense it when I died? Would my mother?

WHEN I MARRIED ANDREW, I tried hard to become a new person. I planned to be devoted, domestic, and responsible. I was, by then, far removed from the strong-willed and angry girl that I'd been when I ran away from the farm. It was Andrew's idea to send Danah's birth announcement to my mother. Lying in my bed, propped up against a wall of pillows, with Danah's small and vulnerable body pressed close against me, I felt a flood of resentment toward my mother that bordered on hatred. She had ruined my childhood; I was determined not to do the same to my daughter.

"Do you want to call your mom?" Andrew asked. Maybe he hoped the baby in my arms might finally bridge what must have seemed to him an unfathomable gap between my mother and me. He tolerated our estrangement, but he never pretended to understand it.

"Why would I call her?" I asked sharply. "That's the last thing I want to do right now." Then I burst into tears. Because I *did* want to call my mother. I wanted to tell her all about my baby and the delivery and how overwhelmed I felt; only I wanted my mother to be different. I wanted some other mother to tell all of these things to.

"Shhh," Andrew soothed. "It's okay. You might change your mind later."

I never did call her, but I did agree to send the birth announcement. When I sealed the envelope with the small rectangle cut out from the newspaper inside, I envisioned one reaction from my mother: remorse.

I wanted the news of Danah's birth to wound her.

ON THE HEELS OF my diagnosis, I was also referred to Niall Patterson. My doctor said, "This is a lot to take in, Lily. Many people in your situation find it helpful to ... to have someone to talk to, someone to help them through ... well, just to help them face things." She looked at me with so much hope in her face, as if I should be excited about the prospect of talking to a therapist about my impending death. "He specializes in cases like yours," she assured me.

Cases like mine. How quaint. Not knowing what else to do, I started seeing Niall in his beige office above Essington Chocolatiers. One of the first questions he asked was what kind of support system I had here in Edinburgh. Family, friends, that sort of thing.

"No family. I have a few friends." Did I have friends? I had people with whom I was *friendly*, but did that make them friends? The kind of friends Dr. Patterson was hinting at — people who would put their lives on hold to help me when I could no longer help myself? Oh, God. In that moment, I felt more alone than I'd felt in a long time. Alone and scared and very, very sorry for myself.

Niall continued to probe on the family question, wanting to know when I'd last had contact with my family. We talked about the letters I'd written. He was curious about my motives. I didn't understand them myself, so I was at a loss to explain to him, but it became obvious to him quite quickly that I had no immediate plans to communicate the news of my diagnosis to anyone.

"You have to do what's right for you," he told me; then he paused, as if allowing the caveat to sink in. "But consider whether or not there might be an opportunity for healing here. What might come of you reaching out? Not for anyone else, you understand. I'm not concerned about anyone else but you right now. What might it mean to *you*?"

"It wouldn't mean anything to *me*," I replied. He nodded and let the matter drop. "Besides, I did reach out. When Andrew died."

When I next saw him, he asked again if I'd given any more thought to contacting my family.

I had.

If what I was supposedly seeking was closure, then maybe Niall was right. Maybe it was possible that there was still a chance for that. Either because I was so lonely or so desperate or already compromised by the tumour pressing on my brain, I decided to send one more letter. I couldn't face a phone call.

I addressed it to my mother, but I wrote it for both of them, for my mother and my grown-up stranger of a daughter. In it I tried, in woefully inadequate ways, to apologize for the way things had turned out. I wasn't brave enough to send the letter to Danah even though I knew she was at McMaster. I didn't think I had the right. Not anymore.

NIALL ASKED ME ONCE, near the beginning, to tell him about Danah. I didn't want to discuss her.

"You don't like talking about your daughter, do you?"

"No."

"Why do you think that is?" Niall asked, sitting back and tilting his head as if he was contemplating all the possible reasons himself. He waited for me to answer, his eyes fixed on me thoughtfully. Patiently.

I knew what he wanted. He wanted me to examine my feelings about my daughter, to line them all up in front of us in a neat little row on the coffee table between our chairs with its convenient box of tissues, so that he could help me dissect them. He wanted to inspect them with me so that I could finally see them for what they were. He wanted to help me understand. It was almost as sickening as the cloying smell of chocolate saturating the air around us.

I must have answered him. I probably said I had no idea, and he probably sighed before trying another approach. Somehow, after, I must have left his office and walked past the chocolates on display in the large bay window. I must have continued to the bus stop one block east, where I would have waited, most likely with my back molars grinding, for bus number 512. When it pulled up, I must have paid my fare, found a seat, and then disembarked at the stop two blocks from my flat, but I don't remember doing any of those things.

What I remember is unlocking my front door and moving through my flat like a sleepwalker, knowing what I was about to do but trying not to dwell on it because then I would feel like a crazy person. Keeping my mind deliberately blank, I walked into my bedroom, reached under my bed, and pulled out the blue shoebox I kept hidden there. Then, sitting on the floor with my back leaning against the metal frame of my bed, I removed an old black plastic film canister from the box. I rolled the canister between the palms of my hands and blew out an unsteady breath. Finally, I peeled back the grey lid and shook the contents into my hand. I stared at the single tiny tooth resting against my pink skin, and then, in one swift motion, I popped the tooth into my mouth. I closed my eyes and used my tongue to press the cracked enamel surface hard against the roof of my mouth until I could feel the tooth's rough edge scraping the thin layer of tissue there.

I probably sat on the floor of my bedroom, sucking Danah's tooth like a Tic Tac, for thirty minutes or more. I couldn't remember the last time I had done this, but I knew that holding that tooth in my mouth was the only thing that could relieve the pressure building inside my head that threatened to push and push until it shattered my skull.

EDITH ❧

YESTERDAY, DANAH BROUGHT ME a jigsaw puzzle. We worked on it for a while together, but there was a strange tension in the air. I got the sense Danah was upset about something, or maybe she was just preoccupied. Sitting at that table, I could just as easily have been back on the farm sliding puzzle pieces over to Jane, the air around us freighted with all the things we could not say. Or would not say.

I remember a night when Jane was twelve or thirteen, sitting on the opposite side of the living room from me. It must have been close to Christmas because the staircase was lined with spruce boughs and the air was scented with peppermint. I was sitting by the window, where we had a makeshift table set up with a puzzle on it. Some cozy winter scene. A horse, I think, pulling a sleigh down a snow-covered trail. Jane was on the sofa, glowering at me, because I hadn't let her go skating the night before.

"Why don't you give me a hand?" I suggested. "You could work on the light from the streetlamp. The yellowish pieces should be easy enough to find."

She came over, although the expression on her face made it clear she was still angry. She wouldn't look at me as she dug through the box.

I'd already told her that I didn't want her skating on the pond. Period. The reasons why should have been obvious enough.

I passed her a few orangey-yellow pieces, and when she found where one fit, she made a small noise of satisfaction. Did I really need to explain to her that all I wanted was to keep her safe? Isn't that what I'm doing with Danah too? I'm only trying to protect her. What's the point in looking back if we can't undo what's been done? When all there is to see is pain.

THE HOURS I SPEND in Danah's apartment are long and lonely. I've run out of projects, and short of sitting and staring or working on the puzzle, there's not much for me to do. This afternoon, my stomach is growling, and since I know better than to wait for Danah when I want to eat, I heat up a small pot of tomato soup, then slice a few thick pieces of cheese for a sandwich. I'm counting on the soup to warm me up since the space heater her landlord provided is about as effective as a kitten blowing out mouthfuls of air. As I am swallowing my last spoonful of soup, I hear a car pull into the driveway. The doorknob at the top of the stairs rattles — Danah keeps forgetting about the new deadbolt — and after a clatter of boots on the steps, Danah walks in and tosses her bag on the floor.

"It's like Fort Knox trying to get in here," she says.

I ignore her comment. "There's soup, if you want it."

Danah serves herself a bowl, takes down a box of crackers, and joins me at the table. She sips at her soup, occasionally trying to place a puzzle piece from her upside-down perspective, saying nothing. I match her silence, fitting one piece after another into the balloon-filled sky.

Eventually, Danah gets up to put her bowl in the sink, then she sits down on the couch with a pile of papers spread out in front of her. "Some light reading for my comps," she says out loud, and whether she is talking to herself or to me, it's impossible to tell.

I watch her as she reads, her eyes narrowed in concentration. Every now and again she pauses to highlight something or to make a note on a separate pad of paper, and I notice that she chews her thumbnail while she works.

Jane used to suck on a strand of her hair when she was upset. A disgusting habit. I cut it short once to make her stop, but instead of thanking me she cried her fool head off for a week. She ranted and raved about me ruining everything and trying to make her ugly. It did stop her sucking her hair, though.

As I stare at Danah, I am reminded that a person can disappear even when they are right in front of you.

EDITH 🐦

THE ZAANSE CLOCK CHIMES out the half hour just as Edith glances at it for the umpteenth time. Eleven-thirty, and still no sign of Jane. Edith's anger mounts with every tick of the ornate minute hand. This is not the first time Jane has openly ignored her curfew. She is losing her head over a boy, and not just any boy either. This one isn't even from Missionville; he's a complete stranger.

The first time Morian came to the farmhouse, he pulled up in a red Mustang and honked the horn. Jane was about to prance out the door when Edith stopped her.

"Where do you think you're going?" she demanded. "If this young man plans on taking you anywhere, he'd better at least have the decency to come to the door and get you. Besides, I'd like to meet him before he drives off like he owns you."

Jane shifted on her feet impatiently, but Edith wouldn't budge. Eventually, Morian climbed out of his car and came toward the front door. Edith pushed it open and stood planted firmly between her daughter and the sandy-haired boy on the step.

"So," she said to him, "you're the young man who thinks he can summon my daughter with his horn like she's some kind of animal."

He didn't even blink. He just stuck out his hand and smiled. "I'm Morian. Nice to meet you."

Jane reached for his arm and steered him away from Edith to the waiting car, no doubt rolling her eyes in shame.

Now the two of them are out again, and apparently neither one of them can be bothered making sure Jane is home on time. Ten o'clock, she told them, which is plenty late for anyone to be out. Edith rubs her temple. She can't very well sit up all night waiting; she has to get up in the morning. Taking one last glance out the window, she makes her way up the stairs to her room. She'll wait in bed. But as soon as she hears Jane come slinking into the house, she'll get up and give her daughter a piece of her mind.

EDITH OPENS HER EYES and sits up slowly. Did she fall asleep? The house is utterly quiet. Her bedroom lamp is on, and when she checks the clock on her nightstand, she is shocked to realize it's nearly three in the morning. She walks down the hall to Jane's room, fear quickening her footsteps. Already she can feel her chest tightening, her breathing becoming tight and shallow.

Jane's door is slightly ajar. Edith pushes it open, and she can see by the light from the hall that Jane is sprawled out on her bed. Safe and sound.

She lets out a breath.

In the morning, that girl will have some explaining to do.

DANAH 🐎

"IT'S NOT LIKE YOU to ignore a message from me," Pauline Sanders says, looking at me closely. We're sitting in her office, and the way Pauline is studying my face makes me nervous. I glance past her at the empty football stadium outside her window.

"I know. I'm sorry. Things have been a little crazy lately. My grandmother is staying with me ... I guess I got a bit sidetracked." I smile at her, hoping she'll give me some pat line about staying focused right up until the finish line and let me go.

She sets her glasses down carefully on her desk, then folds her hands. "I talked to Walter Stone."

Oh. Shit. "Yeah, that was part of the whole crazy thing. I've never been late with my marking before." I fidget in my chair. Could that one small slip-up affect my chances of being considered for her project? I don't like the look on Pauline's face.

Her hands are still clasped in front of her. She leans toward me. "Danah, I don't think I need to stress how important your comps are at this point. I know things have been hard this past year, but if you're struggling, and all of this is more than you can manage right now, we should have a conversation about your options."

My *options?* Oh, God, this is getting worse by the minute. "You really don't need to be worried, Pauline. I'm fine, really." I do my best to look as competent as possible while I say this, not like I am about to burst into tears or throw up on her carpet, both of which seem equally likely.

"You put a lot of pressure on yourself, Danah. I know you're not immune to the expectations people have, given your father's reputation."

I nod dumbly. Just then, there's a knock at her office door, and I turn my head, praying for any excuse to put an end to this mortifying conversation.

Professor Sanders stands up. "I'm here to help, Danah." With that, she motions for the person standing outside her door to come in, and I gratefully slip out, keeping my head low in case it's obvious to whoever is standing there that I'm about to dissolve into a puddle of humiliation.

I head straight for the elevator, my advisor's comment about options tunnelling into my brain. The elevator doors slide open, and Dwayne steps out. As soon as he sees me, he grins.

"Oh, hey!" he says. "I just booked The Stone Oven. Turns out my roommate knows the manager. He pulled a few strings for us."

I try to summon some enthusiasm. "Great!" I say, but even I can hear how phony I sound. "Sorry, I've got to run. But that's amazing. Thanks. You have no idea." I brush past him into the elevator, watching as the doors close on his confused face.

Instinctively, I pull out my phone. I want to find Trevor so he can put his arms around me and hold me together. For the first time, it feels cold in my father's shadow. I stare at the screen on my phone for a few seconds, then drop it back in my bag without pressing a single button.

I GO TO THE gym, and I run hard. Thank God for Dwayne. I can only imagine Pauline's reaction if I had to admit that on top of everything else, I'd also screwed up something as simple as booking a dinner reservation, especially after lying to her about it the other day. I'll definitely have to buy Dwayne a drink the next time the two of us are in the proximity of alcohol.

I skip my usual warm-up, increasing the speed on the treadmill until I'm practically sprinting. I don't have my headphones with me, so the sounds of the gym resonate around me: the thwack of a medicine ball hitting the wall, weights clanging together or crashing against the floor, the steady drone of my treadmill's motor, and the thudding of my rapid footfalls as I push myself to go faster and faster.

My legs and lungs are burning, but I don't slow down. Fuck Pauline and her concerns about me. Who does she think she is, talking about being overwhelmed and needing options? I don't need options. I just need some fucking answers. Is that so hard to understand?

I run and run and run, and when I finally step off the treadmill, I'm dizzy. I should have eaten before coming here. Dwayne told me to be brave, but he's never met Edith. What is it with him and Trevor? Speaking of Trevor, I can just picture him raising his eyebrows and tilting his head, giving me that annoying look he gets when he thinks he's right. Which raises another question: where the hell is he? If he's waiting for me to make the next move, he can keep waiting. I have enough other shit to deal with at the moment without worrying about him.

I take a few wobbly steps beside the treadmill, then lean over with my hands on my knees until my vision clears. Thoughts of my mother drum against my brain in anxious time with my racing heart. And while I'm doubled over like this, trying to catch my breath, I wonder if there was ever a time my mom was happy.

JANE LILY 🐾

NIALL WANTS TO KNOW how I felt when I first learned that Andrew had died. I tell him I can't remember. It was almost a year ago that I found out. He says he didn't realize my memory was that short. I say obviously I was sad to hear it and that I felt bad for Danah because the two of them had always been close.

"It's difficult to talk about death, isn't it?" Niall asks.

"It's difficult to talk about Andrew," I say. "But that was certainly an interesting way to bring him up, all things considered."

I know what Niall is trying to do. But it isn't Niall who has to understand where I made my biggest mistakes. And I already have a pretty good idea. I don't remind him about the letter I sent after Andrew died in case he asks too many questions. Part of me hopes it never arrived. That would explain why no one ever responded.

WHEN I MET ANDREW, I was lonely, isolated, and hurt. I was also young. Just twenty-one, with a host of insecurities that had begun crowding in on me when it became obvious that no matter how hard I tried to be the person I thought other people wanted or needed me to be, I never quite managed. So there I was, a fresh failure, alone in B.C. But Andrew saw something different. He saw only good in me, and I began to *feel* that goodness. I began to see myself the way I imagined he saw me. And I liked that version of myself.

Andrew was the type of person who laughed a lot, and soon I was laughing more too. For a time, I was foolish enough to imagine that *I* was the reason he laughed and smiled so much. I tricked myself into believing I was the centre of his universe.

We met in a park. I was sitting on a bench sipping a chai tea, feeling a little bit sorry for myself, when Andrew, a complete — though rather handsome — stranger, sat down beside me and attempted to strike up a conversation.

"Beautiful day," he said.

I nodded, then turned to stare straight ahead, hoping to discourage further conversation.

He continued talking anyway. "Do you come here often?"

I almost spit out my mouthful of tea as I looked at him incredulously, but I couldn't help smiling.

He caught my look then, as if just realizing what he had said, tried to backtrack. "Oh, God, I didn't mean it like that!" He laughed, and the creases around his eyes deepened. "I really meant that as a genuine question. Do you come to this park often? Not that that sounds much better ..."

I was lonely, so I ended up chatting with him because it felt harmless. He was harmless. Friendly and goofy and sweet. When he asked me if I would join him for coffee the following day, I agreed.

After coffee, we exchanged numbers, and when he called me to ask if he could take me out for dinner, I'd already decided I liked him.

He was older than I was — already working as an associate professor at UBC — and he lived near the campus in a house that he was renting. We went back to his place after dinner. He held my hand as he led me up the front walkway and through the blue front door.

"Did you paint the door blue?" I asked him. It seemed a strange touch on an otherwise ordinary white box of a house.

"No. Must've been the people before me. It came like this."

"I like it."

We sat together on his couch, angled to face one another with our knees touching, and talked. At one point, he reached forward to brush a piece of hair from my face. I knew then that I was going to sleep with him.

After that first time, when I woke up beside him in the bedroom with its matching furniture and thick white blinds, I felt at peace. I felt secure.

My mother's begrudging love and everything that came after had not prepared me for something so solid and honest. Before meeting Andrew, I had been vulnerable and very, very small. He breathed new purpose into me. He made happiness simple.

"YOU SEEM DISTRACTED TONIGHT. Everything okay?" Andrew's concern was genuine, but the attention made me nervous.

"I'm worried about something, but I don't want to bother you with it. Not yet anyway."

Andrew was standing at the stove, stirring the creamy mushroom sauce he'd made to go with our chicken. He set down the wooden spoon. "Lily, you can't do that! Now you have to tell me. What are you worried about?"

I twirled a strand of hair around my finger, assessing him. "I'm late."

"Late? Late, like — oh. As in …"

"As in, I might be pregnant." I turned away from him because I couldn't bear to see the disappointment or fear or whatever else might flash across his face.

He walked over to where I was sitting and put a hand on my cheek, gently turning me to face him. He knelt on the floor in front of me. "I'm going to take care of you," he said. "Whether or not you end up being pregnant, I'm going to take care of you. So you don't have to worry about that."

I buried my face in his shoulder and cried. I think it was from relief, but my heart was pounding out an irregular rhythm. We'd only known each other a few weeks. Yet I wanted Andrew. I wanted to be with him. I know I did.

"What do we need to do?" he said, standing up. "Make an appointment? Get a home pregnancy test?"

"A home test."

"Do you want to go now? We can go to the pharmacy right now and get one if you want."

I wiped my eyes and tried to smile. "No. We can wait until tomorrow. You're making dinner. It will be ruined. Besides, if I am pregnant, I'll still be pregnant tomorrow."

WE GOT MARRIED SIX months after meeting in the park. It was a small civil ceremony, and as Andrew pledged to me his lifelong loyalty, I felt an unexpected stab of claustrophobia. Afterward, we went out for dinner with a few friends (mostly Andrew's) and Georgina, of course, whom I'd met only once before. His parents had died in a boating accident when he was in high school, so apart from Georgina, he didn't have any other immediate family members. I, obviously, didn't invite any family at all.

"Do you plan on telling your mother you're married?" Georgina asked me, carefully avoiding my eyes as she buttered a roll. "Andrew mentioned that you didn't really keep in touch, but I thought something as significant as this might warrant —"

"I plan to send a letter," I said, cutting Georgina off mid-sentence.

Georgina looked up from her roll. "A letter? How nice. Will she be disappointed she wasn't invited?"

"I highly doubt it. Are you heading back to Victoria tomorrow? It's too bad you can't stay longer. I know how much Andrew likes seeing you."

Hearing his name, Andrew turned toward me and took my hand. Then, raising his glass, he proposed a toast: "To my beautiful bride, Lily."

I smiled and took a sip of my sparkling water. Speaking only to him, I said quietly, "To us." The two of us clinked our glasses while Georgina looked on, her thin lips pursed.

"HOW DO YOU THINK your mother reacted to the letter about you getting married?" Niall asks.

"I have no idea," I say. "She probably burned it."

He looks surprised. "Why would she burn it?"

I shrug. "Well, I doubt she kept it. She didn't keep anything that didn't serve an immediate purpose."

"Okay," Niall says slowly, "but how do you think she *felt* when she read it?"

I think about that for a minute. Not that I haven't thought about it before. I've thought about it many times, especially in the weeks immediately after I'd sent it. "I really can't imagine her reaction," I say finally. "Which sort of explains a lot, if you know what I mean."

Not only can I not picture how she responded to the news that I was married, I cannot imagine how she reacted to me running away in the first place. It wasn't as if a bond between us was suddenly broken when I left. By then, any bond we shared had already stretched and stretched until it was too thin to matter.

I never felt it snap, but I always hoped my mother did. I wanted her to mourn my loss the way she did the others.

EDITH 🐟

EDITH STANDS ON THE front step, surveying the sky. A few light clouds scuttle over the fields, but they are thin and white and non-threatening. After three days of unceasing rain, the clear skies are a welcome relief. She returns to the farmhouse and pulls the baby carriage from its corner in the living room, tugging the cumbersome apparatus through the front door and onto the lawn. She goes back inside one last time to scoop Jane from her playpen.

"Off we go," she murmurs.

Jane sits upright in the carriage with her pudgy legs protruding in front of her. Edith tucks a blanket loosely around the baby's waist, then pushes the carriage past the tulips and across the lawn toward the road. She walks quickly. The sun warms her back as she works her way up the steep path that leads from the road to the cemetery entrance. Here, the ground is uneven, and the carriage wheels catch in every muddy rut. Jane clutches the sides as the buggy lurches along. There is a moment, just a brief heartbeat, when Edith imagines her daughter's small body tumbling over the side and hitting the ground with a thud. She waits for the sickening remorse that should follow a thought like that; it doesn't come.

Eventually, the ground levels out, and the carriage begins to roll along smoothly. Jane loosens her terrified grip. Edith trundles through the too-long grass toward the stones in the eastern corner. Now that the rain has finally let up, she hopes someone plans on cutting the grass here. It's unseemly for a cemetery to go untended like this. She'll have to speak to someone at the township about it; otherwise, who knows how long it will take to get someone out here.

Birds chirp in the hedges and in the trees that skirt the cemetery. Jane babbles back, swivelling her head to look for them. The sun, the birdsong, even the healthy daughter in front of her have the opposite of a cheering effect on Edith. She finds them insulting.

God's promises are no consolation either, so she doesn't know why people keep throwing them in her face. *The meek shall inherit the kingdom of God.* Is that supposed to make her feel better?

She turns back to the carriage, where Jane is now sucking her thumb. A shiver of revulsion flits across her skin. She smacks Jane's thumb away from her face.

Jane looks up, startled, and begins to sniffle.

"There's no sense crying about it," Edith says. "You can thank me later when your teeth come in straight."

As the carriage bounces down the hill to the road, Edith notices with satisfaction that Jane is holding on so tightly she couldn't suck her thumb even if she wanted to.

DANAH 🐦

PAULINE SANDERS IS LOOKING at me expectantly, waiting for an answer.

"We're booked at The Stone Oven," I say, meeting her gaze. Why is it so hot in the conference room? I am sweltering beneath my wool sweater, but I'm only wearing a tank top underneath, so I can't exactly take it off.

"I know I said to make the reservation for ten people, but can you change that to twelve? David Leeson and his wife would like to join us too."

"No problem," I say, scribbling a note to myself and casting a quick glance in Dwayne's direction. He smiles, just barely, and gives an almost imperceptible nod.

"What time is the reservation for?"

"Uh ..." I shuffle through my notes.

"You said seven, didn't you?" Dwayne interjects.

"Yes. Seven." Can Pauline sense my nervousness? I take a sip of water, wondering if anyone else is dying from the heat in this room, and then, as my advisor moves on to the next item on her agenda and her attention finally shifts from me, I begin to breathe normally again.

The conversation meanders around the room, with everyone clarifying their duties and promising they are doing their utmost to promote both the departmental talk and the one that's open to the public. It's only a few days now until Arthur Williams arrives. I should be excited. I used to be excited.

After the meeting, I follow Dwayne into the hall, asking him under my breath whether I should call The Stone Oven to change our numbers or if he wants to.

Giving me a level look, he says, "Under the circumstances, I think it might be best for me to do it. Don't you?"

"You don't think I can handle —"

"Danah, I was joking. Relax. But don't worry about it. I'll take care of it."

I'm about to object — wanting to seize back control and also irrationally paranoid that he's gunning for my spot on the project — when it occurs to me that it's possible he's not trying to undermine me at all, that he could actually just be as nice as he seems.

I TEXT TREVOR TO let him know I'm on my way to the Student Centre, where we've agreed to meet for coffee. The shock of cold air when I step outside Kenneth Taylor Hall is a welcome relief after the overheated conference room. However, by the time I reach the doors to the Student Centre, I'm shivering.

It was Trevor's idea to meet up today, and I'm nervous given the strange friction between us. We've never gone this long before without seeing each other.

It's loud in the food court, and busy. I push past a group of students standing around talking in front of Teriyaki Express, and when I breathe in the pungent smell of spice and onion, I realize how hungry I am. I wonder if Trevor's had lunch. I look around for him, expecting to see him in the line at Tim Hortons, but when I do finally spot him, he's sitting at a table with a coffee in front of him.

"Couldn't wait, eh?" I say, slipping into the chair across from him.

"Meeting didn't go well?"

I cock my head in confusion. "No, it was fine. Why?"

"Oh, no reason. So, enlighten me, what's bothering you now?"

What the hell is *his* problem? "What's bothering me now? Actually, at the moment, it's you. Do you even know what's going on with me? Oh, that's right, you're too busy with your thesis to care about me. Or us." I can feel my eyes welling up, and that makes me even more mad. I swing around to look at the line for Tim's again. "You couldn't even wait for me before getting your stupid coffee."

"Danah," Trevor says in a warning tone. "You know I care. I'm sorry I haven't been able to —"

"Then *act* like you care," I interrupt. "*Act* like you actually give a shit. Because from where I'm sitting, it sure doesn't feel like it." I stand up and storm away from the table. I march past the line to Tim Hortons, ignore the aromas wafting from Teriyaki Express, and keep going until I am back outside where the cold air penetrates my sweater and makes my skin sting.

I turn around to see if Trevor's followed me. He hasn't. Fine. I have nothing else to say to him anyway.

MY THOUGHTS SKIP AROUND all afternoon, but as I sit in the library, mercifully alone in my usual spot on the fourth floor, I find myself thinking about a lecture from my undergrad days. It was my first deviance course, and my professor at the time was an animated woman named Professor Platts. She stood at the front of the room one day holding a spoon while we all filed in and took our seats.

"I need a volunteer," she began, and instantly the room quieted and several hands went up. "Okay, you in the blue, front row. Come on up. Before we continue, I need another volunteer, someone who doesn't know this gentleman." She chose a girl from the fourth row and had both volunteers stand at the front of the lecture hall facing the rest of the class. After conferring quietly with the two students to determine their names, Professor Platts set out to make her point.

"Matt, I'd like you to spit onto this spoon." There were several snickers and sounds of mild disgust. "Don't be shy. Get a good amount there. Great." She took the spoon from Matt and turned to the girl, who was beginning to look concerned. "Okay, Lisa, I'd like you to sample Matt's spit."

Lisa laughed nervously. "Are you serious?" she asked.

"Of course I'm serious," Professor Platts replied. "But if you don't want to, that's fine. Do I have any other volunteers?" No one raised their hand this time. There were low murmurs circling around the room as we tried to puzzle out what was happening. Professor Platts turned back to Lisa. "Why won't you taste it?" she asked.

"Because it's gross!" Lisa answered, raising her hands defensively in front of her as if Professor Platts was suddenly going to lunge at her with the spoon.

"It is gross. I agree," Professor Platts conceded. "But why? How many of you have kissed another person where there was an exchange of saliva? Yet, were that same person to offer you their saliva on a spoon, you would undoubtedly be repulsed. Why? What exactly is the difference?"

"Because the saliva on the spoon isn't a direct transfer," one student offered tentatively. "During a kiss, the exchange is subtle. It's not spit — it's just part of the kiss. But on the spoon, well, it's just different."

"Not a direct transfer," Professor Platts repeated. "Interesting theory. So once it leaves the mouth and is exposed to the air, is that when the saliva turns to spit? Is that when it becomes 'gross'? If so, what change has really taken place? Or is the change simply in our minds? And if it is in our minds, why is it we think that way? Why do we all agree that sampling someone else's saliva during a kiss is quite acceptable but taking it from a spoon is — well, we might say deviant? Abnormal? What is it that determines acceptable behaviour? How do we decide when, metaphorically speaking, the saliva turns to spit?"

Sitting in the library, looking out at the busy courtyard, I consider that lecture and the meaning I ascribed to it all those years ago. I understood Platts' point that conceptions of deviance are often arbitrary, but I didn't allow for any mitigating factors where my mother was concerned. Running away from your child is not normal. Loving your offspring is not some random convention that has been normalized by the general population; it's a biological predisposition intended to promote survival of the species. Even if, like the saliva on the spoon, there was something about me that made me inherently objectionable to my own mother, she was supposed to love me anyway.

LATER THAT NIGHT, I replay the scene from the Student Centre again and again in my mind. I watch myself storm away, aware even as I'm doing it that I'm overreacting. What is my problem? Am I intentionally trying to sabotage my relationship with Trevor? He suggested once, when we first started dating, that I have a repressed fear of abandonment that prevents me from getting close to people so that they can't hurt me by leaving.

"I don't have a problem getting close to people," I told him. "I was very close to my father."

"You keep yourself at a remove, that's all I'm saying. And if you think about it, your father left you too."

It was the first time I came close to breaking up with Trevor, but doing that would only have proved his point, so I chose to shrug off his hypothesis, and we agreed to disagree. Still, his comment about my father bothered me. I didn't like him being compared in any way, shape, or form to my mother.

Tonight, there is something else nagging at the edge of my

thoughts. Just before I drift to sleep, I realize what it is. Flickering behind my annoyance with Trevor, I recognize my mother's hallmark of unhappiness: her seeming inability to appreciate her life and the people in it. People who loved her.

I worry that at the end of the day, I'm just like her.

JANE LILY 🐦

SOME DAYS, LILY FINDS it hard to drag herself out of bed. She wakes up already drained of energy. Her whole life, on those days, seems to her oppressive and unfulfilling — despite the evidence all around her to the contrary.

She lives in a beautiful house, has a loving and successful husband, and is the mother of a beautiful little girl. If it's pain and suffering she wants, all she needs to do is go downtown and look around her at the hungry, desperate kids camped out in doorways, begging for spare change so they can get another hit to escape their miserable world. Those are the wasted lives. Runaways, like her, but who somehow didn't make it. Still, she can't shake her own feelings of desolation even in the midst of her blatantly comfortable existence. But it's worse on cloudy days. And Vancouver has plenty of those.

Sometimes she misses Missionville just for its weather. She would rather an icy cold day with the sun reflecting off the snow than the mild, damp weather that is so typical here. The never-ending rain during the winter months is eroding her soul.

THIS MORNING, LILY WAKES, yet again, to the soft patter of rain being blown against her window. Andrew is snoring beside her, snuffling and sighing in sporadic bursts. It is the first Saturday in a long time that they have made plans to do something as a family. Weather permitting, and it doesn't look promising right now, they are packing a picnic and heading to Stanley Park. Danah, almost eight years old, has been looking forward to this trip all week.

At breakfast, Danah eats her cereal too quickly, spilling Cheerios as she shovels in one mouthful after another. "I think it's going to stop raining," she chirps happily. "Do you think I should wear my rubber boots in case there are puddles?"

Lily glances out the window. It *does* look like the sun is trying to break through the clouds. Danah is probably right, but she can't seem to muster up the enthusiasm to match her daughter's excitement. "Yes, you'll have to wear your boots. The trails are going to be muddy."

"The rain will stop, the sun will come out, and we'll have a perfect day exploring and eating sandwiches," Andrew declares. He pats Danah on the shoulder on his way to get more coffee.

Sandwiches. Lily still has to make their lunch, find the picnic blanket, get everything packed, and smile while she's doing it. It's all she can do to lift her coffee mug to her lips. She wants to crawl back into bed and wake up to a different life.

THE TRAILS IN STANLEY Park are lined with trees, opening now and then to allow glimpses of the water surrounding the park, English Bay on one side and Vancouver Harbour on the other. The sun filters through the trees, forming dancing patterns along the sheltered paths. Lily breathes in the scented air as if she has been starved for oxygen. She is glad, after all, that they have come.

They unpack their picnic lunch on a patch of dry sand on Third Beach. There are egg salad sandwiches (Andrew's favourite), grapes, apples, and chocolate chip cookies for dessert. Danah pokes her straw into her juice box and smiles at her parents.

"I love picnics," she announces. "We should have them more often."

Danah looks so happy. Andrew is overflowing with good humour; he has been ever since the Canucks made the playoffs. Everything is perfect, isn't it? The three of them are sitting there on the red-and-black checkered blanket, West Vancouver hazy across the water, the mountains looming in the background, the sun shining. But it won't last; the clouds are already moving in again.

While they are packing up their picnic, a light drizzle begins to fall. Everything is going to be wet, and Lily feels like swearing. Stumbling back to the car, clutching the damp picnic blanket to her chest, watching as Danah and Andrew dash ahead laughing, Lily thinks to herself, *This can't be my life. I don't want this to be my life.*

DANAH ❧

"ARE YOU ALMOST READY?" Edith asks, coming out of the bedroom with her purse over her shoulder. "We need to be there by
seven-thirty."

I haven't had a coffee, but at least I'm dressed. I pull my hair into
a quick ponytail and force a smile. "Ready."

"Good. Let's go then. Alice will be waiting."

We're headed to Gospel Light Church for the pancake breakfast
I agreed to help with days ago, although I can't for the life of me
think why I said yes. I must have been tired when Edith asked me.
There's a light dusting of snow on the ground, and for a moment,
I am buoyed by the sight of it.

The basement of Gospel Light Church is nicer than I expected.
From the outside, the building looks rundown, but the inside
appears to have been recently renovated. The room we're in is set
up with neat rows of tables covered in bright yellow tablecloths.
Every table has a vase of plastic flowers placed carefully in the
centre. It's cheery, in a depressing kind of way.

Alice meets us at the side door. "Oh, I wasn't sure you'd both be
able to make it. Danah, I know how busy you are!"

"I can't stay long," I'm quick to explain. "I have a class at ten, but I'm here to help for a bit."

"Any help is appreciated, dear," Alice says. "We never turn down an extra set of hands, do we, Edith?"

I follow Alice and my grandmother into the church kitchen, where two women are standing at a counter mixing large bowls of batter. A huge cast-iron griddle covers a restaurant-sized stovetop on one side of the kitchen, and on the other, I can see the serving counter, which is where I imagine I'll be standing.

"Here, take this," Alice says, pushing a daisy-patterned apron into my hands. "It gets messy back here."

Soon enough, the first community guests start arriving: mothers with small children, senior citizens, a few teenagers who stare at the walls or the ceiling, anywhere but at the people serving them.

Edith and I stand side by side doling out pancakes. The room is filled with the sounds of multiple conversations taking place at once, punctuated by an occasional burst of noise from a child; there are dishes clattering, chairs scraping, and the quieter but constant hiss of pancake batter hitting the giant griddle behind me. When the line dwindles, and Edith and I are left watching as people sit at the tables, eating, she turns to me and says softly, "Your mom ran away from me too, you know."

What? I open my mouth, but before I can even make a sound, Edith continues. "That's how she ended up in B.C."

"She ran away?" I repeat stupidly. I'm holding my breath, willing Edith to keep talking. Every nerve in my body is on alert. The air around me is buzzing.

"She was seventeen, and one day she just up and took off with some boy named Morian. He wasn't even from Missionville. He was only supposed to be visiting. The two of them went to B.C., and she never came back. I don't know what happened to the boy, though, because the next thing I heard she was married to your dad."

Morian. The name tugs at a string in my mind, a whisper of a memory, but I can't place it.

"I — I didn't know any of that," I finally manage.

"Well, why would you? You said yourself she never talked about me." Edith pauses. "Things were difficult between us. Then all of a sudden, right before she left, she started asking everyone to call her Lily."

"Wasn't that her name?" I say, feeling something heavy slide across my gut. *Don't stop*, I plead silently. *Don't stop.*

"Is there more syrup?" A woman is standing in front of me, holding out an empty Aunt Jemima bottle.

I take it from her as Edith reaches for a new one from the supply beside us on the counter. She hands it to the woman, and I hold my breath. A long silence stretches out between us, and I'm about to prompt her again when she finally answers my question. "Lily was her middle name. Her real name was Jane."

My mind is spinning. I send silent, urgent messages to everyone in the room to stay away. I don't want anyone else to interrupt us. Edith's sudden confession feels as fragile as a butterfly's wings.

Edith busies her hands straightening the rows of Aunt Jemima bottles, turning them all to face the same direction. The sounds in the church hall recede until all I can hear is the uncomfortable beating of my heart.

"But she contacted you? After she ran away?"

Something flits across Edith's features. Before she answers, Alice appears behind us. "There's coffee in the pot if you want some. Might as well have a cup before you leave, Danah."

I turn to face her, flustered. "Thanks." Then, turning back to Edith, blood pounding in my ears, I beg her silently to say more.

She puts out her hand. "Here, give me your apron. You don't want to be late."

I SIT THROUGH PROFESSOR Stone's lecture in a daze. Edith's revelations ricochet around my brain. If I can find out who this Morian was, and who my mother was when she ran away with him, I might finally be able to understand what happened when she ran away from me. My head feels light, and it takes me a minute to recognize the sensation for what it is: relief. I'm on the edge of something new. The answers I've been craving are so close, I can almost taste the truth.

I text Trevor as soon as Stone's class ends, and surprisingly, he agrees to meet me for lunch at The Phoenix.

"I thought you were too busy to see me," I tease in an effort to make light of the recent uneasiness between us. We've just been seated at a table, and Trevor is staring past me at the cathedral-style vaulted ceiling, which makes The Phoenix look like a miniature version of the dining hall at Hogwarts.

"Are we really going there again?" Trevor says, and I can tell by the look on his face that he didn't take my comment lightly, the way I intended.

"I meant that as a joke. But I do have news to share."

He raises his eyebrows.

I order a double rye and coke, then launch into a description of my conversation with Edith. Sitting across from Trevor, discussing things like we used to, infuses me with a pleasing warmth. Or maybe that's the rye. At any rate, for the moment, Trevor is acting like Trevor again, attentive and interested.

"Her name was Jane? Weird. I wonder why she decided to go by her middle name. Did your grandmother say anything about why she ran away? Like, was she pregnant?"

"She didn't say much because we kept getting interrupted. Just that my mom took off with some guy named Morian but then ended up with my dad. You think I have a brother or sister out there somewhere?" I consider the implication of what Trevor is suggesting, and a new thought occurs to me. "Maybe that's why she left me. To be with her other kid. Her first kid." As I say the words out loud, a hole opens in my gut. A dull ache spreads all the way up my chest.

"Let's not get ahead of ourselves," Trevor says. "We're reaching here. It's great that you two are finally talking about it, though."

I take a swig of my drink. "Talking" might be overstating it, but I know more now than I've ever known before. Still, it's not nearly enough. Edith said she doesn't know what happened to Morian, that the next thing she heard my mom was married to Dad. At least she heard something. Mom never once reached out to us after she left. She never once checked to make sure I was okay. The ache in my gut subsides and is replaced by a hard twist of anger.

Across the room, a whole table of people cheer as a woman takes a sip from a silver chalice. The sound of their celebration grates against my nerves. The Phoenix has a tradition of serving you a drink in that special silver chalice when you finally obtain your Ph.D. The chalice itself is stored behind the bar in a hand-crafted box, like some sort of mythical artifact. They also bring you an almost sacred book in which to record your thoughts or thank everyone who helped you achieve your goal. I've been to two of these celebrations, and once, when I flipped through the pages of the gilded book, I saw that someone had drawn a cartoon fist in the bottom corner of one of the blank pages and on every consecutive page until the final drawing revealed the cartoon hand giving the middle finger.

"I wonder if Dad knew about Morian," I say suddenly. "It seems like something you would know about your wife. The fact that she had run away with some guy before you met her."

"I bet your dad knew exactly what he was getting into," Trevor says.

AFTER LUNCH, TREVOR TAKES me back to his place, and the tension between us is erased as he throws me on his bed. Later, while downing a shot of tequila, I promise myself that, come hell or high water, I am going to find out more about this Morian guy. He is, I've decided, the key to understanding pretty much everything.

JANE LILY ✞

MORIAN IS DIFFERENT FROM any of the boys Jane knows. He doesn't belong in their sleepy farm community, where most of the boys spend their mornings in dark barns and their evenings in the fields under the dying light. He can't drive a tractor, and his clothes are clean, new-looking. He's only in Missionville at all because he's staying with his aunt and uncle for a few months while his parents are off in Asia for something to do with his father's work. He tells Jane he's an artist. It's not a hobby, he's quick to point out; he plans to make a living at it.

When Jane danced with him in the hall above the bowling alley, she attributed the nervous flutter in her chest to her fear of being caught sneaking out. The whole time she was at the dance, she kept looking toward the doors, expecting her mother to come bursting in. By the time her friends drove her home, where she sat squished into the back seat with Morian on her left, his knee pressing against her, she knew her nerves had more to do with him than anything else: the pressure of his knee made her whole leg tingle. She slipped into the farmhouse unnoticed and crept into her bed, where she lay on her back, heart pounding, reliving the feeling of dancing in Morian's arms, his eyes on hers, the way he smiled at her, and then, of course, the feel of his knee touching her leg on the short ride home.

In actuality, Morian had only danced with her twice, and he'd danced with plenty of other girls as well, but still she'd felt singled out. When he'd smiled at her across the little round table, the lantern light flickering in his earnest hazel eyes, her whole body had warmed at the intimacy she read in his look.

She was nervous the next morning. Had her mother heard her come in? But Edith showed no signs of being suspicious, and by noon, Jane knew she had got away with it. Still, the thought of what she'd done made her heart pound with a thrilling fear. All day, she was consumed with thoughts of how and when she might see Morian again.

She didn't have to wait long. On Sunday, she saw him at church with his aunt and uncle, and she spent the next hour trying to figure out how to approach him without Edith asking any uncomfortable questions. Reverend Thompson could have been speaking Spanish for all she heard of the sermon. At long last, they sang the closing hymn, and Reverend Thompson gave the benediction before making his way to the back of the church with his wife, where they stood side by side shaking hands with everybody. Jane was impatient to make her way through the painfully slow progression, to get outside and find her friends and hopefully talk to Morian. Had he noticed her? Was he waiting anxiously to talk to her too? Had he been thinking about her throughout the long sermon the way she'd been thinking about him? Her cheeks burned at the thought.

"Jane!" Sarah called, motioning her over to a group of girls clustered on the front lawn. "We're heading to Rebecca's after lunch to play volleyball. Can you come? Stanley can pick you up."

Before Jane could answer, Stanley walked over with Morian and said, "I've found us another player."

That afternoon at Rebecca's house was the true start of things. Morian talked more to Jane than anyone else, and when it was time for her to leave, he offered to drive her. Right before she climbed out of the car, he reached across the seat and touched her arm gently. "I'd like to see you again," he said. "If you want to, of course."

HE TAKES HER ALL the way to Brantford to see *E.T.* When he picks her up, Edith embarrasses her by insisting she meet him in person. On the thirty-minute drive to Brantford, he's quiet, and Jane worries that he's regretting asking her out. It was Edith, she thinks. She scared him off with her stupid questions. But in the theatre, Morian reaches for her hand, and as the strangely sad sci-fi movie unfolds, all she can think about is the feeling of his warm fingers laced with hers. After the movie, in the parking lot, he walks her to the passenger door but then leans against the car instead of letting her in. He pulls her toward him, and she laughs uncertainly.

"I'd like to kiss you," he says.

She nestles against his warm body, then looks up at him. "Okay," she whispers.

He tips her chin upward, and when his lips meet hers, her entire body shivers. He grips the back of her head gently, and his fingers tangle in her curls. "Jane, Jane, Jane," he murmurs.

The whole way home, he keeps one hand on her leg, above her knee, only moving it when he has to shift gears.

MORIAN LIKES TO SMOKE. His aunt and uncle don't care, or at least that's what he tells Jane. The first time she saw him light a cigarette, it made her think of the town boys who hang out behind the drugstore smoking, except with him it is different. She likes the way he studies her with a cigarette between his lips, his eyes squinting slightly. Also, unlike the boys behind the drugstore, he likes to wander while he smokes. They go on long walks together, through town, past the creek that runs behind the high school, even down the rural roads lined with farms. Once, when they are tracing the path of the creek, hidden behind a scrim of trees, he stops and points out a rusting metal bucket along the bank.

"See that?" he says. "How would you describe it?"

"Um, an old pail?"

"It's more than that. Wait, and I'll show you."

She doesn't know what he means, but since he's taken her hand and is leading her along, past the bucket toward a giant oak where they have kissed many times, she doesn't give it too much thought. When they reach the oak, she leans against it, facing him. He pins her hands above her head and kisses her, hard.

His body is pressed against hers, and she can feel herself arching to meet him. Not here, though. The first time she let him touch her like that was in his car, along a dark side road. He pulled over, parked the car, and they spent a few minutes making out. When he slipped his hand under her shirt, she inhaled sharply, but she didn't stop him. Then, with his other hand, he reached for the waistband of her jeans. He fumbled briefly with the button and her zipper before his hand inched its way along the top edge of her underwear. Not much more happened that time, other than her breathing growing shallow. The confines of the car were too restrictive, but the landscape of their relationship shifted. A line was crossed.

The next time they were alone together, at his aunt and uncle's place, it didn't take long for them to find themselves upstairs, in his room. This time, with a bed at their disposal, their explorations went much further.

"We should stop," Jane mumbled, even while she was pulling him toward her on the unmade bed. "Do you have anything?"

"You mean a condom?"

"Uh-huh."

"No, but I'll get some. We can just do this for now. C'mon, don't go all cold on me."

HE SURPRISES HER ONE day with a painting. It's the metal bucket they saw by the creek, half hidden in a patch of bull thistle, the weeds done with such delicate brushstrokes they appear super in-focus while the bucket blurs into the background. It's the first time Jane has seen one of his paintings, and she can tell right away he's talented. That painting makes her suddenly shy of her sketches, her amateur doodling. She decides not to show them to him because she doesn't want fake admiration or, worse, derision.

He pushes the painting into her hands. "It's for you," he says.

She props it up in her bedroom, on her dresser. Edith doesn't understand. When she sees it, she scoffs: "Why can't he paint something nice? He should be doing landscapes or portraits. I don't know why he wants to paint pieces of trash."

Jane ignores her mother. She has been better at doing that ever since meeting Morian. Edith might think he's wasting his time, but Jane believes that there is a lightness and beauty in how he sees the world. When she's with him, she feels as though she is slowly being transformed, and the old version of herself — the old Jane — is fading away. With Morian, she is someone else entirely: she is the girl who snuck out and walked in the dark to a dance; she is brave and beautiful.

She is alive.

THEY DRIVE OUT TO the abandoned mill, which is a popular place for kids to fool around. Morian takes her hand while they're sitting in the grass, leaning against the weathered boards of the crumbling building.

"The name Jane doesn't suit you. You should have been called something more exotic."

Jane laughs. "My middle name is Lily. Is that exotic enough?"

"It's better." He pauses to study her. "My Lily of the Valley. Yeah, I like it."

After that, he only calls her Lily. What he doesn't know is that Jane has always hated her name. When she was younger, she used to make up fantasies about a girl named Lily who had all kinds of adventures. This made-up Lily was beautiful and funny and never got in trouble because everybody loved her too much to get mad at her. And now Morian is turning Jane into that dream version of herself.

She begins to think of herself as Lily, not Jane, and experiences for the first time the freedom that comes with change, with tossing off a layer of herself.

She asks her friends to call her by her middle name, and after some resistance, they do. The only person who refuses to even consider her request is her mother.

"Don't be ridiculous," Edith says. "I named you Jane, and that's what I'll call you."

In that moment, staring at her mother's back across the kitchen, Jane understands with blinding certainty that in order to be herself, or this new version of herself, she will need to cut herself off from her mother.

DANAH ❧

DANAH IS STANDING IN the corner of the playground surrounded by a group of eight-year-old girls. They are all smiling and giggling.

"We should have secret names in our club," one girl suggests.

"Yeah," another one chimes in, "and when we meet, we'll only use our secret names. That's how you become a member, with your secret name."

"We could spell our names backwards. Then mine would be Hanad," Danah says. She's proud of her idea; she thinks it's clever.

"No, that's too easy. It has to be more secret."

"Okay," another one says. "What if we use our middle names? No one knows our middle names."

"That's perfect. Our secret names will be our middle names."

Danah nods her head in agreement. She liked her idea better. But she knows if she disagrees, all the other girls will look at her like she shouldn't be in the club at all. So when they whisper their new secret names to each other and promise to use only them from now on, she lies.

"Ashley," she says. No one gives her a funny look. No one notices her relief when they move on to the next person as if nothing unusual has happened. And so, for a few short weeks, before the club's novelty wears off, Danah becomes Ashley at recess and after school and in secret notes passed between desks when the teacher isn't looking. She likes being called Ashley. It is such a pretty name compared to Danah. It is the name of the type of girl other girls want to be friends with, the type of girl whose mother wants to be around her, the type of girl Danah so desperately wants to be.

WHEN THE GIRLS GROW bored of their club, Danah is disappointed to give up the name Ashley but also relieved that no one discovered her lie. She kept waiting to be found out, and now she can relax.

She feels safe enough to finally ask her mom why she doesn't have a middle name. Her mom is cooking dinner, and as she turns to face Danah, she looks tired.

"Because," her mother says, "I never wanted you to have to be anything other than Danah."

This seems, to Danah, not a real answer at all.

DANAH ❧

THE FAMILIAR TWINGES OF a hangover pull me out of sleep. My head hurts, my mouth is dry, and my stomach is lurching unpredictably. My mind has been spinning all night, but that at least has nothing to do with the tequila I drank last night. Trevor is already up, and the scent of fresh coffee permeates the air.

I drag myself to the bathroom, where I gulp down some much-needed water. My hair is a mess — a few pieces still clinging to a tangled elastic, the rest a snarled jumble above my shoulders. I run a brush through it half-heartedly; it hurts my head to pull too hard. I splash cold water on my face, then stagger, bleary-eyed, to Trevor's kitchen.

"How you feeling?" he asks, handing me a gloriously warm mug.

I grunt, bringing the mug to my lips slowly, unsure how my stomach will react to coffee.

"I can drive you to your car," he says. "Or you can stay here, if you want, but I have to be on campus for nine-thirty."

"I'll go with you. I need to get home anyway." I look at my rumpled clothes, then rub my forehead. Yesterday, I was humming with energy, but now I feel like shit. I need an Advil. And a shower.

I want to know everything Edith knows: the details around my mom running away, her relationship with Morian, her relationship with Edith. If I don't find out the truth, it's going to kill me.

I SQUEEZE INTO MY parking spot in the driveway and spend a few minutes sitting in my car before turning off the engine. I have to brace myself for the heaviness in my apartment, the thick air that constricts my vocal cords and makes it so hard to say the things I want to say.

When I open the door at the bottom of the stairs, I don't wait to confront Edith. If I wait, the words will wilt. "You should have told me a long time ago about my mom running away," I say. It comes out like an accusation. It *is* an accusation. "It would have been helpful to know."

Edith is sitting in front of the space heater, and if my words catch her unawares, she doesn't show it. Her reply is calm and measured. "You didn't need to know."

I take a breath. "How do you know? Don't you think it might have a made a difference to me? Didn't it ever occur to you that I'd want to know she'd done it before, run away?" My voice rises, making my head ache even more. "It establishes a pattern! How can you not see that?"

Edith doesn't bother answering.

"Why does everything have to be such a big secret? Why does no one ever want to talk about her? I'm sick of pretending nothing happened!" I turn toward the bathroom and slam the door shut, then lean against it, spent, my head throbbing.

Armed with the knowledge that my mother changed her name, that she ran away from Edith, I am desperate to revisit the scenes of my childhood and analyze them all over again. If she ran away before, doesn't that change everything I believed about her leaving me? I think back to Professor Platts' saliva lecture, to the point she was illustrating about how we understand and evaluate behaviour based on the subjective meaning we ascribe to it. But what if we are missing context? What if we misinterpreted the meaning all along? What if no one ever told us the whole goddamned story?

Even with these extra pieces of information, the fact that my mother ran away when she was younger doesn't ease the question that's been gnawing at my heart for years: if I wasn't the reason she left, why wasn't I enough to make her stay?

JANE LILY ✐

NIALL UNCROSSES HIS LEGS and leans toward me. There is no dark furniture between us, just the corner of my cheap coffee table, carefully cleared of pill bottles and empty glasses. I liked it better when we had our sessions in his office, in that chocolate-scented space, but since it's becoming harder and harder for me to get there, he suggested we move to home visits instead. So here we are, sitting in my living room, and although the setting is more intimate, I feel less inclined to be honest.

His eyes roam around the room, taking in details. There isn't much to see. My walls are bare, the furniture nondescript, the carpet freshly vacuumed prior to his arrival, the curtains opened to let in light. It's as bright and cheery as anyone could reasonably expect, though the sparseness probably validates some theory of his. *Hmmm, so much ... emptiness.*

"What did you mean," he is saying now, "when you said it was easier than I might think to start over?"

"Just that when you do it, when you actually decide to walk away from something, usually there's not much to stop you." I know, even as I say this, that I'm lying. I don't want him to start probing my memory for instances of regret. His goal, he has clarified, even more so than mine at this point, is acceptance and closure. Maybe we'll both sleep easier if I can convince him I've finally arrived.

He gives me a look that says I haven't fooled him for a second. Although, in part, what I said is technically true. When unhappiness trails you like smoke, moving away from it is a natural reaction. And arriving at a new place, with opportunity stretching before you, *is* liberating. It's like finding a fresh supply of oxygen after you've been starved for air. But I left out the parts where regret catches up with you and tries to pull you back, where it becomes just as suffocating as whatever you were trying to escape. Fighting the pull of regret, the urge to undo what you just did, is anything but easy. You have to be strong. You have to sever your ties cleanly to avoid having them wrap themselves around your neck and start to squeeze.

If I were to say any of those things out loud, Niall would pounce all over them. He would want to talk about severed ties, about regret, about last-minute opportunities to blah, blah, blah. But I don't have the strength for it today. Maybe I never did.

MY FIRST FEW MONTHS in Edinburgh, after the initial thrill had worn off, were the hardest. I struggled to stay rooted in this new place where I had transplanted myself, fighting the tug that threatened to turn me around. I thought constantly about going back. Once, I even started the process of buying a plane ticket, but I knew it wasn't really an option because although Andrew had taken me back before, I was quite sure he wouldn't do it again. After my initial short-lived attempt at running away when Danah was still a baby, he had opened his arms to me, but his heart remained stubbornly closed. I was almost certain that if I came back this time, he wouldn't open even his arms. Worse, I didn't think Danah would either. What would she want with me when she had Andrew?

I was desperate about Danah in those first few months, but not the way you would expect. Not the way a good mother would be.

I wasn't sick with worry about how she was coping. I didn't cry about not being there to tuck her in at night. What consumed me was wanting to know whether or not she missed me. Or how much. I tormented myself with thoughts of how quickly and easily Andrew would fill the hole I'd left behind. That knowledge, that assurance that he would be enough for her, should have comforted me, but instead it opened a new cavern that I was only too eager to slide into.

But that was in the first months. I adjusted. I made my life more permanent in Scotland. I moved out of the room I had rented in the Old Town and into a flat with a woman from Ireland. I never learned Siobhan's story, and she never knew mine. I took the job at the bookstore and eventually moved out of the flat I shared with Siobhan and into my own. The very one where I'm sitting now with Niall, the one with no pictures on the walls.

I convinced myself in those early days that both Danah and Andrew were better off without me. It didn't take much. Niall asked me once if I thought I had been worried that I was going to ruin Danah the same way I believed my mother had ruined me.

"No, it wasn't the same," I said. But I couldn't find the words to explain how my entire childhood was lived under the dark cloud of knowledge that my mother never forgave me for living.

JANE LILY ❧

JANE IS WALKING BESIDE her mother, head bowed, up the road to the cemetery at the top of the hill. They pass Uncle Case's house, and she hopes no one is at the window watching them trudge past. She hates these trips. On the last Sunday of every month, her mother drags her to the cemetery, where she stands and stares at the two graves in front of them, wondering what she is supposed to feel, trying to make her face look sad and serious and sorry because she is sure she has something to be sorry for.

Her mother is saying a little prayer now, mumbling so that Jane can hardly make out the words. Jane lowers her head and pretends to pray too, fulfilling her duty to at least pretend to remember the other half of their family. The dead half.

As they are walking back down the hill, back to the farmhouse, back to their regular lives where no one will mention the dead people at all, Jane finally asks the question that has been burning in her mind for some time now. "Did I kill Anne?" she whispers.

There is a slight pause. "Of course not."

Jane isn't convinced. Ringing just behind her mother's words, Jane hears an echo of accusation. And the fear that she is secretly responsible for her sister's death causes the weight of Anne's absence to settle on her like a heavy stone.

She is only eight years old, but suddenly, she understands why her mother always wants to punish her. For years, she has lived under the shadow of that blame; every single day, she sees in her mother's face all the unspoken recriminations.

What will it take, she wonders, to crawl out from under that blanket of blame?

JANE LILY ❧

WHEN JANE, OR LILY as she thinks of herself now, wakes up, she is surprised to find that she has slept at all. Her sheets are clammy, and already the air in her bedroom is thick and sticky. She spent most of the night in a state of nervous anxiety suffused with excitement.

Morian is picking her up today, this afternoon, and they are leaving. Really leaving. They've been planning it for weeks, and she's been secretly packing for days, setting aside clothes, personal items, and money. She's also stowed away several items from the pantry, things they can eat on the long drive. Everything is hidden in a duffle bag in her wardrobe, waiting to be loaded into Morian's car.

This morning will be tricky. She has to act like nothing is different when her whole life is about to change. She can't let Edith sense her excitement, her skittishness. She heads downstairs, heart beating erratically, and sits down to breakfast. Her mother has made scrambled eggs and toast and set out a bowl of strawberries.

"I'm going over to see Mrs. Knaverly after lunch," her mother says. "It would be nice if you came along. You could help with the babies."

"I would," Jane answers carefully, "but I have a bit of a head-ache."

"Well, see how you're feeling this afternoon. We could use you."

"Okay." Will it look suspicious if she eats her breakfast? Usually when she has a headache she doesn't have much of an appetite. But she wants to make sure she gets one good meal before she leaves, and she's actually hungry, despite the nerves radiating through her body, the energy pulsing just below her skin.

She spends most of the morning in her room, pretending to be lying down, when in fact she is going through the stuff in her bag, wondering if there's anything else she should be taking. It doesn't look like much: her favourite outfits, two pairs of shoes, makeup, hairbrush, toothbrush. Her Walkman and a mixtape to listen to in the car. She throws in a few of her books, then changes her mind and takes them out again. Does this duffle bag really sum up the contents of her life? But Morian has assured her they don't need much.

"We'll have each other," he said. "That's enough."

Finally, after what feels like the longest morning in her memory, her mother calls up the stairs. "I'm leaving. Are you sure you don't want to come? Mrs. Knaverly would love to see you, you know."

Jane walks downstairs to say goodbye. She wants to do it in person. She feels a tug of something — remorse? — as she repeats her excuse from that morning. Then, in one spontaneous move-ment, she hugs her mother. It's awkward, more of a half-hug, but still, she hasn't hugged her mother in years.

Edith gives her a strange look before heading out the door. She must suspect something, Jane thinks. Her breath comes quickly. She's done it. She's said goodbye. And this strange, hollow feeling in her chest will disappear as soon as Morian arrives.

HE TOSSES HER BAG in the back seat, along with her pillow, which she grabbed at the last second, and before she has time to take one last look at the farmhouse, they are driving away.

"Here we go, my Lily of the Valley," Morian says, throwing her one of his heart-stopping smiles.

And she knows in that moment that she will never be Jane again. She turns to face him. "Here we go," she echoes.

They drive for five long days. They spend the nights camped out in a tent Morian brought, and in the dim, bluish moonlight that seeps through the canvas, they make love with a recklessness and abandonment they never experienced during their muffled encounters on Morian's bed at his aunt and uncle's place.

On the Prairies, Lily is hypnotized by the unchanging, endless landscape. She dreams about fields of wheat and a horizon so flat it could have been pencilled into her imagination with a ruler. She wishes she'd brought along her sketchbook to capture this new landscape. She feels so far from Ontario, from Missionville, she might as well be on another planet. Even her friends are becoming a distant memory, something from another lifetime.

As they cross from Alberta into British Columbia, through the Rockies, Lily is awestruck.

"I never knew the mountains looked like this," she breathes. "I mean, I knew they were big, but ..."

Morian pulls over to make some sketches of his own. He's going to paint the mountains later, he explains, after they've arrived in Vancouver. Lily doesn't mention her own desire to draw the scenery around them; her sketches, she knows, would be nothing next to his. At the mention of Vancouver, Lily experiences her first true misgivings. She is anxious about what lies ahead, from a practical standpoint. Where will they live? How will they support themselves? Morian is confident that he can make it as an artist, but what about her? What will she do?

"Trust me," Morian keeps telling her. "We'll be fine." And although his tone is reassuring, she's not entirely convinced.

When they finally arrive in Vancouver, Morian, true to his word, contacts a friend who puts them up temporarily.

"We made it," Morian says, stretching out beside her on the floor of this stranger's living room, where they have once again unrolled their sleeping bags. "Safe and sound."

Safe and sound. She wonders what her mother would think of her sleeping arrangements. Imagines the appalled look on her face. Then, not for the first time, she tries to picture her mother's reaction when she got back from visiting Mrs. Knaverly and discovered that Lily was gone. She'd like to think Edith was consumed with despair, but it's easier for her to imagine her mother being angry. Tight-lipped with fury. So, despite the fact that she is sleeping on a hard floor with no clear idea of how tomorrow will unfold, she finds the vast physical distance between her and her mother comforting.

FIRST WEEKS, THEN MONTHS pass. Morian and Lily move into their own apartment near Granville Island, and Lily finds a job in a florist shop. At first, she only works behind the counter, taking orders or ringing through purchases. Then Donna, the owner, begins to trust her with small arrangements, and when it becomes clear that Lily has a knack for designing bouquets, she is given more and more responsibility in the shop.

Morian celebrates his twentieth birthday by having a loud party at their apartment. He has gathered a circle of friends who like to drink and smoke and listen to pounding rock music. Lily's not old enough to drink, and Morian's friends tease her, calling her a baby because she's only seventeen. She doesn't like the attention. She doesn't like their apartment being filled with noisy, messy people. In Missionville, she didn't have to share Morian. Now, he belongs to so many people that she is lost in the crowd.

CRACKS BEGIN TO APPEAR in Morian's veneer. Where he once cajoled her with assurances, he now snaps with impatience.

"Why is there never anything to eat around here?" he says as he slams the refrigerator door closed. "Is it too much to ask you to get some decent groceries?"

"I don't get paid until Friday. So unless you have a secret stash of money somewhere that you'd like to share, you'll have to make do with what you see. We can barely pay the rent, Morian." Lily hates it when he's like this, when he's frustrated with something he's working on and takes all of his anger out on the world. On her.

"You don't need to keep reminding me that I'm a goddamn failure!" He storms out of the apartment, but Lily knows he'll be back. Full of apologies and affection. And by Friday, when she gets paid, he'll have invited his friends over for drinks so he can bask in the company of fellow starving artists and laugh with them at the hardships that inspire their creativity.

But even if everything isn't as perfect as she imagined, Lily is happier with Morian than she ever remembers being in her other life. At least Morian is real. At least there are no ghosts here.

EDITH 🐦

DANAH STAYED OUT ALL night with her boyfriend, and while she was gone, I hardly slept. This morning, my mind is going round and round in circles. Danah returned full of fire, accusing me of keeping secrets. She thinks she wants to know everything, does she? She has no idea.

I am supposed to visit Alice today. It's our shopping day, and I'd planned to check in on my house when we were done, then spend a few hours crocheting in Alice's bright living room. But I've changed my mind. I don't want to take a taxi to Alder Street, to wander through the aisles in the grocery store reading labels to Alice, to see how slowly my house is being put back together. Even crocheting in the warmth of the sun has lost its appeal. I am overcome instead with a sudden compulsion to do something I've only done once since moving to Hamilton. It doesn't make any sense and will likely cost me a fortune, but I don't care.

While Danah is in the shower, I pick up the phone and call Alice to cancel our plans. Ben can take her shopping today.

Twenty minutes after Danah leaves the apartment, still in a huff, the taxi I ordered pulls in to the driveway. I climb into the back seat and buckle myself in.

The driver looks at me in his rearview mirror. "They said you would give me directions?"

"Yes, we need to get on the 403 westbound. You know how to do that, I expect?"

He nods and backs out of the driveway. "You'll direct me from there, then? When they told me Missionville, I said, 'Where?' I thought I'd heard wrong. But dispatch assured me it's a real place. I don't often have fares that take me out into the boonies like this."

"Yes, well, I'd imagine not." I hope he isn't going to talk to me the whole way. I have too much on my mind. A decision to make.

ABOUT AN HOUR LATER, as we approach the outskirts of Missionville, I begin to sag under the weight of nostalgia. "Turn left here," I say, guiding us onto a rural road lined with farms. We drive past field after field of harvested corn, the leftover stubby stalks protruding like frozen fingers from the ground. Soon, we are approaching the pond where Frank once drowned a litter of puppies, and behind that I can see the long, rectangular turkey barn with its oversize fans spinning steadfastly in the cold air. The air inside will be thick and warm, filled with dust and feathers. I remember all too well wading into that barn, the birds shuffling around my feet, flapping their wings uselessly to get out of my way. The sound, the noise of their frantic gobbling, a thousand throats warbling, used to make me cringe. I hated going into that barn.

Across the road, the grey farmhouse is still standing. The magnolia tree is still there too, beside the front door. When I left that house, I worried that Jane would somehow sense, wherever she was, that she no longer had a home to come back to. She'd been gone for months by then, but within those walls I harboured a hope that was too heavy to drag with me all the way to Hamilton.

I direct the taxi driver past the house and up the hill until the wrought iron fence around the cemetery comes into view. The entrance gates are open, flanked by two hulking stone angels. I always thought they were ugly. Their granite faces are more menacing than welcoming.

"Pull in here," I say to the driver. "If you go back the way we came and turn left on the main road, it will take you into town. You can find a coffee shop. I'll be ready again in an hour."

I wait until the taxi has pulled back out onto the road and is disappearing down the hill before I turn toward the familiar gravestones.

This place has swallowed so many of my imagined tomorrows. I came here regularly in the early days, the dutiful, grieving wife and mother. I planted flowers, offered up prayers, did all the things that were supposed to soothe the sharp edge of loss that had cut through my life like a knife. None of it helped. So, what am I doing here now?

Frank's stone is falling apart. The top left corner is chipped, and there is a long crack running all the way down the side to the frozen ground. Haven't Case or Pieter been looking after things? Who do I talk to about getting this fixed? Anne's small stone, mercifully, is still intact.

The wind lashes at my eyes. What on earth am I going to do here for an hour while I wait for the taxi to return? There is nowhere to sit, apart from the stone benches further down the hill, which will be too cold at any rate. All the strain from the last two weeks must be catching up with me, wreaking havoc with my nervous system and making me insensible. If I'm not careful, I'm going to end up losing my grip on reality altogether.

Danah insists I should have told her about her mother running away. Maybe she's right, maybe it would have been some consolation to her, but despite what the Bible has to say about it, the truth doesn't always set you free. There's plenty Danah doesn't need to know. I think about the letter Danah saw before the fire. What is it Jane, or Lily, wants this time? I never did reply to her last letter, the one she sent after Andrew died. I bet she wants to know if I told

Danah. And if that is why she's writing now, if that's what she's after, what then? What will I say to her?

Danah can shout at me all she wants about wanting the truth. That's why I'm here, isn't it? Standing in this cold graveyard, reminding myself of the losses that have shaped my life. This is my truth. Although I suppose these same losses also shaped Jane's life and, when it comes right down to it, Danah's too.

We are falling dominoes, each generation ruining the next — the sins of the daughter, and on and on and on. I can cast a net of blame as far and wide as I want and still not absolve myself. But even if Jane can never forgive me, maybe Danah can. It doesn't have to be too late for her. We don't need to keep tumbling into despair, one generation after the other.

Danah might hate me, but she doesn't have to hate herself.

EDITH 🌱

AFTER WHAT HAPPENED TO Frank, it is strange how many people tell Edith what a blessing it is that she's pregnant. She doesn't see it as a blessing at all. Contrary to what everyone seems to expect, she is not looking forward with excitement to the birth of a child. So, when she finds out there are *two*, not one, when the doctor confirms a second heartbeat, she does not feel *doubly blessed* thank you very much. She feels a cold sense of dread and disbelief.

Jane is born first, squalling. Then comes Anne, three minutes later, with nothing more than a small cry of surprise at finding herself suddenly expelled into the cold and the light. The room blazes with activity. The doctor is administering to Edith while in the background her mother-in-law offers up a prayer of tearful thanks. Margaret and Isobel each have a newborn in their arms, and in the midst of all the noise, the exclamations, the congratulatory murmurs, the doctor's calm instructions, Edith wants to lie back on the pillow and disappear. Too soon, her tiny daughters are placed in her arms. She holds them against her tired body and experiences none of the boundless love that is supposed to threaten to overwhelm her. She stares down at the red-faced infants whimpering in her arms and is overcome with despair.

ANNE HARDLY EVER MAKES any noise. Jane, on the other hand, is a howling bundle of fury — it's as if she never got over her anger at being born. Anne will lie calmly beside her shrieking, red-faced twin and drift to sleep in their shared crib. She makes no demands. But not Jane. If Jane isn't being fed or rocked or held, she cries and cries — loud, insistent screeches that pierce Edith's ears and grate against her sanity.

During the day, Isobel and Margaret drop by with meat pies and soup and pudding. Margaret never seems to tire of holding Jane and will putter around in the kitchen using one hand to keep Jane pressed firmly against her chest, cooing softly until the child's hiccupping whimpers cease.

"You look exhausted," she says to Edith one afternoon. "Why don't you go upstairs and get some rest? I can take care of the girls."

It's been six weeks since she had the twins, and Edith obediently drags her feet up the stairs, gripping Frank's banister as she goes. She's grateful for Margaret and Isobel and Frank's mother — who even with her bad knee still comes by at least twice a week — but she doesn't like needing their help. She doesn't like the way they speak in soft voices, muffling their grief for her sake, rifling through her cupboards to make tea as if she is wholly incapable of setting out mugs and boiling water herself.

She lies down on top of the floral-print bedspread and stares at the ceiling. The house is quiet. Her breasts are full and heavy; the babies will need to be fed soon. She thinks about the basil that she hasn't planted yet. And the two tomato plants wilting by the back door. They need to be put into the garden. At least she collected the eggs this morning; she did manage to get that done.

What is she doing, lying here on the bed? She should be making use of this time while she has two hands free. But she makes no effort to move; she remains lifeless and miserable, waiting for the inevitable cries of hunger that will force her to her feet.

Margaret eventually goes home, and that night, like every other night, Edith is up again and again nursing the girls one after the other. Jane won't settle. She fusses and squirms and screws up her tiny face in frustration even while she's feeding. Edith hums to her and rocks her, but Jane just arches her body and howls. There's no sense holding her when she's like this, and since Anne doesn't seem bothered by her sister's screams, Edith lays Jane down beside Anne and walks out of the room.

She pulls her pillow over her head and clamps it against her ears. At some point, Jane must cry herself to sleep, and as the house settles into an uneasy silence, Edith finally drifts off too.

THE BABIES AREN'T QUITE three months old when Edith gets her first uninterrupted chunk of sleep. Almost six hours. She wakes up surprised and relieved, despite her painfully swollen breasts. Everyone promised her this would happen, that the demanding nights of non-stop feedings and diaper changes and crying would get better.

"Stuart was colicky for his first three months," Margaret reminded her several times. "This won't last forever; it gets easier."

Edith offers up a silent prayer of gratitude as she makes her way toward the twins' bedroom. When she cracks open the door, she sees Jane staring at her through the slats of the crib. So, she's awake and not crying for once. Will wonders never cease? Anne is lying quietly beside her sister, facing the wall.

As Edith gets closer, her heart stops. Something isn't right. Anne is too still, the skin on her cheeks a sickly grey. Edith reaches into the crib, her mind numb with dread, and scoops up Anne's lifeless body.

"What have you done?" Edith whispers to Jane. Then, hugging Anne tightly to her chest, she murmurs, "What have you done what have you done what have you done," until the words carry no meaning but become a terror-stricken refrain that blocks out the rest of the world.

ON SUNDAYS, EDITH SITS at the very end of the pew, near the stained-glass window with the iridescent image of Jesus dividing the loaves and the fishes. There are other scenes along the sides of the sanctuary: Jesus talking to a group of children; Jesus healing a lame man; Jesus at the Last Supper. At the front of the church, behind the pulpit, a much larger stained-glass window depicts Jesus on the cross.

Edith looks straight ahead during the services and leaves quickly afterward to collect Jane from the nursery with the goal of talking to as few people as possible. It's not hard to do. People avoid her; they don't know what to say. So much tragedy in such a short time.

Her family came down from Kingston for the funeral, and while her mother laid out meals, ironed diapers, and rocked Jane to sleep, Edith felt herself hardening against the anguish that washed over her in waves. When they were leaving, her mother took her by the shoulders, looked her in the eye, and said, "Put your faith in God, Edith. He will guide you and keep you."

Edith nodded dumbly and waved to them as they pulled away. Everyone, it seems, is preoccupied with her faith. Just a few days before, Reverend Bloor sat in her kitchen, explaining to her that while it was sometimes hard to understand God's will, she needed to trust His infinite wisdom. He stroked his white beard while he spoke to her, his mouth drawn into a frown.

She didn't answer because she knew it would be futile to argue, but that didn't mean she agreed.

"It is not for us to know why He chooses to call His children home when He does," Reverend Bloor continued, and Edith felt her throat closing. She stood up, busying herself at the counter, fussing with the teapot, rearranging the lid on the little ceramic sugar bowl.

Today, at the conclusion of the Sunday service, Edith is grateful for the excuse to slip out the door at the side of the sanctuary so that she doesn't have to meet the minister's eyes or answer any questions about how she's holding up. When Edith arrives at the nursery, she is led to one of the cots against the wall, where Jane is sleeping; Jane's eyelids flutter for a moment as Edith lifts her, but she immediately falls back to sleep in Edith's arms.

Edith goes straight home to the silent farmhouse, which only recently, in the days leading to the funeral, hummed with activity: neighbours dropped by with trays of food and soft-spoken consolations; Edith's family bustled about, arranging flowers, clanging dishes, scraping chairs across the hardwood floors. Edith carries Jane — who is awake now — into the quiet house and deposits her in the playpen that has been squished in beside the coffee table. It's hot today. The August afternoon air hangs heavy, and Edith wipes her forehead as she contemplates what to do with the hours ahead.

By dinnertime, Jane has become irritable. This fussy period happens every night around the same time, just after six o'clock. The witching hour, Isobel calls it. Except it doesn't last for an hour: it goes on and on, until Edith could throw something out of sheer frustration.

Edith knows full well that Jane didn't *do* anything to Anne; she understands what the doctor said about infant hearts stopping for no reason at all — crib death, he called it. But even though she is perfectly aware that Jane isn't to blame, she feels something dark and ugly stir within her whenever Jane reminds her, with her unceasing cries, that *she* is very much alive.

JANE LILY ✒

LILY MEANDERS THROUGH THE recently installed art exhibit in the Green Paper Gallery on Granville Island. This particular exhibit is a tribute to marine life and consists mostly of photographs, which do not interest her much. She weaves her way around the room nonetheless, relaxing into the respectful hush that follows each visitor as they admire the larger-than-life prints softly illuminated by the overhanging track lighting. Every now and then, there are soft murmurs of appreciation or whispered comments about a particular image. Lily breathes in the scent of pine needles, which strikes her as odd given the aquatic theme, but she has no one with whom to share this peculiar observation.

Usually, when she comes to Granville Island, where art is celebrated like a religion, she comes alone. On this island, with studios and galleries on almost every street, showcasing both local talent and visiting artists, she can spend hours roaming around, looking and looking.

Danah, who has come with her before, didn't understand why she wasn't allowed to come this time, but Lily remained firm. "This is Mommy time," she explained, looking to Andrew for support.

"You wouldn't enjoy it, Squirt," he told Danah. "Mom likes to look at art, but if you ask me, it's a bit boring. We'll do something fun once we have the house to ourselves."

As always, Danah is easily placated at the thought of spending time with Andrew, leaving Lily free to spend her afternoon alone.

Granville Island is only one of the places she frequents. She has other favourites. The Vancouver Art Gallery and Parrington Galleries both often host visiting artists, and she has spent many afternoons wandering through their exhibits, taking in the beautiful art, wondering if she'll ever find what she's looking for.

Once, with Danah in tow, she saw his name. A binder of his work, prints that could be ordered. She didn't get anything, of course, but the whole experience was jarring. She always thought that when she found him again, she would recognize something of their life together, yet when she saw his work, his name, the sensation that flooded her body wasn't familiarity. It was fear. She's not afraid of him, it's nothing like that. It's herself she's scared of. Because she knew as she flipped through those plastic sleeves that she could be lured away so easily.

She hasn't sketched in years and years, but today, as she wanders along, studying the marine life photography, she thinks about her sketchbooks of drawings. Her childish scribbles. She used to like drawing flowers, she remembers that, which is funny considering her job at Noble's Florist. She doesn't need to work, not with Andrew's salary, but after the incident when Danah was a baby, both she and Andrew agreed it would do her good to get out of the house. With her previous experience as a florist's assistant, back when she had to work, back when her meagre pay was the only thing keeping her and Morian afloat, it wasn't hard to convince Betty Noble to hire her. She may have an artistic flair, but it was always Morian who was the real artist.

She went back once to the little souvenir shop where she saw his prints. The binder was gone by then. They were promoting a different artist, someone who did beadwork: purses, jewellery, designs on T-shirts. She was disappointed, but really, what did she expect to find in a catalogue of his paintings?

LILY LEAVES THE GREEN Paper Gallery and emerges into the bright sunshine. After staring at underwater images for the past hour, it takes a moment for the street to come into focus. She digs in her bag for her sunglasses and finds a bench to rest on. She's not ready to go home. Not yet.

Andrew has never begrudged her these trips to museums and galleries; he indulges her fascination with art. The fact that she prefers to go alone doesn't bother him either. He understands her craving for solitude. He has never questioned her intentions. Not once.

JANE LILY 🐾

THE FIRST TIME I ran away from Andrew, Danah was only fifteen months old. I just left one morning. It was a Saturday, which meant Andrew didn't have to be on campus, but I bet he was banking on me returning before the weekend was over. I should have known he'd call his sister to bail him out. Georgina probably jumped in her car before he'd even finished explaining that I had taken off.

I ended up at the Red Cedar Nudist Resort, and I stayed away for two weeks. Then, unhappy and embarrassed, I made a tearful phone call to Andrew at his university department office and told him I was coming home.

"When?" he asked.

"Now. Today. I'm so sorry, Andrew. I just —"

"Don't," he said. "Don't do that. I'm glad you're coming home. Where are you? I'll come and get you."

"No." My too-quick refusal echoed across the phone line. "I mean, I've already arranged a cab. But will you meet me at the house? Who's ... who's been —"

"Danah's fine. Georgina is taking care of her. But she misses you." A pause. "I miss you."

There was another pause as he waited for me to respond, but I couldn't say what he wanted to hear, so I simply hung up. Then I leaned against the wall and shook.

Niall returned to this moment over and over in our sessions. Why, he wanted to know, was it so hard for me to admit to my husband that I missed him? Because I did miss him, obviously, or why else did I go back? Did I think it was significant that Georgina stayed another three days after I returned? Did I interpret that as a lack of trust on her part? On Andrew's? How did her presence impact my reunion with Andrew?

"I don't know!" I screamed at Niall once as he fired question after question at me. That was when we still met at his office and I still had the strength to scream.

Yesterday, when he visited me at my flat, he didn't ask me to delve into my past at all. Belinda, one of the community nurses who comes daily, made us tea, and I was half-expecting Niall to suddenly pull out a tin of biscuits. It felt more like a social call than a therapy session; yet, in a strange twist of irony, I actually wanted him to push me back to my past. I wanted to relive those moments after I had returned to Andrew, when we both pretended to be happy that I was back. I wanted to explain to Niall that Andrew's easy forgiveness hadn't been forgiving at all. I had wanted my husband to rage, for him to throw furniture, then to hold on to me so tightly I couldn't ever leave again.

EDITH 🦢

THE BILL FOR MY cab to Missionville was over three hundred dollars. I don't know what I was trying to accomplish by going back there. To accrue one more layer of self-doubt and recrimination? Those stones never gave me answers or offered any kind of peace, not for all the dozens and dozens of times I visited them when I still lived on the farm. I arrived back in Hamilton exhausted. But one thing had become clear to me: the past isn't going to go away just because I am so good at ignoring it.

What I need to decide is this: how much am I willing to confess? Not everything, but enough for Danah to see how it was. If I don't, the words will dry up and crumble to dust in the back of my throat, like they have so many times before.

In the meantime, to calm myself down, I methodically lay out the ingredients for an apple-cinnamon loaf. It's a simple loaf and one I can easily make from memory. I set aside one of the apple peels to use later in a cup of tea, which I will sweeten with honey. When I was little, my mother made me apple tea whenever I had a cold. She used to add a bit of lemon if she had any. After my trip to the cemetery, I am thirsty for the comforts of my childhood. I can remember sitting, wrapped in a quilt, on my mother's rocking chair sipping my mug of lukewarm apple tea while reading the cross-stitched axiom that hung beside the stairs: *Be still and know that I am God.*

I took such comfort in that directive. I wonder if my mother placed that particular message beside her rocking chair because it was the only place she could actually sit still long enough to read it. The thought of such simple faith makes me wistful.

I'm sipping my apple tea in Danah's apartment when Steve calls to tell me that his crew will be done on Saturday. "Then you're free to return home," he says cheerfully. His words should make me dizzy with relief, but I feel only the slightest pulse of satisfaction at the thought that by this weekend I'll be back in my own house, back where I belong.

When I open the oven to take out the apple-cinnamon loaf, a surge of hot air escapes. I leave the oven door open partway, allowing the warmth to continue spreading through the kitchen. I doubt Danah is ever going to talk to her landlord about the heat down here. She seems content to simply tolerate the cold, but then she's hardly home to notice it either. And just this morning, she warned me that since that professor from Australia is arriving tonight, I should hardly expect to see her at all over the next few days. Not that we pay each other any attention when we're together anyway.

DANAH RETURNS LATE IN the afternoon, and at one point, I can hear her talking to someone on her phone in the stairwell. Why she feels the need to conduct all her phone calls in private is beyond me, but when she comes back into the apartment, her mood has visibly darkened. She makes a show of pulling papers from her bag with loud, angry sighs.

I leave her alone.

What I have made up my mind to tell her can wait.

JANE LILY ✒

I ASK FLYNN TO pull out my box of Crisp Linen stationery so I can write one last letter. But my mind won't stay in one place long enough to say the things I really want to say. I've written dozens and dozens of letters to Danah, and suddenly they all seem inadequate. Flynn, bless his heart, understands the importance of what I want to do. Of all the community nurses who visit, he's my favourite. I like him better than Belinda even. He doesn't try to talk to me all the time like some of the others. I know they're only trying to be friendly or to alleviate my boredom, but I don't think they realize what a chore it is for me to maintain a conversation I'm not interested in having in the first place.

When he realizes I want to write a letter, Flynn brings me a clipboard so I don't have to sit at the table. Then, once I am set up with paper, the clipboard, and two pens, he leaves the room. My hand trembles as I write, and I hate how feeble my words look. I am still waiting for an answer to my last letter, the one I mailed to my mother, the one where I told her I was dying. But this letter is for Danah, and I've always been more honest in those.

I must fall asleep, because when I jerk my head up, thinking I've only just nodded off, the clipboard and pens have been carefully placed beside me on the coffee table. Flynn is humming in the kitchen, probably preparing my dinner. Did he read my scratchy confessions? What would he think if he saw all the other letters in the blue shoebox hidden under my bed? Are they enough, I wonder, to warrant forgiveness?

It will have to do — this final letter. I will add it to the box with the others, even though it isn't quite finished. None of them are, when it comes right down to it. I could never finish saying whatever it was I was trying to say in any of those letters, which is why I wrote so many.

The blue shoebox is really just a box of inadequate sentiments. It's not enough. But it's something.

DANAH 🦢

I HAVEN'T SLEPT PROPERLY in days. The crappy pullout doesn't help, but it's my mind that won't rest. So this morning, when I wake up sleep-deprived and just as confused as I was before Edith started sharing scraps of details about my mother, I want nothing more than to curl up in my blankets with a hot cup of tea.

I don't have that luxury, though. Today is our first day of events with Arthur Williams, and I have no choice but to pull myself out of bed and brace for a full day. I will find out what happened to Morian, even if I have to hire a private detective to do it. That much I've resolved. Maybe he's with my mom now. Maybe they're together in Edinburgh. I have money from my dad's estate, and while I doubt he'd approve of me throwing it after Mom's shadow, I know he'd want me to be happy. And finding some answers will make me happy.

Right now, though, I have to push aside any thoughts of detectives and fact-finding missions because I only have one shot to make a good impression on Arthur, and I want him to want me on his joint project with Pauline.

As I'm getting ready, I study my reflection in the bathroom mirror. I pull my hair back, then decide to leave it down, taking a few extra minutes to straighten it. When Arthur meets me, I want to appear put-together: confident and capable. The way I used to feel. The way I used to *be*.

My landlord, Bertie, stops me at the top of the stairs just as I'm leaving. "How much longer is your grandmother staying? Not that it matters, I'm just curious, that's all."

Poor Bertie. "Just a few more days," I say. "Her house should be ready soon." I smile at him and inch toward the door. I don't have time to make small talk this morning. I absolutely can't be late for the departmental talk, which Trevor just informed me last night he is no longer attending. When he called to tell me, I was so mad I didn't even let him finish explaining.

"What do you mean you can't make it?"

"Look, Danah, I know you're probably thinking —"

"You have no idea what I'm thinking," I interrupted. I slipped into the stairwell with my phone so Edith couldn't listen in. "Just when I thought you might actually give a damn, you have to go and prove me wrong again!"

He was quick to reply. "Give me a break. That's not fair, and you know it. You're so wrapped up in your own drama you can hardly see straight."

"My own drama? Oh, that's rich. Nice to know how you really feel."

"Danah, don't be like that. I'm just saying —"

"Trust me, I know exactly what you're saying." Before he could continue, I hung up.

BY THE TIME I get to the DeGroote School of Business, where the departmental talk is taking place, I've convinced myself that Trevor might still show up. I feel bad about hanging up on him; I don't want things to be awkward between us tonight in front of everyone, assuming, that is, he's still coming to the dinner.

The room we're using in the DeGroote building is modern, with tiered seating that hasn't been destroyed yet by bored students. The walls are accented with dark wood trim, and there's a large window that lets in a stream of sunlight. It's a far cry from the moldy rooms in the basement of Kenneth Taylor Hall.

"Hey, the place is filling up, eh?" Dwayne has approached and is surveying the room with satisfaction. "Sanders will be happy. Looks like a decent turnout."

"Let's just hope it's this full tomorrow, when the people coming have no idea who Williams is."

Dwayne shrugs. "One day at a time. Is Trevor here? Should we save him a seat?"

"He's not coming." I start to move toward a row of empty seats, then see Navi standing by the door. I wave her over, effectively preventing Dwayne from asking anything more about Trevor and why he isn't coming.

ARTHUR WILLIAMS IS AS entertaining as we've been promised, his presentation an artful mix of academic discourse and quirky showmanship. I find myself relaxing as I fall under the spell of his humour. Leaning against my cushioned leather seat, laughing alongside Dwayne and Navi, I let go of some of the stress I've been carrying around for the past few days.

After the talk, the entire planning committee is having lunch with Arthur at the University Club. We are meant to be there for noon, but the question period following the talk seems like it will never end. Too many people want to hear more, and for every question Arthur answers, five more hands go up. Finally, Pauline intervenes, allowing one last question, then, thankfully, people start clapping and rising from their seats to leave.

"One event down, three more to go," Dwayne says, rising from his own seat and stretching.

"Enjoy your lunch, you lucky bastards," Navi says, poking me in the arm.

I don't end up sitting anywhere near Arthur Williams at the University Club; he is surrounded by faculty members who appear to be just as starstruck by him as us lowly grad students. We're eating in the West Room, specifically set up for our private group, and because I am facing the window, I find myself staring out at the ravine, which backs onto the Royal Botanical Gardens. Trevor and I used to go for long walks along the trails that snake through the gardens, although it's hard to imagine us deciding to step out for a romantic stroll anytime soon.

"I'm nervous being around Williams," Susan splutters. She's been staring down the table at Arthur ever since we got here. "I mean, I have no idea what to say to him."

"I'm sure you'll think of something," I reply. Susan loves convincing people she's the smartest person in the room, and it occurs to me that if she has any thoughts of vying for a spot on Pauline and Arthur's project, my only hope is that she's too annoying to be considered.

LATER, NAVI AND I are sitting in our shared office discussing Arthur. "You have a crush on him, don't you?" Navi says.

"I don't have a crush on him," I insist. "But you have to admit, he's easy to listen to. And not hard to look at either."

Navi slaps Taryn's desk, where she's sitting since Taryn herself is uncharacteristically absent. "I knew it!" she says.

Just then, Dwayne pokes his head in the door. "All set for tonight?" he asks me.

"Pretty much, although I lost my date for the evening." Trevor sent me a short text confirming what I already suspected about the dinner. I hope I sound nonchalant. Navi gives me a questioning look, but I choose to ignore it.

"No date, eh?" Dwayne says, raising his eyebrows. "Well, that's easily remedied. I happen to be going to the same restaurant. And, alas, I'm also flying solo. We can be each other's consolation dates."

I look at him ruefully. "*That's* supposed to console me? But for lack of any better options, I'll take you up on it."

"Ah, you guys make such a cute couple," Navi says, and I can see by the expression on her face that she is dying for an explanation.

Dwayne grins at both of us. "I knew one day someone would succumb to my charms. It was only a matter of time." Then he disappears down the hall, whistling.

"So," Navi says, "are you going to tell me what the hell is going on?"

THE ONLY GOOD THING about Trevor bailing on tonight's dinner is that I'll be in a better position to strike up another conversation with Arthur. After our lunch at the University Club, I was able to corner him for a few minutes, and I took the opportunity to explain my plans for my thesis, emphasizing the role his research on secret deviants had played in selecting my topic. He appeared genuinely interested in the angle I was taking pertaining to secrecy within the family unit, so now all I can hope is that my conversation with him stood out enough to make me memorable. After all, every single person he talked to was likely trying to impress him.

Dwayne said he would pick me up at twenty after six, and when he shows up at 6:19, he points to his watch and raises an eyebrow. "What did I tell you? No, no, you don't need to say it — I know you're impressed."

I roll my eyes. "To The Stone Oven, James," I order curtly. Then, in a more wistful tone, I add, "It would be nice to have a chauffeur, wouldn't it?"

"I wouldn't know. No one's been offering to drive *me* anywhere ..."

That's when I remember Dwayne is supposed to pick up Arthur from his hotel. "Don't you have to get Williams?" I ask, thinking he may have forgotten.

"I do indeed. So, you'll have to relocate to the back seat when we get to the hotel. Although, come to think of it, I do prefer my women in the back seat."

I slap his arm, and we head to the Sheraton, where Arthur is waiting in the lobby. He greets us both by name. I smile to myself. There's no way he remembers the name of everybody that he met today.

We arrive at the restaurant early, and since our table isn't quite ready, the three of us sit down at the bar. I order a glass of red wine.

"I'll have a pint of Heineken, please," Arthur says.

"Shouldn't you be drinking Foster's?" Dwayne asks.

"No, mate. When in Rome … besides, nobody in Australia really drinks Foster's." Then, raising his glass, Arthur says, "I've had enough academic talk for one day, so I'm hoping for more exciting conversations this evening. What are the chances of that?"

"Well, I can't promise exciting," Dwayne says, "but we'll do our best not to disappoint. I won't be held responsible for the turn in conversation when the others arrive, though. Especially Susan. She'll take any chance she can get to show off."

Arthur laughs. "I believe I remember Susan. Short hair, sort of spiky?"

"That's her. If she ends up beside you at dinner, don't say we didn't warn you."

"Are you enjoying your brief taste of winter?" I ask. "We actually didn't have any snow at all a few days ago, so you arrived just in time to see our first sprinkling of it."

Dwayne actually groans out loud. "And you were worried our conversation might veer toward thought-provoking. Next, we'll talk about our favourite colours."

Arthur turns to face me. "I'm not particularly fond of your weather, to tell the truth. I'd rather be surfing. As for my favourite colour, I rather like hazel."

I feel myself flushing. Is he talking about my eyes? Before I can respond, the hostess informs us that our table is ready. Gratefully, I pick up my glass of wine and follow Dwayne and Arthur to the back of the restaurant, where a large table has been set for us in a semi-private enclave. As we sit down, Professor Sanders arrives with Professor Leeson and his wife, followed in quick succession by Carrie, one of the other members of the planning committee, and Susan. Conversation drifts to and from the day's events as the last members of our group arrive, and the waitress assigned to us begins taking drink orders.

I'm sitting between Arthur and Susan, trying to keep my face straight every time Susan leans around me in an attempt to start a conversation with Arthur. I know if I make eye contact with Dwayne, I'll burst out laughing. When Arthur shoots me an amused glance, I am aware of a tiny, bubbling sensation in my stomach.

I drink a lot of wine and laugh a lot. By the end of our meal, my head is buzzing pleasantly, and I'm relieved that I came with Dwayne instead of driving on my own. I look at him across the table, smiling and joking with the people around him. He's so easygoing. He's just such a good guy.

On the way home, I try to explain to Dwayne what a nice person he is. "I'm glad we're friends," I mumble. "You're a good guy. Do people always tell you that? How good you are?"

He doesn't say anything. Then, when we are parked at the end of my driveway, he turns to me and says, "You're a good person too, Danah. Trevor is a lucky guy. Now go inside and try not to wake the living dead."

I look at him, surprised. "That's actually a really apt description of my grandmother!" I fight the urge to giggle, then add, more seriously, "Although I'm not sure she would appreciate the comparison." I thank him again for being my date and, after fumbling for a minute with the new deadbolt at the top of the stairs, make my way into my dark apartment.

When I finally slip beneath the covers on the pullout, I wonder what exactly Dwayne meant about Trevor being a lucky guy.

JANE LILY 🦢

TO A CASUAL OBSERVER, Lily would appear distracted as she wanders through the aisles of the outdoor market on Granville Island. She wants to pick up a few things for dinner but is unsure what to get. For starters, she doesn't know whether she'll be eating alone or with Morian. The kind of meal she usually prepares for Morian is not the same as what she eats when she's on her own. Morian has become a picky eater, and lately he's harder and harder to please. And it isn't just at meals that she finds herself on the wrong side of his moods; sometimes she thinks just seeing her is enough to annoy him.

So while she half-hopes that he won't be home for dinner, she is also worried about how much time he is spending away from her. She wants to grab hold of him and pull him close because she senses him pulling away. At the same time, he can be so frustrating that she's often quite happy to watch him disappear out the door, leaving her in peace. But she is always relieved when he returns. Relieved and angry.

She stops in front of a vendor and listlessly picks out a few vegetables: some peppers, mushrooms, green onion, and carrots. She has decided on a stir-fry for dinner. He can't argue with that. And if he isn't there, at least it's something she likes too.

It isn't even just the fact that he often misses meals, it's the fact that he never bothers to tell her. She always has to guess. Will he be there or not? He's become unpredictable, like a dog that one minute wants you to pet him and the next bites you for trying. But, as Morian is quick to remind her when she complains, his unpredictability is what attracted her to him in the first place.

"You used to like the fact that I was always surprising you," he says. "Now it gets me in trouble. That's hardly fair, Lily."

Fair? He thinks she is being unfair? How about the fact that he can come and go as he pleases, while she is left to take care of everything that needs to be done just so they can keep functioning? She has to make sure the bills are paid because Morian can't be bothered to open them. She has to make sure there is food in the apartment and that the laundry gets done. She has to wash the dishes and clean up the messes that Morian and his friends make. The more she thinks about it, the angrier she becomes. But she loves him. She has to. She has given up so much to be with him.

When she walks into their apartment with her small bag of vegetables, she knows right away that he's home. She can *feel* him. "Hello," she calls out cautiously. "I'm back."

Morian comes to meet her at the door and takes both her purse and her shopping bag from her. He sets them on the floor and wraps his arms around her. "Mmm," he murmurs, his face pressed against her hair, "nice to see you." He pulls away from her, still holding her at arm's length. "Look at you," he says. "Like a flower. My beautiful Lily."

She smiles. "You had a good day?"

"As a matter of fact, it's been a great day. I finished my painting." He pulls her into his studio, which is actually the front room of the apartment, the one with the best light. "Ta-da," he cries as he turns her to face his latest work.

"It's beautiful," Lily whispers. It *is* beautiful. Morian is undeniably talented. How can she not love a man like this?

"So," he says, drawing her attention away from the painting, "what did you bring back for dinner? I'm starving."

Working together in the kitchen, laughing and bumping into each other, Lily feels truly happy. Tonight, she won't have to justify being with him. Tonight, she is reminded of all the reasons she allowed him to sweep her off her feet and away from her life in Missionville. Tonight, things are good.

WHEN SHE WAKES UP, Lily is alone. A familiar heaviness settles on her chest. She pads softly to the front room, where Morian is sitting in front of one of his unfinished paintings. His success of the previous day will now be replaced with a renewed drive to accomplish more. He has dozens of unfinished works: pieces that he can't get right, pieces that drive him to near despair. And as Lily watches him from the doorway, she knows that today she will be a nuisance to him, an uninvited intrusion on his work.

Just like that, she has lost him again.

So, Lily leaves him alone. She makes the bed and washes the dishes from last night's dinner. She retreats to the bedroom and reads a book for over an hour. But she can't stop thinking about last night. She wanted to hold on to those moments a little longer. She wanted to wake up with Morian beside her, then make breakfast together and maybe *do* something, go somewhere. She wanted to feel important, to feel needed, to feel loved.

Finally, she slips out of the apartment and walks down to the beach. She heads in the direction of a giant piece of driftwood where she likes to sit and watch snippets of other people's lives flitting past. Today, there is an older couple with a young girl, a grandchild perhaps, collecting shells. The man strolls along affably, waiting patiently each time his wife or the girl crouch down to pick up another shell. What would it be like, Lily wonders, to have someone humour her whims like that?

Behind the meandering shell collectors, there is a young man throwing a stick into the water for his dog. Over and over again the dog thrashes into the water and then returns the stick to his owner's feet, fur dripping, tail wagging, waiting for that same piece of wood to be thrown into the air one more time.

As Lily watches the stick sink into the gentle waves along the shore, she resolves to stay away from the apartment for the whole day. If Morian wants to withdraw into himself, then let him.

She can disappear too.

"IT'S ONLY TWO WEEKS, Lily," Morian says. "This is what I need right now. If I can't find inspiration in Paris, then ..."

Then what? Lily wants him to finish his sentence. To put exactly what he's thinking into words instead of an incomplete thought that hangs ambiguously in the air, waiting to drop like the blade of a guillotine. They are lying on their bed, on top of the covers, staring at the ceiling instead of each other.

"I wish I could go with you," she says, although they've been over this too. Morian is leaving for France with a friend who knows somebody in Paris they can stay with, but there's really no room for Lily. Not that it matters, because they couldn't both afford to go anyway, and Lily couldn't take the time off without losing her job at the flower shop. They need her pay to keep getting by. Morian's paintings may be exceptional, but even exceptional works by unknown artists don't sell for much. Besides, Morian is not a salesman. He has a terrible habit of keeping his favourite pieces instead of selling them. Lily jokingly tells him that he's his own best collector, but there's really nothing funny about it when it comes right down to it.

"One day, my beautiful Lily, we will return to France together," Morian promises, pulling her toward him, finally looking into her eyes.

They make love, but to Lily, it feels desperate. And sad. There is a sweetness in the way Morian kisses her neck and shoulders, in the way he moves so slowly, trailing his fingers across her skin, but when they are done, and she rolls away from him, she is desolate.

At the airport, when they are saying goodbye, half-hidden behind a monstrous potted plant, Lily cries into Morian's shoulder. They cling to each other tightly, but Morian's friend Jason, an aspiring poet/songwriter, has already gone through security, and Lily knows that, at any moment now, Morian will have to let her go.

LATER, WALKING THROUGH THE rooms in their apartment, instead of the emptiness and loneliness she expected, Lily is surprised to find her shoulders relaxing, to feel her lungs expanding as she takes a few deep breaths. Solitude. She forgot how much she used to crave being alone. She makes herself a cup of tea and takes her brand-new copy of *The Handmaid's Tale* outside to the narrow balcony overlooking the street. But she doesn't read. Instead, she watches the comings and goings of strangers below, everyone on their way somewhere, skimming along, oblivious to all the secrets and mysteries tucked into the hearts around them, passing on bicycles or pushing strollers or sitting alone on balconies high above the street.

Over the next few days, she settles into a rhythm: work, experimenting with different ingredients for dinner, a walk on the beach, then reading on the balcony until the sky is lit with fiery oranges and pinks that slowly fade to a dusty indigo. There are no tricky moods to navigate, no sidestepping or tiptoeing around the apartment, but also no thrilling bursts of passion. She misses Morian, but she suspects that, when he returns, she will miss being alone.

At the end of the two weeks, on the day Morian's flight is scheduled to land, Lily can barely concentrate on the flower orders in front of her. Twice she cuts the stem of a daisy too short and has to select another one from the bucket in the cooler. When she wraps a completed bouquet in paper, her hands are clumsy, and the wrapping is crumpled instead of smooth. She hasn't heard from Morian the entire time he's been gone, so she doesn't know what to expect when they see each other again. Will he enfold her in his arms and kiss the top of her head like he used to after being apart for only a few hours? Or will he be prickly with disappointment and frustration from a failed artistic endeavour? She hopes with all her being that he was right about this trip and that it will have sparked in him a way to allow his true talent to glow so that the old Morian, the boy who whisked her onto a dance floor and across the country, will be the Morian who greets her when she steps through the door of their apartment this afternoon.

The bus ride home is interminably long. Her heart is skipping around near her throat. As she approaches their apartment, she is barely breathing, and she closes her eyes briefly before pushing the door open and stepping tentatively inside.

The air is still, everything exactly as she left it this morning. He's not here. She walks into the bedroom. There are no bags. Nothing. Then she knows. But even as the truth settles heavy as a stone in her gut, she refuses to believe it.

She refuses to believe that he won't walk through the door again, full of explanations and apologies. For days, she returns home from work tasting the expectation that he will be inside, waiting for her. Then, finally, she begins to accept that he isn't coming back, that despite all her longing, he is truly gone.

AFTER WEEKS OF WASTED waiting, Lily gives up on the last tiny seed of hope she had been nurturing. She begins to stop at the park between the bus stop and her apartment. She sits on a bench there and lets her mind go blank. One day, while she's sitting on that bench sipping a chai tea, a man sits down beside her.

"Beautiful day," he says. "Do you come here often?"

In the moments and days and weeks that follow, she begins to imagine a new kind of life where love is reliable and easy and where the promise of stability is an anchor to happiness.

DANAH ✌

I WAKE TO THE sound of Edith throwing up. Even before she
emerges from the bathroom, her eyes ringed with dark circles, her
face pale and drawn, I know she has another migraine. And my
first selfish thought is: *Great, now she won't be able to attend the
public talk.*

She shuffles back to the bedroom without saying a word, and
when I consider for a minute what her day is going to be like, I
try to summon up at least a pretence of sympathy. As quietly as
possible, I find her a bucket, fill a glass with water, then bring them
to the bedroom for her.

"Do you need anything else?" I ask. "A damp cloth, maybe?"
My mind reverts to the image of her lying on her couch the day I
found the envelope in her kitchen, the day before the fire.

"I'll be fine. I just need my pills to kick in."

I do feel bad leaving her like that, but there isn't much I can do.
I have to be on campus at nine for a quick meeting with Pauline
before a small group of us take Arthur on a tour of the university.
I hover around for a few minutes, but eventually Edith shoos me
away.

"Go do your stuff," she says, waving her hand dismissively.

"Sticking around for an extra twenty minutes isn't going to help any."

It's a mild day for December, and sunny. Perfect weather to show off our facilities. Many of the older buildings look like something you'd find on a postcard, a sense of history seeping from their stones. Gilmour Hall, with its ivy-hung tower and grandiose archway, could almost be mistaken for a castle.

I run into Dwayne just outside of Kenneth Taylor Hall. "Are you ready for another day of pulling out all the stops to impress our illustrious guest?" he asks.

"I'm not planning on doing much of the talking," I reply. "Just following along with a smile while Susan goes into excessive detail about every building and its history."

"Do you think Williams even cares about seeing the campus? I can't imagine he's too excited about this tour. Although, if I were in Australia, I might want to have a peek around ANU's campus."

"Yeah, but probably not with Susan as your guide," I joke. If I *do* get selected for the project, maybe it'll be me who gets to visit the Australian National University. Arthur might decide it would be helpful to have me on site to assist with the comparative analysis between the Canadian and Australian data, ignoring, for a moment, the fact that ANU has its own grad students and researchers, of course.

Dwayne and I step into the elevator in the lobby of Kenneth Taylor Hall, and as the doors close, Dwayne nudges my shoulder with his elbow. "You're going to miss our little crew when this whole thing is over," he says, "even Susan."

"I don't know. By tonight, I feel like I'll have seen enough of you all to last a lifetime. What time are you showing up at Chagall's?"

Tonight is our send-off dinner for Arthur at an upscale restaurant that's attached to the Sheraton. After his talk, Arthur will head back to the hotel, then simply walk downstairs to meet us for dinner. I've been to Chagall's once before, with my father. He told me the restaurant got its name from the French painter Marc Chagall and that the artwork on the wall showcased new and upcoming local artists. I never breathed a word to my father, but the restaurant, with all those paintings on display, made me think of my mother and her visits to the different art galleries around Vancouver. She had a strange preoccupation with art.

"I'll be there right at six," Dwayne replies. "Have you noticed yet how punctual I am? It's one of my more endearing qualities."

We walk toward Pauline's office while I fight the urge to text Trevor about today's public talk. He was never planning on attending this one because he was supposed to have come to the departmental talk yesterday, but with Edith sick, I'm tempted to see if Trevor will come. To make up for yesterday.

I hear Susan's shrill voice on the other side of Pauline's door. What are they talking about that has Susan so excited? I lift my chin before knocking on the partially open door and enter my advisor's office with as much confidence as I can muster.

Susan is quiet on the tour, which makes me even more suspicious. It ends up being Dwayne and Carrie who lead our group along the snow-dusted paths between buildings. I am only half paying attention because I'm trying to figure out what's going on with Susan. I could allude to the project and see how she reacts, but I don't want to give too much away. The last thing I need is her asking questions about a project she might not know anything about. Besides, Pauline is my advisor; there's no way she'd choose Susan over me.

EDITH DOESN'T COME TO the talk, but Ben and Alice still show up, which is nice of them. Arthur's presentation is pretty much the same as yesterday's, except this time, given his more general audience, he makes it slightly less academic. I have to hand it to him: he has the crowd mesmerized; there are several times the room erupts in gales of laughter. I'm sorry Edith is missing it, and I'm also disappointed that Trevor didn't show up to surprise me. At least I have Dwayne, laughing in the seat beside me.

When I get back to my apartment, Edith is sitting at the table sipping a bowl of broth. She's still in her housecoat, but the fact that she's out of bed seems promising.

"Feeling better?" I ask.

"A bit. How was the presentation? Did Alice and Ben make it?"

"Yeah, they were both there. I think they enjoyed it. I have one more dinner thing tonight, but is there anything I can do for you before I go?"

"Oh, don't worry about me. I'm used to taking care of myself."

As I turn to get ready, my phone rings.

"Hey, I thought maybe you'd like a ride," Dwayne says. "You know, to save the planet and all that."

I hesitate. "Sure. What time?"

"I'll pick you up at quarter to six. On the dot."

JANE LILY 🌾

"DO YOU SOMETIMES WONDER if maybe you were still waiting for Morian to return?" Niall asks. "Even after you'd met Andrew?"

"No." I am adamant. "At first, I was happy. I hardly thought about Morian at all, except sometimes to be mad about what he'd done. But I definitely wasn't hoping he'd come back, not after meeting Andrew." I shift my position on the couch and adjust the blanket around my legs. It makes no difference; I am always cold. I am stronger today, but my voice still sounds weak. It's good to have Niall pressing me again, though; it's more like our old sessions.

Niall nods his head thoughtfully. "And then when you weren't so happy anymore?"

"Things changed. I developed a bit of a fantasy about Morian rescuing me again."

"Morian? Or just someone like him? Isn't that what you were hoping to find when you were touring all those galleries? Another artist who could redefine your view of the world?" Niall likes the thought of this, I can tell. It does make for a nice theory. But I wasn't looking for someone *like* Morian on all those visits; I was looking for Morian himself. In the flesh. I wanted to feel again the way I felt when we left Missionville together, when the wildflowers had been blooming in the ditches alongside the road, heady with the scent and promise of happiness. I wanted to tell him about Danah.

Niall and I are both silent for a few minutes. Increasingly, when he comes to see me, our conversations are punctuated by these long silences, intended, I guess, as a chance for me to regain my strength from the effort of speaking. It takes a lot of energy to meet with him now, but he keeps encouraging me not to stop yet. Not when he thinks I've finally started being honest. And I do feel lighter lately after our visits.

"I romanticized the way it was with us," I say, attempting to explain. "I remembered how it felt running away with Morian when I was younger, and I wanted to experience that again. I wanted so badly to escape." I am still being only partially honest, but he's happy enough with my answer.

Belinda comes into the room with a cup of water and some pills. The cup has a straw sticking out of it so I am less likely to spill all over myself. Niall looks at his watch. I don't want him to go before I've finished explaining.

"It was hard," I say, my voice a raspy whisper. I clear my throat. "It was really hard." *I took her tooth with me*, I want to add. *I still have her tooth. What does that tell you?*

"I know," he says. He reaches over and takes my thin, papery hand in his. "I know it was hard."

AFTER HE LEAVES, I sleep. And when I awake, hours later, I am trying to hold on to the edges of a dream where Danah was squeezing my hand, telling me with her eyes that she understood. I want to drift back to that moment, where forgiveness seemed possible, and peace, oh peace, that elusive winged creature, was within my grasp at last.

Belinda is in the kitchen, probably putting my dinner together. A soupy concoction that I will again drink through a straw. I call her name, and she appears immediately beside the couch, wiping her hands on a towel.

"Was there any mail today?" I ask.

"Just some flyers and a bill. Your lawyer will take care of the bill. You don't have to worry about any of that now."

I nod. And peace flutters a little further away.

DANAH 🐉

I FEEL A BIT awkward about having Dwayne pick me up again for tonight's dinner. His comment from last night is still bouncing around in my head. Granted, I was tipsy and saying some weird things myself, but I still found his comment about Trevor being a lucky guy strange. And he was sober when he said it. At the same time, having Dwayne drive tonight means I can enjoy a few drinks without worrying about how I'll get home.

The dress I plan to wear is hanging in my closet, and when I go into my bedroom to get it, I glance around at what will soon be my space again. Edith's few belongings are perfectly arranged, everything neatly lined up. Despite the fact that she likely spent most of the day in bed, the covers are pulled up tightly, and the pillow is freshly plumped. I shake my head. Leave it to Edith to make the bed while suffering from a migraine. The box of books she took from her garage is pushed up against the wall by the closet. I only notice it at all because the flaps are open, and that seems at odds with Edith's commitment to absolute order. One of the books on top looks like a Bible. Strange. Edith's made it clear on multiple occasions that she's all but given up on religion.

I open the Bible, wondering if maybe Alice gave it to her, but it's inscribed to Frank and Edith Koestra. Underneath their names, in the space designed to record births, is my mother's name, written in neat blue cursive. Immediately below that, there's another name. My brain somersaults in confusion. I read both names again: Jane Lily Koestra, born April 16, 1965, and Anne Scarlett Koestra, born on the same day. Holy fucking mother of Moses. I flick through the pages until I hit Genesis, but there are no other details recorded. I flip to the back of the Bible, but the pages there are blank.

Holding the Bible in one hand, I march into the living room. Edith is still sitting at the table, sipping her broth, and I don't care how rude I sound when I shake the Bible in her face and demand information.

"Who's Anne? You never told me my mom had a sister! She was a twin?"

Edith at least has the decency to look surprised. She glances at the Bible I'm holding, and I worry that she's going to say nothing, just turn back to her soup and ignore me completely. But she doesn't do that. She opens her mouth and says simply, "Anne died when she was a baby."

I don't know what to say. Edith's silence around my mother, her caginess, the overpowering sensation I have that she's keeping something from me — and now this, another huge secret — it makes my head want to explode. For all the hours I've spent visiting my grandmother, for all the conversations we've had over the years, I actually know next to nothing about her. Why does she think she can't tell me anything?

"How? What happened to her?"

"Crib death. They call it something else now." Edith rubs her temple, and I know she's done. But I'm not.

"Did my mom know?"

"Of course she knew. Why wouldn't she know?"

"Oh, I don't know. Maybe because you don't talk about anything, ever."

I turn away then, defeated, but thoughts are firing through my brain like cannons. I am angry, inexplicably angry, at all the things I don't know. My mother had a twin, and that twin died. I storm back to the bedroom and drop the Bible into the box. The whole time I'm getting dressed, my mind is churning over different ways to shake the truth from Edith. I move into the bathroom, shutting the door firmly behind me. I finish curling my hair and apply one final coat of mascara before checking the time on my phone. Dwayne will be here in five minutes.

I don't expect Edith to talk to me as I make my way to the stairs, but she speaks up anyway. "I was going to tell you, you know. Before you saw that Bible."

I pause, but I don't say anything. I'm past believing her at the moment.

"You look nice," she adds, almost as an afterthought, "but I can see your whole leg when you walk. Your dress is cut too high on the one side." Her voice is tired, but her disapproval rings loud and clear.

"It's supposed to be like that. It's meant to be sexy, Grandma."

I start climbing the stairs just as Dwayne knocks on the outside door. He whistles when he sees me. "Wow," he says, and I feel myself blushing.

"You don't look half bad yourself," I say. He does look good. He's wearing a light grey suit over a white shirt, no tie — a confident blend of formal and casual that he has just enough swagger to pull off.

He leads me to his car, and as he holds open the car door for me, my anger at Edith takes a back seat in my brain. We can talk later. Tonight, I need to be on point. I make a lighthearted comment to Dwayne about his gentlemanly manners, determined to turn my mood around.

"I aim to charm," he replies, closing the door softly.

CHAGALL'S IS PRETTY MUCH the same as I remember. The art on the walls has changed, but they still showcase local artists. The dining room is a soft mix of honey tones: light woods and neutral fabrics in beige and tan and taupe that give off a golden glow. The servers are attentive and serious, dressed in black suits. They don't attempt to memorize our orders; instead, they write everything down in tiny leather-bound notepads, and when they pour the wine, they hold a white linen napkin against the bottle to stop it from dripping.

I'm glad I chose this dress; it suits the formality of Chagall's, even with the side slit that apparently shows too much leg. Everyone here is dressed up, showing off the best version of themselves.

Somehow, I end up sitting between Arthur and Dwayne. Susan is at the far end of the table, no doubt kissing her chances of getting on the project goodbye. Although, to her credit, she also looks really good tonight, spiky hair and all.

"Oh, great," Dwayne whispers as soon as we sit down. "Now I have competition for the evening! With an Australian accent, no less."

I elbow him gently in the ribs, then turn to say hello to Arthur.

"How are you going, Danah? You look lovely this evening. As does everyone." He nods toward Dwayne, as if to include him, belatedly, in his comment. "Ah, I do enjoy your Ontario wines," he adds as one of our servers leans in to fill his glass with a pinot grigio.

Over the course of the meal, I am drawn into the light-hearted banter around the table. Between Dwayne and Arthur, the group is never at a loss for entertainment. Before dessert is served, around the second (or possibly the third) time I am complimenting Arthur on his presentations, he stops me with a mock-serious expression on his face.

"Are you trying to butter me up, lovey?" he asks. "I've been told my head is plenty big as it is, but I'm always keen for more compliments. Go on then."

Dwayne kicks my foot under the table before launching into a description of what he considers the best desserts on the menu. I swallow some more wine, then kick Dwayne back. He gives me a weird look, but I can't figure out why, so I ignore him and turn my attention back to Arthur, who is very good at refilling my wine glass from the bottles that have been left out for us on the table.

After dessert, Professor Sanders apologizes for having to leave so early, but given that she hasn't been feeling well all day, she says she's not up for a late night. She speaks briefly with Arthur before smiling thinly at the rest of us, then heads out the door. Professor Leeson and his wife soon follow, leaving the rest of us to linger over our drinks and desserts. I choose the chocolate soufflé, following Dwayne's raving recommendation. There is a band setting up in one corner of the restaurant, and when they begin to play, Arthur asks me if I'd like to dance. Actually, he asks me if I'd *fancy* a dance.

I studiously avoid looking at Dwayne and instead turn in my seat to face Arthur. "I should warn you," I say, "that I'm a terrible dancer."

"There's no such thing. Trust me." He reaches for my hand, and I allow him to pull me up and onto the small dance floor that has been cleared in front of the band. He smells like expensive cologne and white wine, and his arms feel strong and sure as he skillfully guides me between the other couples spinning around us.

I've barely given any thought to Edith and the dead baby she kept secret. I've also barely given any thought to Trevor, although as Arthur pulls me closer to his chest, I have the decency to suffer a small spasm of guilt. Just as quickly as it surfaces, though, it's replaced with anger. Not only with Trevor, for letting me down, but also with Edith. My earlier outrage begins to creep back into the tunnels of my mind until Arthur leans toward my ear to whisper something.

"Sorry?" I say. "I didn't catch that."

"I said your friend Dwayne is sure keeping a close eye on you."

I glance back toward our group and notice that more people have left, enough so that the long table looks almost deserted. Susan raises her eyebrows at me when we come back to take our seats, and within minutes she is shaking Arthur's hand, saying how nice it was to meet him. Brad and Carrie follow suit, leaving just the three of us at the table: me, Dwayne, and Arthur.

"I can get a taxi home," I say to Dwayne. "You don't have to wait for me." Arthur's hand is on my knee under the table, and the sensation of it resting there is ringing through every nerve in my body.

I can see Dwayne hesitate, but then he stands up and wishes Arthur a safe flight in the morning. He looks back at me once before disappearing through the doors of the restaurant. That leaves me. Alone at the table with Arthur.

MY HEAD IS SPINNING as Arthur leads me out of the restaurant and toward the bank of elevators in the lobby. I know where he's taking me, and I am following along like a sleepwalker. When the elevator doors shut, enclosing us in the tiny space, my brain tries to argue with my body. My brain loses. I am leaning against Arthur, and he is kissing my hair. The doors open, and I stumble into the carpeted hall. He steers me gently down the hall, around a corner, and to a door. It wobbles in front of me. He swipes his key card, and I watch the tiny light turn green while my brain makes one last feeble stand by repeating a series of annoying instructions: *Turn around. Walk away. Turn around. Walk away.*

I follow Arthur into his room.

Before I can slow down my racing thoughts, he has a hand on either side of my face. He's kissing me, gently at first, then more and more hungrily. My mind is reeling. My thoughts scream for my attention, but my hands are around his neck, and my mouth matches his urgency. We stumble toward the bed, and when I feel the edge of the mattress at the back of my legs, I collapse onto it, pulling Arthur on top of me. He begins kissing my neck while his hands work at the straps on my dress. I sit up awkwardly so he can reach the zipper at the back. My brain has finally stopped its pointless protests. As my dress slips from my shoulders, Arthur traces a finger lightly down my arm, sending an avalanche of shivers cascading in its wake.

Slowly, so slowly, he caresses my skin, watching my face, my eyes. I sink back onto the mattress and exhale with pleasure as he gently tugs the dress over my hips and lets it fall to the floor. When he tries to reach behind my back for the clasp on my bra, I stop him.

"It's your turn," I mumble, half sitting up. "Take off your jacket. And your shirt."

While he's unbuttoning his shirt, I lean forward to unbuckle his belt. My fingers won't work properly, and I can't get the buckle undone. Laughing, he takes over and steps out of his pants. His shirt is still partly buttoned, so I reach for it and pull it open. The last two buttons pop off, bouncing like Skittles on the floor.

"Well, that worked!" I say. Why are his clothes so complicated? I just want them off. Now.

He bends down to remove my shoes, then begins a trail of soft kisses up the inside of my leg. I couldn't stop him now even if I wanted to.

JANE LILY ❧

LILY IS HOLDING A flyer in her hand advertising an exhibit at Westerly Hall to celebrate the work of Morian DeWeir. These are not the same prints she saw in the souvenir shop. These, she can see by the thumbnail images on the flyer, are paintings of a different calibre. The elusive masterpieces he couldn't create while working in their cramped apartment. How long, she wonders, did it take him to find this kind of success? The kind he promised to share with her? Lily rereads the flyer to make sure she read it correctly the first time. He's actually going to be here. In Vancouver. It's as if an electric current has just shot through her chest. She stares at the glossy slip of paper in her hand and wonders what she should do.

Of course, she already knows what she's going to do. Has known since the very first time she went skipping out to a gallery with a bubble of expectation in her throat. But at the same time, she wants to be logical about this; she wants to be in control of how she handles this thing. Because this is exactly what she's been waiting for, right? This is why she never stopped haunting the galleries around Vancouver. She'll go to the exhibit; she has no doubt in her mind about that. But what will she do when she sees him? What will she say?

THE EXHIBIT IS DONE well. His paintings are mounted under rows of track lighting along dark burgundy walls. Waiters dressed in tuxedos circulate unobtrusively with their trays, offering wine, champagne, and platters of artfully arranged canapés. There's an impressive crowd.

Men in dark suits speak in hushed voices to women wearing dresses just shy of evening gowns. Lily herself chose a deep blue dress that hugs her body. The last time she wore this outfit was to a dinner function at the university with Andrew, and she remembers being complimented on it, remembers even Andrew raising an eyebrow in appreciation when she first stepped out of their bedroom. Her heart stalls for a second as she stands uncertainly in the midst of the muted movements all around her, but then it jumps nervously as soon as she spots Morian. She knows it's him right away. His sandy hair is shorter now and interspersed with grey, but his stance, the tilt of his chin, they flood her heart with recognition. He's mingling with the crowd, about twenty paces away, shaking hands and smiling. She walks toward him on unsteady legs.

He doesn't notice her, or if he does, he doesn't recognize her. She should have worn her hair down. His eyes skim past her, and he turns to greet someone who has approached from the other direction. He lets this girl — for this beautiful, young thing is hardly more than a girl — lead him away from where Lily stands. Lily remains frozen in place, as if her legs have turned to ice.

She is light-headed. Her legs could melt to nothing at any moment. She needs to lean on something or, better yet, to sit down. She glances toward the nearest wall, wondering if it will be enough to support her or if she is going to collapse right here, in front of Morian and all his guests. She can feel herself falling. Somehow, she makes her way to the exit and slips outside.

LATER, AT HOME, SITTING on the edge of the bathtub, shaking, she makes up her mind. She has to get away from here. Maybe if she goes far enough, away from everything and everyone she knows, she'll be able to breathe again, to start over. Alone. A plan begins to form in her mind. And even though she loves her daughter — she does, she knows she does — she experiences a thrill of anticipation at the thought of walking away.

Besides, Danah has Andrew.

LILY CLIMBS INTO THE taxi that has just pulled up in front of her house. The driver puts her two suitcases in the trunk and slams it shut. She winces.

"Going off on a little vay-cay-tion?" he asks, drawing out the word.

"Yes," she answers. She turns her head to the window, hoping he gets the hint that she's not interested in talking.

He persists. "Good on ya. I say more people should do things for themselves, you know. Take a little time, a trip, or sumthin' — just sumthin' to —"

"Yes," Lily interrupts, "people should." Her head hurts. She can feel herself slowly splitting in two. One half of her is staying behind, while the other is pulling away in this yellow taxi, trying not to look back. Trying not to think.

At the airport, Lily nearly changes her mind. She climbs out of the taxi on wooden legs. Her hands fumble with the heavy suitcases as she lifts them onto a cart. But she pushes forward. She keeps moving. Through the automatic sliding doors into the hum of people and energy, down the polished corridor, toward the Air Canada counter. As she checks her baggage, watches it slide away from her on the conveyer belt, she knows she has committed to going through with this. When she walks through security and down the long hall to her boarding lounge, her feet become lighter. Her heart begins to beat again.

She focuses her attention on finding Gate 49. Once there, she lowers herself into one of the plastic seats that is welded to the others in the row. Through the giant window beside her, she can see pieces of luggage being unloaded from a cargo train and tossed onto a conveyer belt that disappears inside the bottom of a plane.

Not for the first time, she shakes off the constraints of a previous life and prepares to meet a different future.

She is one of the last people to board the plane. She waits and waits, half-expecting something or someone to stop her. Thinking maybe she might stop herself. But eventually, she follows the others down the boardwalk, finds her seat, and sits there, heart pounding. As the plane taxis down the runway, she closes her eyes and takes deep, even breaths. The woman beside her pats her arm reassuringly.

"You'll be fine once we're in the air, love."

The air in the cabin has a smell to it — slightly stale with an undercurrent of sweat. A flight attendant stands in the aisle, demonstrating how to clip and unclip the seatbelt while over the loudspeaker, someone else drones on and on with the rest of the safety instructions, first in English, then in French. There is a roaring in her ears as the plane accelerates then lifts into the air, making Lily's ears ache from the pressure. The woman beside her touches her arm again, this time to offer her a piece of gum.

"Keep chewing and swallowing," the woman advises.

Lily concentrates on those two simple tasks. Chew, then swallow. Chew, then swallow. Her ears pop over and over. The woman beside her smiles; Lily smiles back weakly, but her lips feel trembly, and she is worried that the sob building in her chest will bubble out at any minute.

She faces forward and closes her eyes. As the plane levels out, Lily dozes. At one point, she awakes with a start. The plane doesn't appear to be moving — time and motion are suspended — and with a lurch, she thinks this must all be a dream: the woman beside her, the ticket she kept hidden for so long, the suitcases she packed just this morning. Slowly, the sounds in the cabin reassert themselves. She becomes aware again of the rush of recirculated air, the low murmur of conversations, the rumble of the plane's engines.

She is on a plane, flying away. Yet the wonderful liberating release she has craved for so long eludes her. This is what she wanted, isn't it? To escape.

So why isn't her soul soaring, along with her body, high above the Atlantic? She knows why. Because really, only a part of her is leaving. She left too many pieces behind this time. And, thinking this, she begins to panic. It's possible that she will never be able to pull herself together and feel whole again.

Only her own tight grip on the armrest beside her anchors her to anything at all.

DANAH 🐲

EVEN BEFORE I OPEN my eyes, a deep dread has settled on my chest, where it sits like a heavy, fire-breathing dragon. I am in my apartment, on the pullout, and someone is running water in the bathroom. I want desperately to convince myself that last night never happened. That I have nothing to do with the person in this body, lying under the blankets, cringing in shame.

How did I get home? My mind is filled with hazy half-remembrances. Arthur holding me in the elevator. In his room. Oh, God, I am going to be sick. What have I done? *What have I done?* Then, somehow, getting dressed again. Tripping over my own feet. Arthur, watching me with an amused smile. Trying to fix my hair. Not being able to put my shoes on. Finally, picking them up and walking barefoot down that hideously carpeted hall. Standing there crying in an elevator that wouldn't move because I hadn't pushed any buttons.

Edith emerges from the bathroom and glances at me with a slight frown. But if she heard me come in last night, she doesn't say a word about it. Instead, she offers to make me a cup of tea.

"Yes, please," I say weakly.

DWAYNE CALLS TO CHECK in on me at one point. He sounds concerned, but also distant. "I just wanted to make sure you were okay," he says. "You were in pretty rough shape last night."

"I know. Thanks. I didn't do anything in front of Sanders, did I? I hope I didn't embarrass myself while she was there." *Shit. Shit. Shit.*

"No, she was gone before things sort of ... went downhill." He pauses, then adds, "Take care of yourself, Danah."

I drag myself out of bed and join Edith at the table. We sip our tea in silence. Later, in the shower, I let the hot water rain down on me while I cry. Then I force myself through the motions of getting dressed and putting my living room back in order. Edith is supposed to be leaving today, but she hasn't mentioned it at all this morning. It seems strange to think that my apartment will be empty tonight and that Edith will be alone again in her house, each of us existing separately, unaware of the other's movements. I stand at the sink and wash our mugs, scrubbing them longer than necessary. If my mind settles too long on the events of last night, I will fall apart. I'll think about it later when my head has cleared, when I can gain some perspective. Right now, it's too confusing and terrifying.

"Steve's given me the all clear," Edith suddenly says, interrupting my spinning thoughts. "I can go back any time today."

"Oh, okay. That's great. When were you thinking of going?" I set the mugs in the drying rack but don't turn to face my grandmother. I actually don't want her to go, despite all the moments I spent resenting her presence. Despite how angry I was with her yesterday. Or, I do want her to go, but not yet. Just for tonight, I want company. Suddenly, impulsively, I say, "Why don't we do something together tonight? I've been so busy the past few days ... then I could take you home tomorrow and help you move everything back in?"

Edith studies me for a moment. "I suppose one more night won't kill me."

Before I can think too hard about what it means that Edith is willing to stay an extra night, a knock at the door at the top of the stairs startles me. I open it to a delivery man holding out a bouquet of flowers. "Danah Calsley?" he asks.

"That's me," I say, taking the bouquet. I carry it to my kitchen, aware that my fingers are trembling with guilt. I cut open the cellophane wrapper and reach for the small white envelope inserted into the greenery.

The flowers are from Trevor.

HOW DID I END UP here? With a bouquet of flowers in front of me and the sickening knowledge that everything around me is about to unravel. Has been unravelling, in fact, for a while now. I read Trevor's card, and my mouth goes dry.

Edith watches me as I move sluggishly around the kitchen. "Where are you going to put those? You need to make sure they get enough light, or they won't last long."

I nod, but we both knew there isn't anywhere in my apartment that gets much light. "Maybe you should take them," I say. "To put in your new kitchen."

"Oh, no. Those are for you to enjoy."

I CHANGE INTO A pair of faded flannel pajamas after dinner. My father gave them to me for Christmas the first year I left for university, and whenever I wear them, it's like I'm wrapped in comfort. Tonight, I don't think even these pajamas can slow the jittering of my heart.

Edith and I settle onto the couch with pillows and blankets and steaming mugs of hot chocolate to watch *Gone with the Wind*. Edith's never seen it before, and although I've already watched it at least half a dozen times, as Scarlett's world crumbles around her, I find myself empathizing in a whole new way. By the time the movie ends, I am echoing Scarlett's famous words as a balm to my own wounded soul. *Tomorrow*, I repeat to myself, *tomorrow is another day.*

Edith and I sit there for a few minutes after the final scene, not moving. Then, turning to face me, Edith says, "Sometimes things just fall apart. Out of nowhere, the future you envisioned just slips out of your hands and shatters. You can stand there and look at the mess, or you can bend down and start picking up the pieces."

I don't know whose life she is referring to, hers or mine.

SITTING IN DELI DIVINE, a place where Trevor and I have shared a thousand breakfasts, I nervously pull on a strand of my hair. I've chewed the skin around my thumbs until they bled, and now they are raw and ugly. When Trevor walks in, I find it hard to swallow. I lower my chewed-up hands to my lap and try make my face look normal. The restaurant is warm, but my hands form icy fists. Trevor suggested this meeting, and after the flowers, I have a pretty good idea why.

He slides into the seat across from me and smiles apologetically. I've seen that sweet, boyish smile before, and while it usually works to break down my defences, today its obliviousness sears my heart. Trevor looks so innocent. So hopeful.

"Hey." My voice is scratchy.

"I miss you," he says, placing both hands on the table as if reaching for me.

I keep my cold fists in my lap.

He continues talking, but not before dragging his hands back toward his side of the table. "Danah, I know you're upset with me, but —"

"I'm not ..." I fumble. How can I even begin to explain? He thinks we're here to talk about him bailing on me. Of all the ways he's let me down. "Trevor," I start again, "I want things to be right between us, I really do, but —" I break off, unsure how to continue. Part of me wants to pretend nothing happened, but I know he'll find out sooner or later anyway. Besides, if I really want things to go back to normal between us, I can't very well start by lying to him. At the same time, I know with a frightening certainty that what I did could be the thing that severs us as cleanly as a surgeon's scalpel. Trevor's face remains bleakly hopeful as I struggle for a way to admit what I did.

"I want that too," he says. "So where do we go from here?"

I stare into my milky tea. I haven't managed to swallow even one small sip. My stomach is churning. "Trevor, on Friday night ... I had too much to drink, and I did something really stupid." I watch his face transform from bleak to apprehensive.

"Danah —"

I continue, resolute. "I went back to Arthur's room with him. And ... and things got out of hand."

Trevor's eyes are wide with incredulity. "What do you mean 'out of hand'? For God's sake, Danah. Don't tell me you —"

I nod as the tears I've been holding back spill over. Trevor is silent. I try to wipe my eyes as inconspicuously as possible. Finally, he speaks again. "So you slept with him."

I can't look at him. His words hover in the space between us, wavering uncertainly for a moment before dropping like lead bars to the table. From the corner of my eye, I see Trevor pick up his mug, and I think for a second that he's going to throw it at me. Instead, he takes a long, careful sip. Then another. He sets the mug down gently on the table and stares past me. He is nodding his head slowly.

I finally reach for him. I lift my hand toward his, but he is sliding out of the booth, standing up. He looks at me then. He looks straight down into my pleading eyes and says, "That was one hell of a way to decide where we go from here." Then, grabbing his coat from the bench, he walks away.

I can already hear Aunt Georgina's voice resounding in my skull. *You need to get down on your knees and pray!* Trevor turns around at the door, and I lock eyes with him, willing him to come back. To just come back to me.

"Thanks for the coffee," he says. Then he steps outside into the swirling snow.

JANE LILY ❧

FLYNN IS THE ONE who tells me. He holds my hand and says he's sorry, but I'm not going to be able to stay at home much longer. My lawyer, Joseph Doughton, has already made arrangements for all the legalities around dying, but I have one more thing to take care of, and I want Niall's help.

I nod when Flynn tells me, then I ask him to please ask Dr. Patterson if he can come and see me again. Soon. Before I am moved to the hospice. Niall comes right away. He probably thinks I have some deathbed confession to make or that I've received a response to my letter just in the nick of time.

"Lily," he says, placing a hand on my arm, and I can see the sadness in his eyes as he looks at me.

There is so much I want to say to him, but I don't have the energy. Lately, when I try to talk, half of the sounds that come out of my mouth are a mixture of incoherent syllables and grunts. Somehow, I manage to tell him where to find the shoebox full of letters to Danah. I never did finish the last letter, but all together, I hope they say enough: pages and pages crammed with all the things I couldn't say in person. Years of emotions spilled out in ink.

Niall and I have talked about these letters often. He knew about them from the beginning. In fact, he returned to them over and over in our sessions. He was the one who gave me permission to splurge on expensive writing paper even though I wasn't working anymore and didn't have money for extravagances.

Now, as he holds the box in his hands, I explain, through a series of false starts and jumbled words, what I want him to do. But first, I ask him to remove the black plastic film canister from the box. I hold out Danah's cracked and brittle baby tooth for him to see.

"Tell her," I rasp, "I never stopped —"

Niall pats my arm. "I know, Lily," he says. "I know." He holds the box almost reverently against his chest. "And she'll know too."

I fall back onto my pillow, weak but grateful. And relieved. So relieved. He will send the whole box of letters to Danah.

After.

DANAH ❧

SOMEHOW, AFTER TREVOR WALKS away from me in Deli Divine, I drag myself back to my apartment, where Edith is waiting for me to drive her home. Her bag is packed and ready to go by her feet, and I can see through the open bedroom door that the bed has been stripped. The sight of the bare mattress, waiting to be remade so I can sleep on it again, is discomfiting. I am so empty and numb that I actually wish Edith were staying longer. Even though she's still standing in the living room, waiting for me to finish brushing my teeth, my apartment already feels silent and lonely — an echo of how hollow my life has become.

"I told Steve not to bother having his crew put anything away," Edith says as we drive toward Alder Street. "I know I'll just end up having to move it all again anyway. And before anything goes in those kitchen cupboards, I need to give them a good scrub. Who knows how many people have had their grubby hands all over them."

We go in the side door, by the garage. The kitchen is unrecognizable. I glance toward the spot on the counter where I dropped Edith's mail so many days ago as if expecting to see the pile sitting there again. This kitchen is not the same place where the world shifted under my feet. Everything is new and modern and shiny, but as I admire the appliances and the cabinets and the floor, I realize that there was something comforting about Edith's previous outdated kitchen. This new kitchen is cold.

The living room, too, feels strange. The furniture is all the same but shabbier somehow. I wonder if Edith senses it too — this foreignness — like she's home but not really *home*.

Ben and Alice come over to help. Edith is puttering around, putting things away as we carry in the boxes and loose items from the garage.

"That one can go to my room," she tells me, indicating the box I'm about to set down in the living room.

Obediently, I carry it to her bedroom. I think about the bits and pieces of Edith's former life that have cropped up over the past weeks: the photo of my mother as a little girl; the Bible with its record of her dead daughter's name. And as I listen to Edith barking orders at her neighbours, I am confronted with the disheartening certainty that I will never find the answers I'm looking for.

Ben pokes his head into Edith's bedroom, where I am sitting on the as yet unmade bed staring into space. "Alice made up some sandwiches for lunch. Come and get something to eat before they disappear."

"I can't stay," I say. I need to lie down. My limbs are aching with fatigue, and my temples have been pulsing with a steady pain ever since leaving Deli Divine. I know this feeling well; it comes from holding back tears. What is Trevor doing right now? What is he thinking at this precise moment?

"Take one for the road then. Alice will be disappointed if you don't."

"Okay, thanks."

After he leaves, I sink onto Edith's bed and close my eyes against all the stupid, stupid shit I can't fix in my life. I want Trevor at that moment more than anything. And as crazy as it is, I feel a tiny connection with my mother as I sit in my grandmother's bedroom contemplating how badly I've messed everything up. Did she feel the same cold, knife-edged pain when she walked away from me? Did regret pummel her heart until she could barely feel it beating?

AS SOON AS I get home from Edith's, I pour myself a stiff rye even though it's barely past noon. I'm just getting ready to sit down and sink into a hole of self-pity when my phone rings. My heart lurches in hopeful anticipation, thinking maybe, just maybe it will be Trevor. But it's only Dwayne.

"I just wanted to check in with you. Make sure you're all right," he says.

"Things are a little ugly right now," I admit. "What about you? Still on top of the world?"

Dwayne waits a few seconds before he replies. "I have this friend that I'm a little worried about. She hasn't been herself lately. And I'm not just talking about Friday night, Danah. Although I will admit, you did surprise me a bit there." There is an awkward pause. "Seriously, though," he continues, "I'm here if you ever need to talk or whatever. Or if you just need some help getting your shit back together. I mean, Danah, people like me rely on people like you to have it together, you know?"

I try to mimic his tone, but I don't really have it in me to joke. "I'll do my best to get up and dust myself off so you can get back to marvelling at me," I say. Then, because that sounds kind of mean, I add, "I've got some stuff to sort out, but I'll be fine. Thanks for checking on me, though. It's nice to know I still have a few friends."

"Yeah, well, don't be a stranger."

It's too late for Dwayne's advice. I already am a stranger. Sitting in my empty apartment, gripping my glass of rye, even *I* don't recognize myself anymore.

JANE LILY ✒

I NEVER SAW MORIAN again after the exhibition at Westerly Hall.
I've often thought about what might have happened if I'd spoken
to him that day. Would he have recognized me right away, or
would I have had to go through the awkwardness of introducing
myself? Niall suggested once that I play out the scenario: imagine
the conversation we could have had. I never get past the part where
I tell him about Danah, but even the pretend lead-up offers some
consolation.

I imagine him turning and noticing me at Westerly Hall as I
approach on my unsteady legs.

"You look familiar," he says, extending his hand in greeting,
studying me with his head tipped slightly to the side, eyes searching
mine.

"I should hope so, Morian." At the sound of my voice, or maybe
hearing me say his name, recognition flashes across his features.

"Lily? My God, Lily!" He clasps my hand, then releases it suddenly. We both laugh. Nervous, giddy laughter with smiles frozen
on our faces.

"Your work — it's magnificent," I offer, gesturing to the paintings around us. "It was always magnificent, but this, this is amazing. So, are you living — are you back in Canada now?"

Morian doesn't flinch. "I'm living in Europe, actually. Amsterdam. But a friend of mine has arranged a Canadian tour, so I'm revisiting some of the places where I've found inspiration in the past."

"I suppose you have a few memories here."

"I do, Lily. Great memories."

Now that the small talk is out of the way, I barrel ahead. "When you left, Morian, you didn't just leave me. You left a daughter. I wish you could see her; she has your eyes."

I NEVER BREATHED A word to Andrew. It all happened so fast. Meeting him, discovering I was pregnant. I knew, though. I suspected I was pregnant before I slept with Andrew. At first, I didn't notice the signs. I was too caught up waiting for Morian to come back. But after meeting Andrew, after tumbling headfirst into his warm world, everything seemed to fall into place so easily. The way he embraced the idea of starting a family together; the way he promised to take care of me. I wanted the fairy-tale ending. I really did.

I DON'T KNOW IF Danah and my mother ever got to know one another. It seems likely they've met, especially given that they live in the same city. Knowing Andrew, after I left he would have reached out to her, tried to make up for all the years I stubbornly refused her overtures. He would have wanted Danah to have a grandmother, especially since she no longer had a mother.

After Andrew died, I wrote to my mother and told her the truth about Danah's father. I don't know why I trusted her with that information, but I didn't know what else to do with it, and she was always good at managing other people's problems. If she knew Danah at all, I hoped she would know what to do with that long-held secret. When Niall convinced me to write to my mother, to tell her about my diagnosis, I didn't tell him about the unanswered letter I'd already sent. I didn't tell him that I had a pretty good idea my mother wouldn't care about the fact that I was dying because, in the end, I was dead to her long ago, wasn't I?

EDITH 🐍

EDITH STARES DOWN AT her daughter's sleeping face. Jane looks so innocent, so peaceful, lying there with one arm flung above her head, her cheeks flushed with the heat still permeating the July night air. Although she has just turned ten, in these stolen moments when Edith tiptoes into her daughter's moonlit bedroom, Jane looks childlike and pure, with none of the scowling insolence that so often defines her expression during the day.

It is easier, when she looks like this, to do the thing that Edith has secretly been doing for weeks now: telling her daughter that she loves her. Each night, hovering beside her little girl's bed, Edith whispers the words into the still, dark air. Once, she leaned down and kissed Jane's damp forehead, but when Jane stirred and mumbled something in her sleep, Edith drew back stiffly, and that had been the end of that.

Edith notices now that Jane's brown curls are sticking in places to her neck. It's too hot for all that hair. Tomorrow, she will tell Jane to keep it braided, even at night. Edith leans closer to her little girl and resists the temptation to brush the heavy hair away from the skin of her neck. The words she wants to say are so simple, but her tongue trips over each syllable, making her declaration sound stilted and unsure.

"I love you, Jane," she tells her sleeping daughter. And she is glad that Jane is not awake to hear how unnatural those four words sound. How forced.

JANE LILY ❧

I ASK ONE OF the nurses at St. Joseph's Hospice what is happening to my mail. My voice comes out in a feathery whisper, but she understands me just the same.

"You don't need to worry about that," she says. "Someone will take care of it for you."

"Who?" I croak.

She doesn't know. But she doesn't want me worrying about it. She promises to look into it for me, and later that same day, she stops by my room to tell me she talked to Flynn and that he will collect the mail from my flat for me.

I close my eyes in silent gratitude, too weak to thank her properly. How strange the whims of the dying must seem to those who are busy living.

I am still waiting. For a reply. For the end. But it seems as if the end will come before a reply ever reaches me.

Perhaps I deserve as much.

EDITH 🦥

I WAKE UP IN my own house on Monday morning and walk around the rooms, examining for the umpteenth time the work that's been done. There's no evidence of the fire unless you count the renovated kitchen and the freshly painted walls. My carpets, drapes, and furniture have all been cleaned — scrubbed so that there's no indication they were recently coated with smoke and ash.

Wash me, and I shall be whiter than snow.

I am a little girl again, standing beside my mother and my brothers and sisters in church, singing with my whole heart. I remember wanting so badly to be made pure, to be made whiter than snow like the song said. Those words made me feel light. Reverent. Yet, from where I stand now, my whole life smoulders behind me, smudged with the residue of a million mistakes. All that holiness I felt as a little girl didn't do me one jot of good in the end.

"Humph," I snort, returning to the kitchen. I need to go shopping, that much is clear. I don't even have the ingredients to make a decent batch of cookies. Perhaps I should make something to share with Danah. She didn't stay long yesterday, and she looked like a wreck. We never talked about Anne or about Danah's anger at finding out about her like that, so unexpectedly.

I won't make cookies. I'll make a cherry angel cake, light and airy with a simple glaze. Maybe then, sitting face to face with my granddaughter, I can at last explain to her what happened, starting at the beginning. With Frank. And Anne. And how I raised her mother under a cloud of grief so thick we hadn't been able to see each other properly. How in the end, I know I was the one to blame for her leaving. I'm not a fool. I don't think knowing any of that will be any real comfort to Danah, but at the very least it might help her understand. Because isn't that what we all crave? Just to understand? Or to be understood?

I will reply to Jane's letters too. The one she sent when Andrew died and now this last one, the one Danah saw. I'll tell her I never had the chance to read it because of the fire. I'll explain that it was destroyed before I even opened it. Perhaps this is how we will begin again. Although I'm not going to be the one to tell Danah about her father. If Jane wants her to know, she can tell her herself. Maybe that's what this last letter was about. Maybe my daughter is finally ready to be found. Perhaps it took her this long to make peace with her past.

The Good Lord knows I'm still making peace with mine.

I do wish Jane that. To live out her life in peace.

DANAH 🐾

EDITH'S ONLY BEEN GONE one day, and already she's invited me over for dessert. I agree to go because I want to get out of my apartment, where I'm sitting around hating myself. Her invitation is a welcome reminder that I'm not as alone as I feel right now. Just as that thought crosses my mind, my phone buzzes again with a text.

It's Trevor, saying: *Let's talk.*

I sit there reading those two words over and over until they stop making sense. He wants to talk? What does that mean? Is he going to break up with me, or does this mean something else?

When? I type back.

You home now? I'll come get you.

I pick myself up off the couch and start getting ready. I am more nervous than I was on our first date. I try on three different outfits before settling on jeans and a knitted shawl. I want to look casual but also like I am trying. Like I am making an effort. For him.

He comes to the door, and he looks so good standing there with his hair all mussed up. I want to run my fingers through it and pull him inside so I can fall into him the way I have a thousand times before. I want to feel his arms wrap around me, strong and solid and comforting. Instead, I follow him awkwardly to his car, where I sit beside him, quivering with undisguised hope.

"I thought we could go to cottage-land," he suggests.

Cottage-land is our corny name for the neighbourhood of quaint little houses located just beyond the eastern edge of campus. Made from stone, with stubby chimneys, every house looks like a cottage straight from the pages of a fairy tale.

I nod, wondering whether or not his choosing our fairy-tale place is a good sign. But why else would he choose somewhere that's special to us?

He drives to Langley Street and parks beneath the empty branches of a towering maple at the edge of a cul-de-sac. We both climb out of the car and take a few faltering steps toward each other. It's started to snow lightly, and there is a raw wind blowing against our faces, but neither of us comments on it. I tuck my chin into the collar of my coat and, with my hands pushed up into my sleeves, plod slowly alongside Trevor. At first, we don't talk at all.

I want to take his hand, but there is about a foot of space between us that might as well be a gaping canyon. I don't know what it will take to bridge that gap. How I can ever cross it without feeling forever as if I am teetering on the edge.

As the light slowly leaks from the sky, I tell Trevor that Edith moved back into her own house.

"That must be a relief," he says, but his voice lacks any enthusiasm.

"I'm actually going over there tonight. I think she misses me."

We walk in silence for a little longer, and his next words bite into my heart like teeth. "About us."

I nod. I knew this was coming, but I'm not prepared at all.

"I don't know how to fix things, Danah." His voice is soft and so sad.

I turn to face him then. "Neither do I," I whisper, but I hope that just admitting that fact implies, for both of us, a willingness to try.

JANE LILY ❧

MY THOUGHTS ARE SCATTERED like petals on the wind. I am trying to catch one in particular, to hold on to it, but it keeps flitting away on wings of pain and confusion. There are figures, shadows of people, walking in and out of my vision. Cool hands on my hot cheeks. Soft murmurs.

I am floating. Drifting on a current of peace.

I can feel myself growing fainter. Slowly dissolving.

I am good at leaving.

ACKNOWLEDGEMENTS

As with almost any book, there are countless people who touched aspects of this story during its journey and it would be impossible to name (or even remember) them all, but I am immensely grateful to everyone who read early drafts, chapters, or scenes; who offered support, advice, and encouragement; who either believed in me when I said I was writing a novel or feigned polite interest. This particular book has been a long labour of love! I started it before I had children. My oldest is now fifteen.

I do need to thank a few people in particular: Dave Ribble, for his firefighter insights; Steve Cassidy, for details about the restoration process; my writing groups (BAM and TARTS), for motivation, advice, laughter, wine, and so much more; and my book club peeps, for listening to me blather on about possible plot points and character arcs. Dorothy Pawluch, thank you, thank you, thank you for reading the whole manuscript and unraveling the parts of the story that needed unraveling.

Carrie Sanders, you propelled me forward with this story from the beginning, and I will never forget the day you showed me around Kenneth Taylor Hall, introducing me as "an author", like it was a foregone conclusion. If anything sounds right about Danah's graduate student experience, it's because of you. And if anything doesn't, I'll take the credit for those parts.

Merilyn Simonds, I knew I wanted to work with you from the first words of yours I read, and I am so fortunate to have you as a mentor. You guided me through the final shaping of this story with such wisdom and a seemingly innate understanding of what I was trying to do. Without you, this book wouldn't be a book. Without you, I would likely still be "raking stones."

To Marc Côté, and the rest of the team at Cormorant, my eternal gratitude for seeing potential, not only in this story, but in me.

Finally, the biggest and most important thank you of all, to Scott, Hannah, and Jacob, for everything.

We acknowledge the sacred land on which Cormorant Books operates. It has been a site of human activity for 15,000 years. This land is the territory of the Huron-Wendat and Petun First Nations, the Seneca, and most recently, the Mississaugas of the Credit River. The territory was the subject of the Dish With One Spoon Wampum Belt Covenant, an agreement between the Iroquois Confederacy and Confederacy of the Anishinaabe and allied nations to peaceably share and steward the resources around the Great Lakes. Today, the meeting place of Toronto is still home to many Indigenous people from across Turtle Island. We are grateful to have the opportunity to work in the community, on this territory.

We are also mindful of broken covenants and the need to strive to make right with all our relations.